QUINDARO

A Novel

A A Johnson

Alden Lane Publishing
Lenexa, Kansas

Copyright ©2019 by A. A. Johnson

All rights reserved. No part of this publication may be reproduced, stored or transmitted in any form or by any means, electronic, mechanical, photocopying, recording, scanning, or otherwise without written permission from the publisher. It is illegal to copy this book, post it to a website, or distribute it by any other means without permission.

This novel is a work of fiction. Characters, corporations, institutions and organizations mentioned herein are either the product of the author's imagination or, if real, used fictitiously without any intent whatsoever to describe actual events or conduct.

Alden Lane Publishing

Lenexa, Kansas

First edition, 2019

ISBN: 978-1-7340509-0-5 (e-book)

ISBN: 978-1-7340509-2-9 (paperback)

To the Mojo 5

ABOUT THE TIME PERIOD

The Kansas Territory of the mid to late 1850s was violent and volatile. The Kansas-Nebraska Act of 1854, drafted by Senator Stephen Douglas of Illinois and sitting President Franklin Pierce, all but reversed the Missouri Compromise of 1820 and allowed for the potential spread of slavery north of 36°30' latitude and west of the Mississippi River. The bill permitted each territory to decide by popular sovereignty whether they would adopt or outlaw slavery. There was little doubt Nebraska would be free, so Kansas would become the battleground.

Floods of pro-slavery men, mostly from Missouri, crossed the river to vote for Kansas to become a slave state. Northeastern and midwestern abolitionists inundated the area as well, hoping to sway the vote toward freedom. Elections were held but the results were habitually unreliable. Between the considerable intimidation at polling places and the blatantly obvious fraud, the losing faction, whomever that may be, never agreed to the final tallies. On most occasions, the total number of votes for the winning side was greater than the total number of registered or even qualified voters in the district. Cheating was rampant, brazen, and expected. Therefore, it was only a matter of time before the fervent discourse gave way to physical confrontation.

Both sides claimed sanctity and believed they acted in the best interest of both God and country. Middle ground was hard to find as lines were clearly drawn and dangerous to cross. Small local arguments led to skirmishes, which led the indignant to retaliate causing full-fledged firefights and soon, battles. In 1856 alone, a group of nearly 700 pro-slavery enthusiasts attacked the city of Lawrence, burning a hotel, smashing the newspaper presses, and killing one man. Soon after, the Reverend John Brown and his sons used broadswords to murder five pro-slavery men just outside of Pottawatomie.

Weeks later, Brown led a contingent in the Battle of Black Jack near Baldwin City, a battle some consider the first of the American Civil War.

The fighting was brutal and unusually personal. The wounds and divisions created would last for generations, continually driving an invisible wedge between the states of Missouri and Kansas as most found it difficult, if not impossible, to forgive or forget.

The era would be labeled as "Bleeding Kansas" by the *New York Tribune* and looked upon as merely a time of change or unrest in a small area of the country. But it was more than that. The area and its people would be the first casualties of a disastrous civil war that would cost America more than $5 billion and 620,000 lives.

1.

With 65 milligrams of morphine sulphate per fluid ounce, Mrs. Winslow's Soothing Syrup was a magic potion. It was used to rid the body of pain, be it physical or mental, and it worked famously. In fact, it worked so well, doctors frequently prescribed it to heal ailments, big and small. Patients found that initially, tiny sips did the trick. However, over time, more was needed, almost craved, just to maintain a sense of normalcy. Therefore, empty bottles like the one on Sarah Murray's nightstand were common and helped to reinforce what some said when discussing the syrup—an open bottle is an empty bottle. Later, as medicine advanced and the effects of the use of morphine on the human body were better understood, Mrs. Winslow's syrup would be labeled a "baby killer", among other things, and its use banned outright. But in 1857, for a patient like Sarah, peppered with tumors and such, Mrs. Winslow's was her only remedy.

Nighttime was the worst for Sarah, and it had just settled in. The visiting nurse cracked the seal on a new bottle of soothing syrup and helped Sarah take a pull. The nurse then checked the bedding, the curtains, and the lamp, finding it all satisfactory. She leaned down and whispered to Sarah, explaining her plans to return soon and any other comforting notions she could think of. It was difficult to tell if Sarah heard anything, but the young nurse thought it was Christian to at least try, so she did. Occasionally Sarah would look into the girl's eyes and smile, giving the nurse an inkling someone was still in there. But not tonight. The medicine must have been working, and of course, the cancer was shutting down the organs. The end was near.

The young nurse turned to leave and gently pulled the door closed behind her. Sarah was floating, fuzzy from the medicine but aware enough to notice the figure hidden behind the door. She saw him sneak in earlier but said nothing. She could have if she wanted but it would have taken everything, and she needed to save her strength. She needed it to dispatch this fool once and for all. For his own good.

The figure, the shadow, the man, wasn't supposed to be there. Not just in the room but in the city. He was to have left yesterday or the day before. She had been assured of it and yet here he was. Stupid!

The man walked to her slowly, trying not to make a noise, fighting the creaking wooden slats of the floor. He could see the anger flash in her but he came close anyway. He noticed her teeth clench and she tried to speak, but he stopped her with a whisper as he knelt beside her bed, grabbing her hand.

"Shhh," he said quietly. "Don't talk, Mother, save your strength." He stared into her eyes between checking the door after each tiny sound he heard. "I know you're angry, but I had to see you." She squeezed his hand and reached her neck out for him to come closer. She spoke gently into his ear, tiny words, tiny sounds. He listened with all his heart.

He straightened again, nodding as he went, a silent affirmation that he heard the orders and would follow her direction this time. He held the tears only long enough to say, "I love you, Mother." Then they gushed. He hugged her and she hugged back as best she could. She felt his tears as they fell onto her cheek, dripping down and around her neck and wetting her hair in the back. She never wanted to let him go. Her baby, her boy, her man, was in shambles. It broke her.

A door shut loudly on the floor below and reality returned. She grunted loudly—their time was over, and he needed to move. Now. She let go of his hand and stared into his eyes.

Strong. Proud. With her head up she chopped the side of the mattress three times, spitting, "Get...your..." She couldn't finish, but her boy knew. He clenched his jaw tight and nodded to her. Not as strong. Not as proud. But the best he had. He knelt and kissed her forehead one more time, for as long as he could before she pushed him away. He tucked her covers and with one more "I love you", he was gone.

Walter Pomfrey, Sarah's brother, lingered at the bottom of the stairs, peeking just outside the back door. The waiting carriage a few yards away was ready, ready to move, ready to escape. All it lacked was the passenger. Walter checked his pocket watch, then the carriage driver sitting atop the wooden box. He gave Walter a grouchy shrug, asking without words, *What's the hold up?* Walter raised a finger in reply, *One moment, please.* Turning back inward, Walter looked up the stairs and swore. The boy was taking longer than he should and the getaway was at risk.

Just as Walter turned again toward the alley, a figure appeared at the top of the stairs. *Thank God!* Walter pulled his watch out, showing it to the boy as he cleared the last step. His whisper was angry, "Goddammit, Charlie, you should have been gone ten minutes ago!" He scolded the kid under his breath, ushering him toward and into the carriage. He shut the door between them and started to run through the plan.

"Now remember," Walter said. He stopped, noticing the tears filling Charlie's eyes. The poor kid was a mess. Who could blame him? Walter reached out to him and touched his shoulder. "This is not permanent, understand?" he said.

Charlie replied, "That is," looking upstairs.

Walter nodded, that's all he had. "I know, Charlie. There's nothing we can do about that. I promise I'll take care of everything here, alright?" Time was wasting and Walter needed to get the kid back on task. "Now remember." He grabbed Charlie's chin, turning it so they were face-to-face. "Hey, look at me. Remember the plan. Yes?" Charlie nodded. "Stick to the plan."

Walter went through it again, quickly, stopping every once in a while to make sure Charlie was still there. It was pretty basic, just travel arrangements, really. How to get from one safe place to another without getting lost or killed. The where was not the important part. The principal design was to get Charlie as far away from the city of Boston as possible. And now that Sarah was about gone, the boy needed to go too. Quickly.

Walter made it to the end, pausing to make sure he covered everything. Then he finished the way he liked to end any conversation, with advice. He spoke slowly, explicitly. "Keep your head down, stay as invisible as you can. Blend, yes? Blend in. I'll send for you when it's safe to return but until then, stay away. And stay alive."

Charlie nodded.

"Alright then," Walter said. There was nothing else to discuss. It was a good plan.

Walter stared at Charlie, only now seeing this for what it was. Goodbye. In all the planning, all the preparation, Walter never anticipated the finality of this moment. The details had taken so much of his concentration, it never dawned on him he would have to stand here now and physically send the boy away. For God knows how long. It hit him suddenly and he swooned, grabbing the wooden door of the carriage for balance. Walter choked, his throat sore as hell, trying to keep from breaking. He had to show he was strong and able lest Charlie lose his faith in him. But it took more than he had and his eyes started to drip.

The driver broke the silence from above, leaning over the side, whispering loudly, "Mr. Pomfrey, we gotta get going."

Walter's eyes never left Charlie as he responded, "Indeed."

Walter reached through the carriage window again and grabbed Charlie's shoulder with his left hand. He shoved the right one through as well, holding it out for a gentlemanly farewell shake. It was all he could think to do. Charlie grabbed his hand and Walter squeezed like a vice, feeling every bit of the kid he could touch. Before he was gone. Taking a step back, Walter wiped a tear from his face then bowed slightly. Regaining a touch of composure, Walter called to the driver, "Sam! Godspeed."

As the carriage started down the alley, the coach dog, a small female Dalmatian, took her place under the back axle. Walter watched until the team turned the corner onto the main avenue and was out of sight. He inspected the alleyway one more time, even checking the windows above to make sure some nosy local wasn't watching the escape. Folks around here would tell lies about their own mother for a nickel, maybe less, so he didn't need a chatty witness running about. Feeling secure, he took a deep breath and headed back inside. Climbing the stairs to Sarah's room, he was pleased everything went well. Unfortunately, there was still a lot that needed to be done.

2.

James Murray had three sons. Well, four if you counted Kyle, but he didn't, so no one else did either. Daniel was the oldest, Boyd next, both from James' first wife, Eugenia. She was a raving bitch by most accounts and the boys carried the family crest proudly, chipped from the old block, you might say. Kyle was next, from his second wife, Mary. She was a delight but rarely seen, and Kyle was her clone. Consequently, Kyle never really had a chance. He was much too much like his mother, drifted from the rugged Murray path and ended up floating in the bay. That's another story.

Then came Charles, from the third and current wife, Sarah. Although James was the only paternal figure Charles ever knew, he was not his real father. Sarah was a widow and from a wealthy shipping family. James, good-hearted as he was, did her and her father a favor by taking her hand. It was more of a business deal than a real love affair, and both parties knew it. Sarah's father needed someone capable of running the family business when he passed, so he thought James, who owned a smaller local shipping company, would be a good fit. He courted James more than James did Sarah and she, being much younger and a widow with a young boy, accepted her fate gracefully. James adopted Charles as a final condition of the arrangement, changing Charles' surname to Murray.

James liked Charlie as much as he was capable of liking anyone who was devoid of proper Murray blood. Daniel and Boyd were really all the older Murray cared about, and that was no secret. Luckily, Charlie was easy to tolerate. He was smart but not too smart. He spoke only when spoken to and went mostly unseen. As far as James was concerned, the kid was average in every respect, except maybe his looks. Charlie was lucky and inherited most of his mother's soft features. He was considered by most to be a very pretty man and fortunate as far as James was concerned. He would often tell Charlie he should thank heaven every day that he didn't look like his father. "That man had the face of a goat after a mule kicked it," James would say. He and his boys thought that was hilarious.

Charlie would get his allowance at Sunday dinner and then be seen only a couple of times during the week. While Daniel and Boyd helped run the business, learning from their father, Charlie stayed away. The boy knew his place and James appreciated that. There was an equilibrium in the blended family maintained by distance. James and the boys on one side, Sarah and Charlie on the other. The family business was the only link.

Over the last week, however, things had fallen out of balance and not in a good way for James. Sarah died five days ago. James had buried wives before, that in and of itself wasn't much trouble. C'est la vie. Charlie had disappeared four days ago, even missing the fancy funeral yesterday. This by itself wasn't a problem either; Charles being gone probably worked best for everyone. However, after the reading of the will today, James learned Sarah had done something no one alive had the guts to do—screw James Murray.

It seems the attorney lying on the floor at James' feet had helped Sarah amend her Last Will and Testament shortly before her health turned completely. Before, Sarah and James had agreed to a simple plan. As the majority stockholder of her father's company, Sarah would divide her shares of Pom Shipping between Charles and James. Charles would get enough to give him a nice income but nothing too extravagant. Fifteen percent is what they decided. That would help him on his way and once he earned his own living, his total income would be well above average. The remaining thirty-six percent would go to James and allow him to have complete control over the direction of the company. However, at the reading, the numbers were reversed.

At first, James chuckled and mentioned to Howard, the attorney, that he had read the document incorrectly. When Howard informed James that the numbers were indeed correct as he read them due to the changes instigated by Sarah, James lost control. The beating was swift and severe. The language was caustic and piercing, continuing as blow after blow fell. It didn't take long for James to pummel the attorney and leave him rolled in a ball on the floor. Now, James stood over him, collar popped free, hair disheveled, snot running clear to his chin. He was trying to catch his breath but was struggling. It had been a long time since he did his own bidding and it showed physically.

James pulled the handkerchief from his front pocket and wiped his face of the snot, spit, and blood mixture. The ringing in his ears subsided and his mind cleared. This was certainly a setback and his immediate plans would have to wait. Nevertheless, his goal for Pom Shipping did not change at all with this news. It may be a bit more laborious now, but he would have his way no matter what.

He turned around to speak with his sons, who were the only other parties present for the meeting. Daniel stood at the door. He had sprung quickly to lock the only way in or out once the thrashing started. Boyd remained seated on the brown leather couch in the corner of the room. He had a cigarette in his mouth and a pistol in his hand.

James' voice was higher than usual, still gaining his faculties. He asked, "Has anyone seen Charlie?"

"Sorry, Father, no one has," said Daniel. "We have people looking all over Boston for him but so far, nothing." Daniel walked to a walnut bar on the far wall of the office. He helped himself and asked, "You need anything while I'm here?"

His father answered, "Yeah, but just a little. I'm supposed to meet with the Temperance League in an hour."

"You?" Daniel asked his brother. Boyd said nothing, just shook his head no and continued to stare at the man on the floor.

"He was at dinner on Sunday, then poof, gone," said Daniel to his father.

"Where else are you looking besides Boston?" asked James, tossing back the drink.

"I sent a message to Joseph in New York so he knows we're looking for him, but I didn't tell him why. I just told him to lock Charlie down if he sees him," answered Daniel.

James handed his glass back to Daniel and said, "One more." Howard was coming to and James looked him over as he continued. "This doesn't change anything. We were getting rid of him anyway, for the fifteen percent. This just raises the stakes. Find him. Soon."

"We will, Dad," replied Daniel.

James shook his head. "I'm probably going to be planning another wedding soon, so this needs to get wrapped up. What is it with these young girls nowadays? They just have to get married as soon as…"

"You know, he would have needed money to run." Boyd finally spoke up, cutting his father off in mid-sentence as he stared at the man squirming on the floor.

Daniel started to answer, "We checked with his friends but no one…" He was cut off too. Boyd had more to say.

"His friends don't have any money. He runs with trash. The only people he knows with money to disappear is his family. We didn't give him any money, did we?" Silence. "There's no one else on our side. So, who's that leave?"

It didn't take the other two men long to come to the

same conclusion Boyd had. There was an uncle, Sarah's older brother, who really didn't like the boys much and their father even less. The only one on this side of the family he did like was Charlie, but he probably hadn't seen him in ten years. Or had he?

"Go see your uncle," James said to Daniel. He gave a glance toward Boyd. "Go alone."

"I'm going too," Boyd somberly stated. "It'll be nice to see our old uncle again."

Daniel looked at his father, slightly shaking his head no, hoping he would keep Boyd's leash tighter but was given the opposite response. "Give your uncle my regards. And whatever he deserves."

Daniel looked at the attorney on the floor and asked, "What about him?"

"It's not that bad, just a lot of blood," answered James. "He'll make it."

Boyd stood with his pistol and shook his head. "That's a bad idea."

Howard didn't make it.

3.

Walter Pomfrey entered his downtown Boston office. He arrived like most days, early but not too early, carrying nothing but his cane and humming a tune that was stuck in his head since yesterday. He had made the mistake of walking by Mrs. Gill's house on the way to lunch and heard one of her piano students playing something from Stephen Foster. He couldn't remember the name or the words, but he couldn't shake the melody for almost a full day now. A Stephen Foster song was a demon that way. The door stuck when he first opened it, and he thought about getting one of the young law students who rented the office upstairs to file it down. They had to do this occasionally as the building swelled and contracted with the changes in the weather. He usually saw Gordon leaving for court in the afternoon, an able fellow, and Walter made a note to mention it.

Without looking up, he said good morning to Mrs. Wedge, the woman he paid to open and clean the office every day. When he didn't hear her usual reply, he looked up and instantly knew something was wrong.

"Mrs. Wedge?" He repeated her name only, eyebrows raised, waiting.

"There are two gentlemen waiting in your office, Mr. Pomfrey," she said. "I told them they should wait out here until you arrive, but they insisted on going in." She paused. "I wasn't sure I could stop them so…" Her voice trailed off.

Walter could tell she was anxious, borderline afraid, even. He chuckled to try to ease the tension. "Well," he said and rapped his cane on the floor for dramatic effect, "did they give you a name, Mrs. Wedge?" he asked.

"No, sir," she replied. "But one of them called you 'Uncle Walt'."

Walter knew that was Daniel, James' oldest boy. He was the only nephew that called him "Uncle Walt", and certainly the only one who would go into his office as if he owned it. Walter had been expecting a visit from him. The next thing he needed to find out was who came with him.

"And the other one, did he call me anything?" Walter asked her.

She glanced over her shoulder toward the door to make sure no one was there. Then she quietly answered, "The other one," she paused, "didn't say anything."

Shit. That was Boyd. It was no wonder Mrs. Wedge was troubled. He was scary when he was a ten-year-old boy. As a man, he was terrifying. Walter had hoped he could meet with Daniel alone, convince him he knew nothing about Charlie, and avoid being in the same room with Boyd at all. Evidently, James was desperate to find Charlie after the reading of the will. Desperate enough to let Boyd loose.

Walter had gone over this meeting in his head a couple hundred times since he helped Charlie get out of town. He came up with a few options but wasn't sure which way he was going to go. He had decided he would make his decision when his hand was forced and he had all the details. Now that he knew Boyd was in there too, he knew how he would play it. It was a risk but it was better than being caught in a lie right off the bat.

"Thank you, Mrs. Wedge," said Walter. "Would you mind running down the street to Mr. Kamp's and picking up the items he has set aside for me?" He was trying to get rid of her just in case the meeting turned ugly. "He has the list but he may still need to pull it all together. Go ahead and wait for it, and I'll see you in an hour or so."

Mrs. Wedge knew what he was up to but knew him well enough not to argue. She grabbed her things and made her way to the door. She paused when she came near him and gave his upper arm a light squeeze. "I will be back soon, Mr. Pomfrey," she said. "And I will see you then."

Walter gave her a smile. "Indeed."

She shut the door behind her and left Walter alone in the waiting area. He took a deep breath, readied himself, and turned for the door of his office. He opened it and spoke. "Good day, gentlemen. I assume you are here to talk about Charlie."

4.

Daniel started. "Well good morning to you as well, Uncle. I guess we'll get right to it then. I gather you've spoken to our young brother?"

Walter walked around his desk to have a seat. Daniel sat directly in front of him, leaning back in a chair, legs crossed, cigarette burning. Boyd sat on a couch in the back of the office near the door. Walter avoided looking toward the couch, instead busying himself with items on his desk and answering Daniel. "I did, a few days ago. He came in the evening asking for money. The nerve."

"Did you give him any?" asked Daniel.

"I had only a few coins on me at the time so I gave him all I had. Not much, maybe a few dollars. I had the feeling he wouldn't leave me alone until I acquiesced," Walter answered, feigning annoyance.

"And I take it he hasn't been back," Daniel stated more than questioned. "Did he mention where he was heading, if he had any plans? Anything?"

"No. He had a bag with him, but just a small one," replied Walter. It was time to gain the moral high ground. "We discussed the untimely death of his mother, my sister. He was upset, as am I. We will both miss her greatly." He paused. Daniel didn't seem moved. "He never mentioned where he was going and I never asked. I gave him the money and off he went." He hung his cane on the edge of his desk, reached into his drawer and pulled out a file, pretending to be preparing for the day. He continued, "I don't have a great deal of time this morning, gentlemen, is there anything else?"

Daniel stood up and walked over to the fireplace. It had only been lit twice since spring ended but still smelled like smoke. He looked at the number of items his uncle had displayed on his wall—photographs, awards, and various acknowledgements. He read them as he talked. "Walt, we need to find Charlie, in the worst way. We're sure he left town because he wouldn't have missed the funeral if he were here. We're just not sure which way he went. We've talked to the boys down on the docks to see if he got on one of Father's ships, but no one saw him. And they see everything. We're still looking for a couple of his friends but the ones we talked to, they hadn't seen him in weeks."

Walter didn't answer.

"I'm sure I don't need to tell you how bad it looks for a newly christened major shareholder of Pom Shipping to be inaccessible," Daniel continued. "It reflects poorly on the company and frankly, on the Pomfrey name." He looked at his uncle in the reflection of a photograph in front of him. He wanted to see if that comment touched a nerve. Walter was hunched over his desk, writing.

Walter spoke without looking up. "He's not a Pomfrey anymore, he's a Murray."

"You know what I mean," Daniel said, disappointed by the lack of reaction. *Let's try this one.* He continued, "The Pomfreys have a track record of making decisions that are, what's the word, irrational?" He looked again in the reflection and thought he saw his uncle flinch ever so slightly. "I think people know that's not a Murray trait." He turned to face his uncle, took a deep breath, and shook his head slightly for dramatic effect. "People are talking, Walt..."

"I don't care what people are talking about, nephew!" Walter interrupted. "I have no doubt my name has scars, but my name is not the same name that hangs on the docks and hasn't been for most of my life. Everyone on the East Coast knows I'm not *that* 'Pomfrey'. They may think me a fool for it, but I have never been confused with the lot that runs that mess of a company. I have built my name separately, my way. Therefore, if people are talking, then they are talking about you and yours, Daniel. Not me."

"Touché, Uncle," Daniel replied happily. He touched the nerve he was aiming for. He continued. "Nonetheless, we both want the same thing, don't we? For Charlie to be here. We need him to demonstrate the stability of the third largest shipping company on the East Coast. That's very important to us."

Walter interjected, "You need his shares."

Daniel ignored the jab. "And I'm sure you would gain some sort of twisted satisfaction knowing the last, the only, true Pomfrey heir was in a position of influence at Pom Shipping. Finally. If it can't be you, I'm sure Charlie is the next best thing, right?" He paused. "Do you want to see him run the company, Walt?"

"I don't care," he replied.

"'Cause no one else does," Daniel added.

"I don't care," Walter repeated.

"He's not smart enough, Walt. And doesn't want to anyway."

"I don't care." That was all Walter could muster the strength to say. Over and over again, his only answer to Daniel's venom was "I don't care."

Walter knew Daniel's strategy was to push him, spur him on until he lost focus and revealed a secret. Something, anything the brothers could use to find Charlie and prove Walter had helped in some way. If that happened, his goose was cooked. Walter knew it was a ploy but still found it difficult to stay under control. After all, Daniel was great at finding buttons and even better at pushing them. He could push and push, finding more and more joy the higher his victim's frustration rose. And when he pushed far enough and things moved to the next level, like a coward, Daniel would turn it over to his brother to finish things. That was what Walter had to avoid right now.

Unfortunately, it was getting harder by the second. His "I don't care" response was getting louder and seemed to contain more and more anger. The sad truth was, he did care. The sadder truth was that most of what Daniel was saying about the Pomfrey name and Charlie was true. And Walter had no defense.

His final "I don't care" came with a fist slammed hard on the desk. He reached for his cane to stand up, leave the room, something. Instead, the gun pointed at his head held him in place. The monster had been awakened. Boyd was standing, pistol aimed toward Walter, waiting for the tiniest movement to end the argument for good.

"Take your hand off the cane, Walter," Boyd said, barely audible.

Walter slowly raised both hands in the air and spoke as softly as he could. "Take it easy, Boyd. I was just going to take my leave. I would rather not talk to your brother anymore today."

"I assume it's loaded. Kick it over," Boyd commanded.

Walter followed the order. He had forgotten the cane was loaded, two shots worth, .22 caliber. A friend had given it to him thinking someday it may come in handy, an old man walking around alone in the big city and all. He didn't plan to use it on his nephews despite his anger but Boyd didn't know that. Oddly enough, he knew it was a gun somehow and was quick to make the first move.

Daniel moved behind the desk and picked up the cane. He started his inspection while his brother continued. "We're going to find Charlie and get what's ours. We'll find out who helped him too, and they'll get what's coming to them. If you hear from him, Walter, do not help him again. Understand?" Walter gave him a nod. Boyd turned and walked out.

Daniel unloaded the cane, dropping the two shells on Walter's desk. Handing him his cane, Daniel leaned down and spoke softly, right in Walter's ear. "If your story doesn't check out, Walt, *I'm* not coming back. *He'll* be back," said Daniel, pointing at the empty doorway. "That won't go well for you." With a light pat on the shoulders, Daniel turned toward the door and finished with, "Good to see you again, Uncle Walt."

5.

Walter had not moved since his nephews left. He was leaning back in his chair, eyes closed, trying to get a grip. Being both angry and terrified simultaneously had taken a toll on him. He felt weak and dizzy. He could use a shot of the bourbon on the other side of the office but he lacked the strength to go get it. His deep breaths were helping and he felt his body starting to work again when another jolt went through him. The outer door opened, someone came in, then closed it behind them. Walter, hands starting to shake again, reached for his cane and the two shells on his desk. He knew the loading wouldn't happen fast enough and started to panic. Then he heard a voice.

"Mr. Pomfrey, I have returned. Is everything alright?" It was Mrs. Wedge, her voice cracking ever so slightly, fearing the answer.

Walter took a deep breath and felt his shoulders lower and relax. He yelled to her, trying to sound as normal as possible. "In here, Mrs. Wedge."

She opened the door quickly, her hand obviously on the knob before she bellowed. She saw Walter sitting in his chair and the color begin to return to his face. She looked around to make sure they were alone, that the danger was gone. She asked, "Are you alright, Walter?" She rarely called him Walter.

"Peachy, Mrs. Wedge. Just peachy." He looked toward the liquor bottle, and she got the hint. Normally, she would give him the business if he had the notion to imbibe the evil liquid during the day. Her temperance meetings gave her plenty of ammunition to use on him, and she did so whenever necessary. The bottle was for the sinners he worked for who needed the poison to forget all the miserable things they did to each other in the name of business. She held Walter to a much higher standard and expected him to resist the temptation. Never really knowing why she thought better of him than his associates, he played along and used his coffee mug instead of the glasses whenever he did choose to partake.

She filled a glass and brought it to him. He thanked her with a nod and chugged it down. He handed her the empty glass and while the burn subsided in his mouth, pointed her back to the bottle. He let out a scratchy "Please" as he did so. Walter was surprised she accommodated without any prodding. He figured he must look worse off than he felt. She brought him another full glass and retreated to the couch where Boyd had sat earlier. She wanted details and made it clear she was done serving Walter liquor.

She waited for him to chug the second drink and began. "I have your items in the front..." Her voice trailed off. "I was so scared."

He interrupted her. "I apologize, Mrs. Wedge, for putting you in that situation. I knew there was a possibility that they may pay me visit, and I should have taken more care. It is completely my fault and I am very, very sorry."

She asked, "Does this have anything to do with your nephew Charlie? He was here a lot over the last month or so, but I haven't seen him in..."

Walter interrupted again. "No, no, no, Mrs. Wedge." He stood up and walked toward her. He knelt in front of her, grabbed her hands in his and spoke quietly. "You must never mention that. Never mention Charlie. Never mention he was here. We must keep that between us for now. Do you understand? That is imperative." She nodded. "This will all blow over and everything will return to normal, but for now, mum's the word when it comes to Charlie." She nodded again.

He stood and walked toward the bottle for one more swig. "I'll fill you in on everything as soon as I'm able. I have a couple meetings today, but we'll get together soon and fix our stories. In the meantime, it would be best if you stayed away from the office for a day or two. Just in case. I will reimburse you as usual per our agreement. Yes?"

All she could muster was a "Thank you, Walter."

He made it to the cart, poured another glass and looked up at the wall where Daniel had stood staring. The pictures moved a bit as Walter swayed slightly. The liquor was working! He smiled to himself, hiding it from Mrs. Wedge. This feeling right here, not drunk but not sober either, was the sweet spot. He often thought that if he could stay here indefinitely, he could take over the world. Everything made sense to him in this state. Or maybe it was here that he realized everything was nonsense. That all the so-called important things he had to deal with every day, in the grand scheme of life and the universe, didn't really mean shit. After all, no one will care about any of this in 100 years and...

Wait. The picture on the wall. It was of him and Cara Mead standing next to the British Ambassador in downtown Boston. Ah, Cara. How he wished that could have worked. But she was too young, too full of life for him. She also had crazy ideas about life and politics that just didn't fit into his slice of society. And her language. Oh God! To call her blunt was an understatement. Filthy was more like it. They were just too different.

He didn't deserve to feel young anymore, his time had passed. And he certainly didn't need a woman speaking her mind and trying to change the world, making him look like a lazy fool. And that mouth! That filthy, raw...beautiful, wonderful, talented mouth...

Stop it, stay focused! Daniel was looking at this picture,

he was almost sure of it. And his nephew would most certainly know Cara, at least know of her. They were both well-to-do, after all. Her connection to the Immigrant Aid Society was no secret, nor was Walter's, for that matter. The Society constantly recruited the area for folks to move to the next big, important town to do battle in the fight for freedom. No doubt, the Murrays had been approached several times about investing in the West. Daniel would know there was a blossoming new town or city gaining traction and that a free trip would be the perfect escape for his stepbrother. A visit to the Society would be a reasonable next step for the Murry brothers, wouldn't it?

Walter paused and tried to calm his mind. Did his thought process make sense or was he just creating an excuse to go and see Cara? Or was he just crocked and confused, giving the Murrays too much credit? He and Cara hadn't talked in months, but then, they had nothing to talk about. Now they did. Didn't they? Oh hell! He needed to go see her and make sure she kept the small town of Quindaro a secret for a bit longer, at least until he and Charlie could plan their next move. It was a business visit, nothing more. Unless... No! Nothing more.

He gulped his third shot of liquor and excused himself from Mrs. Wedge. As he hurried out of his office and onto the street, he turned and checked his reflection in the glass. Why did he wear this tie today? It never hangs right.

6.

The Blackstone Block, where Walter set up shop, was a bustling business district filled with offices, restaurants, and taverns, many older than the country itself. Atwood & Hawes had been selling oysters for decades and would forever after. Jimmy Wilson, the last town crier, moved his fifty-year-old tavern, the Bell in Hand, to the area in 1844. Jimmy's place, the Green Dragon Tavern, and many other establishments in the district served some of the most famous dissidents in history including Paul Revere, Samuel Adams, and John Adams. The Great Orator was a more recent patron of the area. He could eat his weight in oysters and drank enough Daniel Webster punch to destroy a human liver.

Walter was flying by these joints without giving them a second thought. To the locals, including Walter, the rebel ghosts had faded and not enough time had passed to consider them the sacred icons they would become. Veneration takes time and history moves slowly. Mr. Webster was old news as well. He had passed five years ago, a fall from his horse beating his failing liver by a nose. And most Bostonians with an abolitionist lean still hadn't forgiven him for his "Seventh of March" speech in which he gave his support to the Compromise of 1850. He was a traitor too, but not the good kind people adore.

He could have taken a carriage from Union, down Hanover to Tremont, but Walter thought the walk would give him time to settle. He needed to get his thoughts together. He wasn't sure how he was going to play it with Cara and was running scenarios in his mind as he walked. He knew she was the person who would receive and file the final list of folks sent west by the Society. She had been elected secretary, and it was her responsibility to keep the records. Charlie's name would be on that list, so Walter's goal, his quest today, was to make sure Cara, if questioned, would not share the list with the Murrays. Or anyone else snooping around, for that matter. If the Murrays got ahold of that list, things would get ugly fast.

There was a time when all Walter would have had to do was ask Cara for the favor and it would have been done. She would have altered the list in a moment, and Charlie's trip would be erased forever. Now though, after the way he left things, she may just publish the list in the paper with Charlie's name at the top, in all capital letters! It's not that she was a trivial woman who would hold on to petty grudges or make things hard on someone out of simple spite. Some of her victims may not have believed this, but Walter knew her better. It was not spite. It was a warrior's conviction that wrongs, offenses to her and her name, brought punishment. Punishment at such a severe level the offender would be left scarred. Damaged forever. They would never forget her and would, from then on, show her the respect she deserved. This is what he was afraid of and why he must tread lightly.

Walter ran a few scenarios in his head and finally settled on a plan. There was a chance she wouldn't open the door, and he may never get to speak at all. Then what would he do? He would cross that bridge when he got to it. For now, if she allowed him access, he had decided to tell her everything and see how far that got him. She could read him like a book anyway and would sniff out any shenanigans. She would respect the truth. Probably. Maybe. Hopefully.

Walter finally turned onto Tremont Street and could immediately feel his environment change. The avenue, lined with American elms and walled off on both sides by gorgeous two- and three-story brick structures, was home to some of Boston's wealthiest citizens. Dark green grass grew in small front yards, usually surrounded by black wrought iron fences. The gates were closed but rarely locked. Police patrolled the area frequently, collecting tips from the homeowners for running off any who didn't belong and producing a feeling of security appreciated by all. The surnames on the street included Higginson, Howe, Lawrence, Mann, Holmes, and Browning. Six of the last seven mayors owned property on Tremont. Cara's family had a place here, one of the biggest. Walter's father had a place too, but when he died, it went to Sarah. Now, the Murrays had a place here. Luckily, it was around the corner past the park, and Walter wouldn't see it on his way to Cara's house. It would break his heart.

At the end of the sidewalk, Walter fixed his tie again and peered toward Cara's doorway. He shivered, noticing a man at the door, standing on the top step. It was Daniel. Walter looked to the street and saw a carriage. Boyd was inside. The driver took off the brake and the carriage started away, coming right toward Walter. He jumped behind a thick elm before anyone could see him, standing straight as a board, back pushed against the decorative tree. The carriage turned off Tremont, taking Boyd with it. That was a relief. However, Daniel was inside, and that was a huge problem.

Walter didn't know what he was going to do, but he found himself sneaking toward Cara's house, down an alleyway between her place and a neighboring building. Her study, located on the side of her home, had a large window, and Walter headed towards it. This is where Cara handled her business callers. It was as good a place to start as any.

Under the window, hiding between two large trash bins, Walter caught his breath. He heard the study door open and Daniel's voice through the panes of glass. Walter turned around and peeked in from the lowest corner. Daniel and the housekeeper were the only two in the room, him sitting on a couch, and her getting him a drink. As she handed it to him, his other hand went to the back of her thigh and down her leg.

He whispered something, too quiet for Walter to hear, and she pulled away. She hurried toward the door, never looking back, and slammed it shut on her way out. Daniel was entertained. Walter was repulsed. God, he hated this kid!

A moment later, the door reopened and Cara came in. She looked beautiful! Daniel stood and bowed as Cara crossed the room, then he sat back down. She asked about his drink, went to the cart, refilled his glass and made a drink for herself. They were talking too low for Walter to hear everything, but some words made it through. It was small talk for now, nothing to fear.

Cara brought the drink back to Daniel and stood above him as the housekeeper had. This time, Daniel didn't take the drink. Rather, he leaned forward with two hands outstretched, giving both of Cara's legs the disgusting caress. Cara said something and backed away. Good for her. Now he's going to get it!

She walked across the room toward the door but instead of leaving, she locked it. She walked back over to the couch, again standing over him and again, he leaned in. She spoke but very low, intimately. He answered in the same way and it seemed natural. She held the glass to his lips and he took a sip.

Walter wanted to run but he couldn't. His body was frozen. He knew what was happening. He was familiar with the look on her face, he had seen it many times. He couldn't believe this was real and happening right in front of him. He felt like he was watching his own funeral. When the first piece of clothing came off, it jolted him back to life. He jumped, trying to get away and knocked over one of the bins serving as his hideout. He whispered "Shit!" as he backed up against the house under the window. He tried to be as little as possible, but he was sure if Daniel looked out, the jig would be up.

He sat frozen, waiting. He thought for a moment that being caught now would not be the worst thing that could happen to him. He'd just witnessed the queen mother of all nightmares. Hell, if that's where he ended up after the Murrays were through with him, would be a picnic in the park comparatively speaking. Hearing a muffled laugh, Walter looked above him but saw no one. He didn't dare look into the study again, but he looked at the window to see if it was safe to go, and it was. They never heard a sound.

He stumbled down the alley to the street, picking up speed as he went. He crossed the road and cut through a yard, using any shortcut he could find. It was all a blur until he came to a cross street he recognized and stopped to catch his breath. Just down the block he saw his destination, a small tavern run by a man Walter used to know. He hadn't been there in years but tonight, once he was there, he thought he might never leave.

7.

Walter's head was pounding. He had not tried to move yet, but he knew it was going to be a tough day. This is why he didn't drink...much. He lay there trying to figure out if he had anything today that couldn't be pushed to next week. It was Friday, he was fairly certain, so he should be ready to go by the next business day, Monday. He could only remember one meeting with a young man he was mentoring. His name was... something. Whatever. He should get used to being stood up.

Just to be safe, Walter reached toward his nightstand to get the backup version of his itinerary and maybe try to put on his glasses. However, where the nightstand should be, there was nothing. He grimaced as he tried to open his eyes just enough to keep out the extra light that would surely be torture.

"You're not going to find your glasses there, Walter," a voice spoke. A woman's voice, Cara's voice? "I put them on the table down by your feet, but I'm sure you're in no shape to reach that far."

It was Cara. Through his squinted eyes, he could tell he was in her sitting room, on the couch. That couch.

She continued. "You look like you're in terrible shape this afternoon. Like your head is going to explode. That's good. That makes me happy. You deserve to be the most miserable man alive."

He could barely get a sentence out. "Not so loud. Why am I here?"

She answered, "That's a great question, Walter. Why are you here?" Cara took a drink of bourbon and, just to be a bitch, blew the smell from her mouth into Walter's face. He gagged.

"You stumbled here last night," she continued. "Poor Walter Pomfrey, drunk as a sailor, pounding on my door in the middle of the night, screaming and cussing, calling me all sorts of foul names and airing every little bit of dirty laundry for everyone on the block to enjoy." Walter grimaced. "You were so offensive, the reverend across the street wanted to let the police beat you senseless and drop your body down at the docks where God knows what would happen to you. A reverend, for crying out loud! That's how much of an ass you were. I only let you into the house to shut you up and buy some time before someone could come and take you away. Luckily for everyone, you tripped and hit your fool head on the coffee table. Hilda covered you up and left you there to die. Wishful thinking, I guess."

Walter sighed deeply, shaking his head. "I'm very sorry, Cara…" She cut him off.

"I'm not a whore, Walter. Or maybe I am, but that never bothered you when we were together." Walter buried his face in his hands. He was an ass. She continued. "You are the one who wanted out, remember? You are the one with the 'complications', not me. You being ten years my senior with no prospects is enough of a reason for you. But that's you, Walter. That's how you are. It's not how the rest of us have to be. I'm ten years older than Daniel and I'm not bothered by that at all. Nor is he. And judging by your angry rhetoric last night, you've seen proof of that."

That was low but he deserved it. Walter rubbed his head and said all he could, "I'm very sorry." He wanted to say more. Much more. Of course, he didn't think she was a whore or anything else he called her last night. He was just drunk. And mad. And jealous. And drunk! She was wonderful and he let her get away. He gave her up and although Daniel was a dagger, anyone with her would cut him deeply.

Cara stood and said, "You should get your things and go. Now. He will be here shortly."

Walter agreed. He grabbed his glasses and his head spun. Then the "he" sank in and Walter remembered what started all of this. "Oh, Cara. By chance, did your *suitor* happen to mention anything about the small town in the Kansas Territory? Quindaro, I think it's called?"

"As a matter of fact, he did," she replied. "He didn't mention it by name, but he did ask if there were any investment opportunities in the West. Seems he and his brother are thinking of getting involved with the Society. To help their fellow man in the battle for freedom and such."

Walter rolled his eyes. *Yeah, I'm sure.* Cara noticed.

"I didn't buy his story seeing that there isn't a giving or caring bone in any Murray I've ever met," she continued. "I got the feeling Daniel had an ulterior motive to his line of questioning, so I kept Quindaro to myself." She glared at Walter. "You know how I dislike ulterior motives."

"Don't we all," he agreed.

"Why do you ask, Walter?" She was on to him, too.

Walter started in on his script. "I just thought it prudent for the Society to keep *all* the newest towns, Quindaro in particular, quiet for just a little while longer." *Smart opening.* "I've heard there have been issues with the survey and the lot dimensions, naturally, due to the hilly terrain and whatnot. And investors…new investors…the wealthier lot…especially those of the Murray ilk, may not understand the…idiosyncrasies involved in developing a new area." He started to wobble. "As I'm sure you're well aware, there are so many behind the scenes functions…and whatnot…and new money, I mean, new…what's the word? People? No. Interests? I mean…" Cara stopped him before he could hurt himself.

"Cut the shit, Walter." That mouth! "I know you're lying. I

can always tell. You start to babble like an idiot." She stopped and thought for a moment. Then hit him right between the eyes. "Did you send Charlie to Quindaro?" She knew the answer by the look on his face.

Walter didn't bother to deny it either, he just rubbed his head and stood up. "I should be going," he said.

She grabbed his arm and laid into him. "You are so stupid!" He tried not to look her in the eyes as the scolding escalated. "The Kansas Territory is a cruel place, Walter! And Quindaro is in the thick of it, you know that. People there are fighting and dying every day. It's not a game, Walter, it's a war."

"Please, Cara." He tried to stop her tirade but couldn't.

 "A sheltered, spoiled kid like Charlie will be dead in a week. If he's lucky," she continued. "The odds are better he'll be tortured for months before he hangs from a tree like a common criminal. Nice job, Uncle. You sure took care of things for your sister. Jesus, Charlie would have been better off taking his chances with the Murrays."

Walter knew the risk he took sending Charlie to Kansas and the trouble the boy was in. He didn't need to hear it from Cara. He had had enough. "Are you done?"

"No," she snarled. "I have you now, Walter. I have the list. If I show Daniel, well, you know what happens. But I'll keep your secret for now, for Charlie's sake. And I'll help him if I can. But I don't want to see you around here again. You don't get to judge me or decide what I should be doing. You don't have me, Walter Pomfrey. I have you. Understand?"

"Can I go now?" he asked sourly.

"Please do."

He left the study fuming and got a dirty look from Hilda the housekeeper for good measure. His head was still spinning, and his stomach was churning. He wasn't at his best or even anywhere near it. But he was pretty sure he heard the word, "Asshole!" as the front door closed. Oh, that mouth!

8.

The bluffs were higher than he imagined. He had heard folks describe the view, the height, the angle of the hill. "It's like the town goes straight up," one old man told him. Another man he met in St. Louis told him he'd never go back. "I'm scared I'll fall down and won't stop rollin' till I end up in the river." He saw mountains on his way west and wasn't impressed. So a tall hill with a few buildings on it, especially in Kansas Territory, didn't sound remarkable. He had no perspective.

However, when the ferry rounded the sharp bend and the Missouri River slowed, Charlie couldn't help but stare in awe. The channel ran right up to the shore, a rock ledge creating a natural dock. Directly behind the dock was a hill, stretching nearly a half mile vertically. On the hill were a hundred or so buildings of different sizes, shapes, and colors. And walking around these buildings were people, like ants in the sky, moving here and there as if they had no idea they were floating as high as they were.

He felt the ferry hit the dock with a crack, a hard landing, but no one else seemed to notice. The driver mumbled a curse or two checking the damage to his craft, then threw the ropes to two young men waiting on the dock. He didn't want to be the first passenger off nor the last, so he waited his turn and snuck in behind a man with a pair of oxen and in front of a group of Presbyterians. The passengers exited between the two dock men standing on the rock ledge. One smiled and nodded to each new traveler like they were old friends. The other stood looking at nothing and probably wouldn't have noticed if the oxen were zebras and the Presbyterians were Catholics. He tried not to make eye contact with the friendly greeter, but that proved to be rather difficult. The welcome wagon was relentless.

He put some space between himself and the river, walking slowly toward the bottom of the hill, looking up the whole time. His eyes went from building to building, scoping out the town's layout and plotting his ascent. It was steep, no doubt. In fact, most structures built on the incline had stilts on the front side to keep them level. He was amazed at what an organized group of people could accomplish. He didn't know where he was going but figured he would decide his route from here rather than after he started his ascent.

"You got two options. The blue building is a hotel and the white building behind it is another hotel."

He turned to see the fellow from the dock, the greeter. "Both cost the same, both are nice enough. They'll be full so you may end up in the hallway or a closet or something." A chuckle. "The other option is the clearing down yonder, see them tents?" A head scratch. "A couple grifters may hit you up for rent, but you don't have to pay no one to stay down there. Tell 'em to go to hell and they usually do."

Charlie thought about the two options, trying not to let on that the man had read his mind. He nodded a little and started to say "Thanks" but was interrupted.

"There are ten or twelve places to grab a bite, all over, really. I'd stay away from that shack over there, the Russian fella. Food's cheap but terrible and he's crazy. Carries a big knife, says Tsar Nichols gave it to him himself, for valor or something, I forget." He paused, thought for a second. "There's a story but I can't remember how it goes. Good story though, if you ever get a chance to hear it."

Silence.

He continued, whispering, "Only two places to get something to drink in town. Neither one's that hard to find once the sun goes down. The clearing is full of it, but the town's drying up. Lots of temperance folks coming in lately, wanting to do away with the sinning and whatnot. Probably be completely dry by the end of the year but for now, you can still get it. Those places get a little dangerous after dark. If you end up going, let me know and I'll come along. Introduce you, make sure you don't get shot or something." A smile and a pat on the back.

Shot?

"I'll be right there, down by the water, in that red building, see it?" he asked, pointing back to where the ferry docked. "Me and my cousin stay there till the last ferry comes, 'bout 8:30 or so. Come get us, we'll show you around if you want." Silence. "All right then. Welcome. Welcome to the Hole in the Hill," he said, waving his hand like a magician. Silence. "Welcome to Quindaro."

9.

What a difference a couple of weeks can make. Not long ago, Charlie Murray was sitting at Sunday dinner, listening to his stepfather discuss how Sarah's passing would affect business affairs. Charlie had nothing to add to the discussion. He quietly listened as his stepfather gave him direction and laid out the best plan for the family going forward. He heard a little but didn't care. His mother was very near death and he was completely alone in this world. The Murray's world. Uncle Walter was putting together his plan, therefore Charlie already knew he would be gone soon. Walter told him he would need every penny he could get, including his last weekly allowance. That was the only reason he was there. He didn't feel the danger that night like Walter thought he would. It was cold for sure. They were cold to him—James, Daniel, and Boyd. But they were always cold. He was the odd man out and everyone at the table knew it. Nevertheless, Walter seemed to know for sure that Charlie needed to go. So, he ran. That was the worst Sunday of his life.

However, today, another Sunday, maybe his best Sunday, he was, of all things, sitting in a tree, hiding with a couple of fellows he met just a few days ago. They were each in their own tree, waiting quietly. They could see each other and every now and then, signals were passed. Charlie really didn't know what the signals meant, but he played along anyway. He felt a tiny bite on the back of his neck and swung an arm around to remedy it. A mosquito. Looking at Lee, one of the two men he had met, he received a snarl with a finger to the lips. A silent "Shhh!" flashed his way. Charlie understood that sign and returned a shoulder shrug and a mouthed "Sorry!"

Leland Melville—Lee—was the greeter at the docks. Turns out, he was the same age as Charlie, twenty-one or so, but gave the impression of being much older. He was wise. He could do things too, like cut down trees, tie knots, trap, and hunt. He grew up on a farm in South Carolina and came to the territory with his cousin to try to make a living doing something other than farming. He worked at the docks, supplied game to the hotels and restaurants in town, and acted as the de facto welcome wagon. To a spoiled city kid like Charlie, who really couldn't do anything, Lee was a marvel.

Lee's cousin, Lucas Norris or Luke, was a bit older. He was bigger too, and stronger. He lacked Lee's personality and sense of humor, so he usually let his cousin take the lead. He was also good at things like Lee but had to work a bit harder at it. The added muscle helped. He was hard to impress and tended to have a sour look on his face most of the time.

Charlie liked both men and appreciated the hospitality they had shown him in such a short amount of time. They had a cabin outside of town and allowed Charlie to stay with them as long as he pulled his weight. Knowing that was impossible, Charlie agreed anyway and did what he was told as best he could. Luke was not impressed and thought Charlie a lost cause. Lee, however, took everything in stride and helped Charlie along the way. Charlie thought it was nice to have friends again.

They had been in the trees for some time. It felt like forever to Charlie and he had just about had enough. His legs were sore and he had a broken tree limb stabbing him in the ass. When he turned to find a way down, he noticed movement under his tree. He froze. He slowly tipped his head down and saw the reason for all this madness. A giant deer had walked up and was standing against the oak he was sitting in. Its antlers were huge and the deer looked to Charlie to be as large as a cow. How the hell was he supposed to kill this massive beast? He had a gun, but where should he aim? The thoughts came quickly and he started to panic. Luckily, the tension was broken with a giant *BOOM* followed by a second *BOOM* almost right on top of the first one. Charlie flinched and almost slipped out of the tree. Fortunately, the limb stabbing his butt caught his pants and his fall was halted. He steadied himself just in time to see the animal take two small, quick jumps and then fall flat. Dead.

"You were early!" Luke yelled.

"Like hell, you were late. I counted like always," replied Lee as he started his descent. "And you're lucky I hit him square, or we'd be tracking him all over these woods."

Luke started down too, mumbling curse words under his breath. The two met at the deer, looking over the bounty. Luke said, "Get down here and help us roll him over, Charlie, you might learn something."

Charlie made it to the ground, feeling proud he hadn't fallen to his death. That alone was a victory. He reached down, grabbed the huge animal's leg and helped roll it onto its back. It was so heavy. The three stood silently, taking it in. Luke knelt and with his right hand, scraped away the blood and guts blocking the view of the kill shots. Charlie grimaced. Luke stood back up and smiled at Lee. He put out his hand and said, "Nice shot."

Lee grabbed Luke's hand and shook hard, replying, "Right back at ya! We're gettin' there." The two men continued to discuss the kill in terms Charlie barely understood. What he gathered by looking at the wounds was that both men had shot at almost the same time and hit within inches of each other. The poor animal never stood a chance. The fact that the cousins didn't consider the outcome perfection took Charlie by surprise. If they could do better, God help whatever they took aim at.

Luke started to prepare the deer for travel while Lee grabbed rope and bossed Charlie around. Charlie moved as fast as he could, following orders and loving every minute of it. This was fantastic! His mother would have gotten such a kick out of the stories of her boy's exploits in the Kansas wilderness. She probably would have compared him to the great Daniel Boone and made him and Charlie seem like equals. She had a way of building him up and making him seem better than he knew he really was. But that's a mother's duty.

He had to look away from the boys as the emotions came with the realization that he had no one with which to share this. He and his uncle Walter had gotten closer as his mother's health deteriorated. However, for most of Charlie's life, Walter was estranged. They knew very little about each other, in fact. They both tried to change that with the little time they had together at the end, which was nice. But now Charlie was gone, making it difficult—darned impossible—to bond with his only living blood relative. He felt defeated.

Speaking of Walter, Charlie remembered he was supposed to check in once he settled into the new town. He hadn't done it yet but felt like he had news now and should send it to Walter. There was also a chance Walter had sent word from his end regarding the happenings back East and what their next move would be. He waited for a break in the work and asked the cousins about the post and if there was an office in town. Naturally, Lee was the one giving the answers.

"Quindaro doesn't have a post office. Yet anyway," he said. "A few of the town founders are working on it but it's slow going on account of their 'political leanings.'"

"How do you receive notices and such?" asked Charlie.

"The city of Wyandotte, a few miles to the east collects for this area," replied Lee. "I'll point you in the right direction once we get back to town and settled."

"Thanks," said Charlie.

"You should be relatively safe as long as you leave early enough and come straight back," Lee added. "There are a couple other things we should go over too, but I'll fill you in later. We'll try to keep you alive a while longer." Charlie couldn't tell if that was supposed to be a joke. It didn't feel like it.

10.

The city of Wyandotte sat at the confluence of two rivers, the Missouri and the Kansas, or Kaw. So, too, did the Town of Kansas, soon to be known as Kansas City. Only it was on the other side of the Missouri River, looking down on its smaller neighbor from its own high bluffs. The general area became known as Kaw Point and was a documented campsite of Lewis and Clark on their epic journey across the continent.

Wyandotte's population consisted mostly of pro-slavery voters who usually sided with their more well-to-do Missouri neighbors to the east. Most were not the staunch supporters of slavery found across the river, as they themselves never had the means necessary to own another human being. But they voted that way and that was what mattered.

The town shops and hotels actually offered services to anyone who could pay. This made their politics fluid and a bit confusing. Missouri raiders were welcomed in Wyandotte as well as their Kansas counterparts, as long as they were paying customers. Any disagreement or violent outbreak between the two sides must be handled outside the city limits. If the peace was broken, punishment took the form of tariffs or outright confiscation of goods. Both sides honored the decree making Wyandotte safe, for the most part, and a lot of money.

One of the most successful businesses in Wyandotte was Stan's Place, a part-time dry goods store, full-time saloon and weapons depot. It was owned by a man named Stan, of course, whose only devotion, political or otherwise, was to his bottom line. Most in the area hated him more than smallpox. They used him anyway because he could get things no one else could. He was a magician.

David Sorter, who sat alone in the outdoor portion of Stan's, was not like most in the area. He liked Stan because he could count on him. Give him money, he gives you bullets, or whiskey, or whatever. Stan was simple and David liked simple.

The sun was shining brightly today, causing David to choose a seat under the covered area to enjoy his cigar, water and whiskey. He had given his crew instructions and had already paid Stan, so he had a moment to relax while they loaded up. The goods were sorely needed, especially the bullets and powder. He and the men who rode with him had been busy. It seems he had shot more bullets over the last couple of months than he had during the entire Mexican war, and from the local chatter, it was only going to get worse.

The opportunity to relax was rare, and David tried his best to clear his mind and enjoy it. He watched the people of Wyandotte, or "Y &" as some called it, come and go. He nodded hello to folks walking by. Some kids chased a dog down the street, and it made him happy. The dog more so than the kids. He was off duty and loving it. Hell, he even ignored the stranger who came into town a few minutes ago. He barely even noticed the kid wandering like he was lost, head down, hat pulled low, in a hurry, out of place, wearing strange boots. City boots. Why would this kid sneak into the post office? Who sneaks into a post office? David couldn't stop it now, his mind, a machine, started to work, assessing every detail. He was saved only by a large glass bottle slammed down on the table in front of him.

"A special gift for my best customer," yelled Stan, breaking David's concentration.

"Right. What did I pay for this?" asked David, holding up the bottle to the sunlight for inspection. "You're not the gift-giving type, Stan."

"Just take it and let me know what you think. It came in

with a load last night. Seems a new place opened just north of here, close to Weston. I can get plenty more and cheap, but I want to make sure my customers approve before I buy more." David was reading the label when Stan finished, "It may be shit, but try it anyway."

"Anything for you, my friend," David replied, tapping Stan's chest with the neck of the bottle.

David's right hand man, Colonel William Tough, joined the conversation. "Am I interrupting something special?"

"Maybe," David joked. "Stan gave me a gift."

Colonel Tough feigned surprise and took the bottle from David for his own inspection. David let him and Stan discuss the new product while his eyes scanned the street for the stranger he saw earlier. Back to work. There he is!

"Who is that?" David interrupted. His stare pointed the colonel in the direction of his quarry, and Tough picked him up almost instantly. He and David had ridden together for so long, they could communicate without words. Stan was left scanning the entire street, finally settling on the stranger after David and Tough had already started to move. Stan had never seen the stranger before either and told David as much as he and Tough gathered their things. The three men said their farewells as Tough went out the back way and David exited straight onto the street. "Keep me in the loop, gentlemen," hollered Stan. "And let me know about the whiskey."

David and the colonel heard every word Stan said but only replied with nods. They moved separately but as a unit through the town, between buildings, keeping out of sight of the stranger who, by the looks of it, wouldn't notice them anyway. They watched as he stopped and peered into a couple shop windows, only to turn and continue his tour. They followed as the stranger made his way toward the riverfront where the ferryboats docked and watched him pay the dockhand the price of a ticket.

David hid behind a coach that was preparing to leave town and waited to see which way the stranger would travel. If he went west up the Kaw, he would be heading into Kansas Territory and may not be a threat. North on the Missouri would take him between the Kansas Territory and the state of Missouri. No way to know if he was heading to Quindaro, Parkville or Leavenworth. However, if he went east on the Missouri into enemy territory, the stranger was marked. And the next time David saw him, he would be sorry.

Colonel Tough waited as well, across and down the street with an eye on the same target. As the northbound ferry docked and the stranger approached to board, he and David shared a look. David thought for a moment, then shook his head. No need to follow this one. For now. Tough, who was preparing to take the chase to the next level, stood down.

11.

The Missouri River is the longest river in North America. It travels from western Montana to the city of St. Louis where it drains into the more famous Mississippi, then vanishes. The water is muddy, filled with silt swept up from the deep bottom. Jetties appear out of nowhere and create whirlpools capable of spinning small boats sideways. It flows south for the most part, makes a sharp left at Kansas City and travels through the entire state of Missouri, cutting it almost in half.

From the city of Wyandotte, you can travel north against the current six miles to Quindaro. It is in the Kansas Territory so will be on the port or left side. A couple miles farther, you will come to Parkville, a small Missouri town. It will be on the starboard or right side. Still farther, Leavenworth and Atchison, both in Kansas Territory. And much farther, St. Joseph, Missouri. The river twists and turns at roughly five miles an hour through this area, so a small trip from Wyandotte to Quindaro may take an hour or more depending on how fast the current is working against you.

Charlie had taken this ferry ride before, though not on this vessel. *The Lightfoot* brought him to town the first time, if memory served. With so many ferryboats on the river, it was hard to know for sure. Today, he would ride the *Otis Webb*. He knew that because of the giant sign hanging below the wheelhouse. It read, "Welcome aboard the *Otis Webb*. Otis Webb, Captain." He felt more comfortable traveling this way than the shorter three miles over land. The boats never went the wrong way and ended up lost in the woods or captured by Indians or Ruffians.

He boarded early and sat alone waiting for their departure. He sat on the boat's floor, leaning against the cabin wall, and tried to stay out of the way of other travelers as they boarded. Just as he got comfortable and contemplated a quick nap, the engine started and the craft began to move.

Captain Otis Webb yelled from the deck, giving instructions to the crew and shouting estimated times of arrival to the passengers. Charlie could hear the captain yelling but could hardly make out anything he said. That was fine. This time, he knew where he was going and about how long it would take. No surprises. He felt the engine begin to work harder and assumed they had made it out into the main channel and started to climb the hill.

Charlie was satisfied with the day so far. He made it in and out of Wyandotte without incident and was able to send the letter he had written his uncle. They had worked out a plan whereby Charlie would send the first letter by way of his uncle's business partner. This way, if the Murrays were to intercept the mail deliveries to his uncle's home, they wouldn't find the letter and trace it back to Charlie. Uncle Walter had discussed the situation with his partner and found him sympathetic to the ordeal. He, too, was no fan of the Murrays and was a hardline abolitionist. His partner would look for a marker—a small star—on the envelope. And when he saw the mark, he personally and discreetly would deliver the correspondence to Walter. Uncle Walter would then reply within a couple days and deliver his letter to his partner, who would send it on its way via the post office located near his home. The plan was perfect. Probably. This would be the first go, so its worthiness would be tested soon enough.

He reached into a small satchel wrapped around his shoulder and pulled out an apple and a few roasted hazelnuts. Quindaro was lousy with hazelnut trees and Charlie had already acquired a taste for them. Lee advised bringing a snack for the journey and as usual, he was right. Charlie was hungry. He had dinner plans with the cousins, but that was hours away. They had also invited him to help with an "important assignment" later in the evening. They wouldn't give him details but it felt like he was being accepted into something. Like they were finally allowing him to be a complete part of the group. He was honored and would do all he could to prove himself worthy.

Deep in thought and halfway through his apple, Charlie noticed the engine starting to slow. He watched a couple of other passengers ask the crew what was happening. He stood up and walked to the side of the ferry to see if he could make out the issue himself. He looked up the river but didn't see anything. They were traveling very close to the right bank for some reason. Charlie walked back across the boat to check out that side and saw the problem.

About a quarter of a mile ahead, three men sat atop horses waiting for the ferry to come to them. One of the men was waving to the captain, calling him to come closer to the bank. The other two men held rifles aimed in the general direction of the boat. Captain Webb steered the ferry as close as he could to the bank without running aground but tried to stay just far enough away that the men could not board easily. He turned and whispered instructions to one of his men, who climbed down toward the passengers and delivered what the captain had ordered. They were to stay toward the rear and, if spoken to first, say as little as possible. The deckhand gave the orders as quickly and quietly as he could, then slipped back upstairs to the cabin.

Lee warned Charlie about the possibility of a confrontation on his trip to Wyandotte. He had given Charlie the same basic advice the deckhand gave except Lee's advice was to say nothing no matter what. Lee also offered him a gun for the trip, but Charlie had passed. Although he really didn't know what he would do with it now, he wished he had tucked it in his jacket. Instead, he stood with the other passengers, unarmed and feeling extremely vulnerable.

The three men on the bank had expected the captain's maneuvers, and each tossed a rope onto the ferry, hooking it and pulling it closer to them. The bottom of the boat scraped as they pulled it right up next to them and secured it to a couple trees farther up the bank.

"Hello, Captain Webb," said one man, the obvious boss. He walked to the edge of the bank and took a seat on a large stone overlooking the ferry. He made himself comfortable.

The two other men jumped from the bank onto the ferry. They circled like jackals, searching for the weakest and most exposed. The captain reluctantly descended the stairs and walked to the edge of the ferry to converse with the leader sitting high above on the bank. The two belligerents patted Webb on the back as they passed him, a more aggressive gesture than polite, and then made their way toward Charlie and the rest of the riders. As they reached the group, they stood still, silent, coiled. After a brief moment, one spoke. "Who's first?"

12.

On his way west, Charlie had read newspaper articles about the problems in the territory. At the time, they seemed to be wild tales from some far-off land full of ignorant barbarians. Men like John Brown existed only in newspapers and the exploits, undoubtedly embellished, were blissfully publicized in order to sell copies. But now that he was here, he knew better.

People here weren't just telling stories about men like John Brown. They knew men like John Brown. They traded with them, helped them. Were like him themselves. Hell, Luke told him about a man he once met in town who claimed to have been present when "Reverend Brown hacked up those pro-slavery dogs in Osawatomie." He claimed to have helped toss the bodies on the funeral pyre, for Christ's sake. The stories were real. The people were animals. And now, looking into the eyes of the man standing in front of him on the ferry, Charlie knew he was being threatened by one for the first time.

The other passengers took their turns and all had similar stories. They were from Missouri for the most part and heading north to Parkville or Leavenworth. They intentionally avoided the words "Kansas" or "Quindaro", knowing the words alone were triggers to these men. Charlie listened carefully, making sure he could tell the same story when his time came. That time was now.

"And you there, where are you from?" asked the man. This one did the talking when it came to the passenger interviews.

"He's from down south somewhere, that one," yelled

Captain Webb, walking toward the group. "He's heading to Leavenworth, looking for work. Rode up the other day. Thus far, a non-combatant."

The captain looked over his glasses at Charlie and nodded his head slightly, so as not to be noticed by the interrogators. Charlie took Lee's advice and neither confirmed nor denied the statement.

"Is that right, son?" asked the talker.

Charlie knew he had to go with it. He just hoped the captain would continue to guide the conversation and that they could stay on the same page. Before he spoke, luckily, he remembered Lee's last piece of advice: "Oh and if you have to say something, don't talk like you're from Boston. There's a bounty on Massachusetts tongues. They pay fifty dollars each."

Charlie tried his best to sound like the cousins and replied, "Yeah."

"Yeah?" repeated the talker, stunned. He turned and looked at his quiet partner. Charlie looked that way too. The quiet man was staring at Charlie, right through him, it seemed. His face looked like he was working on a puzzle. Charlie got a chill from this one, as if he was talking to his stepbrother Boyd. He changed his tone.

"I mean yes, sir," said Charlie.

The talker turned back to Charlie. "That's better. Where at down south you from?" he asked.

Charlie picked the first state that jumped into his mind —Lee and Luke's home state. "South Carolina," he answered, hoping it was far enough away to be a safe bet.

The questions continued, "And you're heading to Leavenworth, huh? For work?" Charlie nodded. "What kind of work you do, boy?"

Good question. Charlie never really had to work at all therefore any answer would be a lie. However, he needed the right one. Farmer, lawyer, banker, blacksmith? He couldn't decide on a reply that didn't paint him into a corner. If they asked details about any job, Charlie was screwed.

"The boy can't do shit," said Captain Webb. "Just a laborer. No real skill. Hell, I'd put him to work on the ferry if I didn't have to have my sister's boys here. He'd be damn cheap. Almost as cheap as a slave." The captain turned and shot a defiant look at the leader, still sitting atop the rock on the bank.

The man on the rock smiled back at the captain, his eyes warning "tread lightly." He spoke to Charlie. "Probably hard to compete down there in Carolina, huh? All them strong black backs running around, doing all that work free of charge," he chuckled. "A poor, dumb, white bastard like you might starve."

The leader and the talker burst into laughter. The quiet one was still working on the puzzle. "I'll tell you what, boy," said the leader. "We take care of our kind around here. As long as you toe the line. Understand?"

Charlie peeked at Captain Webb who nodded slightly, giving him the answer. Charlie nodded his head yes.

The leader continued. "There's a man in Leavenworth named Harris. If you can find him, tell him I sent you, he'll put you up and give you some work. Some food too, maybe. But you gotta find him. Think you can do that?"

Charlie nodded again.

"My name is Cook, Henry Cook. Can you remember that?" asked the leader.

Another nod, yes.

"And your name is?" he asked.

"Charlie," he replied without thinking. Stupid! He should

have made something up.

"Well Charlie, we're gonna be in Leavenworth in a week or so, I'll expect to see you again when we pass through. You can repay me for my help. Understand? You remember my friend's name, don't you?" asked the leader.

Charlie kept nodding yes to everything. He didn't plan on going to Leavenworth or looking for the man there, whatever his name was. He would go along with anything to get out of the situation he was in right now. Unfortunately, he wasn't listening closely enough.

"Do you remember the name, boy?" asked the talker.

Hell. He didn't remember. "His name is…um…" Shit!

"How 'bout I help you?" The silent one finally spoke. He walked close to Charlie, splitting the crowd of passengers like the Red Sea. He reached down his leg, unsheathed a large Bowie knife and started to pick his teeth with it. "The name is Harris." He paused. "Harris. Say it." Charlie repeated the name. "If you don't think you can remember, I can carve it right here above your eyes." He stared intently at the blank canvas that was Charlie's forehead. "That way, you don't have to ask around when you get there, right? You can just walk down the street, and point up at your head," he pointed to his own head with the large blade, "let people read it. Then they can say, 'Oh yeah, I know Mr. Harris, he stays straight over there.' And they can point you in the right direction. Think that would work?"

Charlie swallowed hard. All he could muster was "I'll remember."

The quiet man said nothing and headed back toward the bank to join the leader. The talker was beside himself. He had never heard a better idea in his life. The three men thanked the captain for his cooperation and saddled up. Henry Cook gave one more glance at Charlie and with a tip of his hat, said, "Good luck, son, see you soon."

13.

Captain Webb stood beside Charlie as his boys pushed the ferry back into the main channel. They both watched as the three men on shore mounted their horses, chatted a bit, then began to move.

"It's over, son, relax," said the captain, putting his arm around Charlie. "We made it another day." He took a deep breath, then hollered to the crew, "Hit it, boys, we have some time to make up!" He walked toward a set of stairs that led to his wheelhouse.

Charlie finally awoke from the dazed state he was in and yelled to the captain. "What the hell was that?" he asked. "And who the hell was that? I thought they were going to kill me."

The questions came fast and furious until the captain finally cut him off. "Oh, for Christ's sake, shut up! Take a breath. Jesus, you sound like my wife." He pulled his pipe from his shirt pocket. "Come up to the wheelhouse and I'll fill you in."

Charlie followed the captain up the stairs and waited patiently for the details. His heart was still racing from the incident, but he kept his mouth shut so as not to irritate the old man. He seemed to have a short fuse. Once settled on a course, the captain turned to Charlie and started talking.

He explained that the man they just encountered, Henry Cook, led a small band of Missouri Ruffians who patrolled the area. Their job was to gather intelligence for a much larger group headed by General Atchison. Cook's men rousted the ferryboats, wagon trains and the lot, castigating any Free

State pioneers they came across. They were on the lookout for weapons mostly, caches sent from back east to help in the fighting. However, they would often confiscate anything of value. Money, luggage, supplies, sometimes even the clothes the travelers wore. They made it clear to the poor, unfortunate, naked bastards that they were not welcome in the territory.

Cook's men were a rowdy bunch. He was a fair leader, demanding complete loyalty, but never requiring an oath of any kind. And he never needed it. Desertion or insubordination were capital crimes in his regiment and all the men knew it. But they joined anyway. Some were beckoned by the cause, others by the high rate of compensation for what was considered a low output of effort. Thievery and intimidation come naturally to some men, and these qualities were just what Cook needed. He tended to let his dogs run wild as long as they obeyed when he needed them to do so. And for the most part, they did.

However, there was one story the captain loved to tell. During the Mexican War, Cook was a trusted lieutenant of Captain Philip Kearny and was issued a dapple-gray horse for being a 1st US Cavalry Dragoon. Kearny demanded all his men ride the same gray horse so he and everyone else would know the men who made up his elite unit. Since then, Cook still rode the grays. Some time ago, one of Cook's men decided to take his horse for a ride just for the fun of it. Cook happened upon the man as he returned to camp and told him he looked stunning atop the noble gray steed. The man tipped his hat in gratitude, for the moment proud of his leader's appreciation. However, the moment didn't last. Cook pulled his pistol and emptied it into the man, the last two bullets as he lay on the ground. That night, a drunken Cook wrote an apology to his men and posted it in camp. In it, he offered them the opportunity to ride his horse, shoot his pistols, drink his whiskey and sleep with his wife. But only if they came to him first and asked. Smartly, no one ever took him up on that.

The inquisitor riding with Cook was common muscle who most people referred to as "Blue." No one knew for sure if that was a first or last name or just a nickname given by his compatriots. But he tended to answer to it so whatever it was, it worked. Blue had been in the area since 1855, came from the South with 400 or so men promised land and money in exchange for a pro-slavery vote in the territory. Jefferson Buford, the leader of the colonization effort, had already returned to Dixie. But many of the men who journeyed with him in what came to be known as "Buford's Expedition" remained and fought proudly for the cause. Blue was one of these men. He wasn't all that mean or smart, for that matter. But he was loyal as hell. And Cook rewarded that loyalty with a leadership position within the crew.

One of the men Blue was in charge of was called "Happy," the other man on the boat. He didn't have a name that anyone knew, so Happy was what people called him. Actually, no one called him Happy except Cook, and even he didn't do it that often. Cook had asked Happy his name early on and was rebuffed with silence. Cook, never one to quibble and being a bit of a satirist, pronounced him "Happy" and it stuck. Others would use the moniker when talking *about* Happy, but never when talking *to* Happy. To his face, he would usually be referred to as "Buddy" or "Friend." The captain was pretty sure Happy was born in the area, but he wasn't positive. Also, he had what seemed like an older brother and either a sister or wife who would sometimes follow behind him in town. They were a weird lot, to be sure. Maybe hill folk from Southern Missouri. Or Arkansas. Hard telling.

The captain seemed genuinely surprised that no harm had come to Charlie during the ordeal. He figured Charlie would have at least taken a little beating for being new to the area and an unknown. It was smart to cover the northeastern accent that he had when he boarded the ferry. Webb had heard it earlier and that's why he decided to intercede on Charlie's behalf. He hated seeing bad things happen to his passengers.

Rather than a beating, it seemed like Cook had another thing in mind. Charlie, being an able-bodied young man from the South, must have piqued Cook's interest, and the mission turned from intelligence to recruitment. Being offered employment around these parts was a big deal. Having the offer come directly from a man of Cook's status was unheard of. The captain paused. Then he looked at Charlie with sadness and said, "You're in real trouble, son. You need to go to Leavenworth."

Charlie's reply came quickly, "I'm not going to Leavenworth."

"You have to, boy," the captain interrupted. "They know your face. And your name. Wait, is Charlie your real name?" he asked with hope.

Charlie nodded yes, shamefully.

"Stupid, stupid, stupid," the captain mumbled. "You got to get smart, like quick, boy, you hear? These men are not to be trifled with. They will kill you like you're one of these squirrels running around here. Understand? They probably have you on some list now, and if you don't show, they'll come looking for you. Hell, they'll probably come ask me! Goddammit!" Charlie was right. No sooner had the fuse been lit than the bomb went off.

Charlie tried to calm the old man down, but nothing seemed to work until he said, "Alright, I'll go up there. To Leavenworth. Alright?"

The captain asked, "Today?"

"Not today," Charlie answered. "But I will go. I promise. I don't want to cause you any trouble, so I'll go and at least make an appearance. Then when I leave, it'll all be on me." He paused and tried to lighten the mood. "And when I go, the ride up is on the house."

"The hell it is! There's no free rides in this life, boy," Webb replied.

Charlie felt he made a connection, that the old man might actually like him. He slapped the captain on the shoulder and said, "Come on, Captain, cut me some slack. I almost died back there."

Captain Webb shook his head but couldn't help the smirk on his face. "Half fare."

Charlie replied with a wink, "Deal."

14.

Charlie saw his mother for the last time two nights before she passed. She knew the time was near and the threat her death would bring to her son. She and her brother Walter had made plans for her estate, but if anything happened to Charlie in the meantime, it would all be moot. Walter heard through several business associates how devastated Charlie was with his mother's sickness. The story also included the notion that no one should be surprised if Charlie were to do something rash once his mother was gone. After Walter heard the same story on separate occasions, he figured someone was laying the groundwork for Charlie's eventual breakdown and probable "suicide." There was no doubt the Murrays were behind it and that Charlie needed to get as far away from Boston as possible.

Every detail of that night stuck with Charlie. The smell of the sickness in his mother's room. Her in bed, lying under a mountain of blankets but still freezing. Her strength gone, she couldn't even talk, only mumble. However, Charlie was able to make out a couple words. "Go" and "love." He left that night.

Unbeknownst to him, she held on for two more evenings just to give Charlie the head start he needed. When the last breath left her body, a wry smile lay upon her lips. Her nurse called her the *Mona Lisa*.

Charlie saw that same smile as he looked at his mother, Sarah, standing in front of him. The sunlight made her glow. The tall grass of the meadow covering her to the knees made it look like she was floating. Then again, maybe she was floating.

She was dead, after all, and dead people could probably float if they so choose. Hell, dead people could probably do all sorts of wonderful things. That would explain the smile on Sarah's face. She knew she had powers now, or at least fewer limitations. Death looked good on her.

She looked healthy, happy. And that made Charlie happy. He hadn't felt like this in so long that he almost laughed out loud. He started to talk, to tell her how much he missed her and loved her. He wanted to tell her about his journey west and all the adventures he'd had thus far. She would be so proud. But Sarah cut him off by placing a silent finger to her lips. He waited for her to speak but she didn't. She came closer, smiling. She placed her hand on his cheek, and it felt like she was holding him in her arms. The caress was magical.

Charlie wanted only to say, "I love you." He needed to say that to her in the worst way. It felt like his life depended on it. He tried to speak, but nothing came out. His mother shook her head and put her finger to his lips this time, but he moved away. Charlie tried again to talk but had the same result. Oh God, something was wrong.

He couldn't speak. He couldn't move his arms or his legs. He felt like he was on fire. His eyes burned. His throat too, clear down to his lungs. The pain came out of nowhere and overwhelmed him. It had a taste too. What was that? Fish? Mud? What the hell?

His mother moved closer still, reaching out and holding his shoulders as they shook. He tried again to speak but still couldn't take the necessary breath. He began to panic. His mother leaned in face-to-face and spoke. "Breathe, child. You can, you must. The river is in you but you can fight it. Get your bearings."

That expression, "Get your bearings," was Charlie and Sarah's secret weapon. A personal hymn only they would sing, and it got Charlie through several difficult moments as a child.

Sarah used to say her father would look into her eyes and slowly utter the phrase, making a chopping motion with his right hand with each word. "Get. Your. Bearings." It meant nothing more than the literal "find your position relative to other things," but it had a powerful effect on Sarah as a child and wielded the same influence over Charlie. It brought calm. Clarity. Focus. It made everything around them slow down and gave them time to put things into perspective. That's what Charlie needed to do right now, quickly.

He began to retrace his steps, find the last thing he remembered. He was on the ferryboat with Captain Webb. They argued about something. Not really an argument, a squabble, at the most. What about? Well, the captain had decided he wasn't going to make the normal stop at Quindaro because "they had eyes on them." What the hell did that mean? Oh, the men, the wild-eyed Missourians who stopped and boarded the ferry were still around, trailing from a distance, watching. The captain didn't want to stop in Quindaro because everyone was supposed to be heading farther north, at least that's what he told the Ruffians. No one was traveling to Quindaro, so he couldn't stop there or they would know he had lied. "You don't let these men find out you lied to them, you understand? It'll be the end of you!" the captain screamed. The next stop was going to be another couple of hours in Parkville, on the Missouri side, and there was no changing that.

Two hours up, an hour or more wait for another ferry coming back down the river, then a two-hour trip back? That wasn't going to work. Charlie was to meet Lee and Luke that evening to help with a task, a secret task about…something. *Why do you think Lee wouldn't just say what it was? Focus!* Anyway, the trip north to Parkville was not in the cards, and Charlie decided that once the ferry rounded the bend and the men couldn't see them anymore, he would jump and, oh hell, swim for it.

That's why he and the captain were fighting! He didn't

want Charlie to jump. Webb called him a "damn fool" and grabbed his arm, but Charlie swung away and went for it. After all, he was a strong swimmer, went swimming in the harbor all the time. The last thing he remembered was Captain Webb yelling, "You're gonna drown, stupid ass!" Apparently, the captain was right.

Charlie's eyes widened as he put the pieces together. He reached for Sarah, for help. She let him grab her, smiling, relieved, glad Charlie had finally solved the riddle. She was so proud. Her voice sounded almost like a laugh when she spoke.

"Oh, my brilliant son. My beautiful, bright Lazarus." She hugged him tight until the struggle left him, then pushed him away, her arms super strong.

She looked into his eyes and continued. "You have your bearings now, Charlie. All you have to do is breathe, silly, and everything will be fine."

She waited. He tried. He tried again. Nothing yet.

Sarah sighed and said, "Very well, you poor, sad creature. I will help you. Just remember, in case I don't see you for a while, I love you. I love you more than anyone has ever loved a person or thing since the beginning of time. You are my beautiful son, the reason for my life. And I will be with you always."

Sarah dropped her arms to her side and the smile went away. Her head cocked to the side a bit, her jaw tightened. She took a deep breath. Then, as her right hand smacked the side of Charlie's face, she shouted, "Now breathe!"

The river water exploded from his chest, left his mouth and flew at least eight feet in the air. He rolled onto his side and choked the rest out, filling his waterlogged lungs with thick, fresh air as quickly as he could. It hurt, to be sure, but he was alive and never felt better.

Charlie rolled over onto his back again and slowly, carefully tried to open his eyes. He blinked again and again, removing bits of mud with each round. As his vision began to clear, a shape started to take form, kneeling close to him. It was a person, a real one this time. He knew because it was holding his hand. The sun setting low behind the stranger made it tough to make out much detail, but from the distinctly feminine form of the chest, he assumed it was a woman. She was dark, and not just from the backlighting of the sun. She was black. And she smelled like coffee and smoke from a fire. She smelled like heaven.

15.

Captain Webb ran to the wheelhouse as soon as Charlie hit the water. He had to slow down, and if Cook and his men noticed, he would just have to face the music. Luckily, the ferry had turned a corner and the men were out of sight. The harassment was over. At least for today.

He slowed the boat the best he could without letting the current take him backwards. The kid was back there somewhere, and the captain didn't want to run him over. He screamed orders to his deckhands to start tossing the floats and ropes over, but he feared they were already too far away to help.

He was scanning the water and trying to drive at the same time when he noticed a splash near the shore. If they were back home in Florida, that splash would spell the end for the kid. Lucky for him, gators didn't troll the Missouri. There were things to fear in the river, no doubt. Water moccasins, copperheads, even gigantic catfish. However, nothing as deadly as a fifteen-foot gator.

He noticed movement on the shore near the splash and saw Dux, a local woman, coming out of the timber, getting close to the riverbank. She was looking at something, and it didn't take him long to figure out what it was. Cuff was in the water. This stupid kid is the luckiest son of a bitch in the entire world! First, Cook and his boys didn't lay a finger on him. Then, he jumps in the river when Cuff, the only person within a hundred miles who could swim in this river, happens to be nearby.

Cuff disappeared under the surface for a moment, then came back up, holding the kid. Then he used the current to get back to the bank, downriver where Dux was waiting to pull them out.

Dux pushed on the boy's chest and put her mouth to his a few times. Cuff sat nearby catching his breath. Soon enough, the boy rolled over on his own and Dux raised her hands to the sky, thanking God for his help. Cuff stood up and gave a wave to Captain Webb, a sign the kid was alive and would probably make it. The captain tipped his hat to Cuff and revved the engine to get going again.

"Next time I see that goddamn kid, he's gonna wish he died in the river." Then he burst into laughter.

16.

Clarina Nichols was the editor of the Quindaro newspaper, the *Chin-do-wan*, which took its name from the Wyandotte Indian word meaning "leader." She arrived in Quindaro shortly after the town incorporated and was a pillar of the community's leadership. She was a widow and had an adult son named Tom. They lived together in town, taking the upper story of the newspaper office and turning it into a two-bedroom suite.

Clarina was a powerful force, being close friends with some of the most tried and true abolitionists and suffragists in the country. She knew and was known by the Anthony family, Susan B. and her brother Daniel. Daniel happened to live just north in the town of Leavenworth and was one of a few brave enough to rail against slavery in the mostly pro-slavery village. Other friends included Elizabeth Cady Stanton, Thomas Wentworth Higginson and William Lloyd Garrison. She was also very close to the founder of the New England Emigrant Aid Company, Eli Thayer, and the Beecher family—Henry, the preacher/arms dealer and Harriet, the author.

In Quindaro, she held several posts in the town council and worked diligently to perform the duties assumed by her positions. However, the role she was most proud of was being the second in command of the Quindaro stop on the Underground Railroad. It had taken some effort, but over time, Clarina had earned the trust of the local engineer, a black woman named Dux who lived down the hill on the delta. She had proven her worth and, more importantly, her loyalty to Dux and the cause. Now she used every resource available to help move people to freedom.

Tonight, a "package" was being moved from the Parkville, Missouri area, through the dangerous woodlands of the delta, across the river and into Quindaro. Once there, the traveler would stay an evening or two in a fruit cellar below Clarina's building. It was outfitted with an emergency exit through a false well dug in the side yard. Clarina and Tom would care for the traveler, providing food, water and occasionally medical services. Then, when the time was right, lying flat and quiet in a wagon loaded with hay or bags of hazelnuts, the traveler would start the next leg of the journey.

Seldom did anyone know the entire route an escaped slave would take. It was dangerous for anyone to have that much knowledge. In these parts, folks knew a stop or two but that was about it. Clarina, however, because of her standing, knew the entire route, clear to Nebraska. First the Grinter House, where Moses Grinter operated a ferry across the Kaw River. Then to John Stewart's property just south of Lawrence. Stewart was a Methodist minister and a fiery abolitionist. Not as hard lined as John Brown but not far off either.

The road then went north through Lawrence, with stops at either John Doy's house or Joseph Gardner's cabin. North of there, a traveler could find safety at the Nemaha Half-Breed Indian Reservation. This was the last stop before making it to Allen and Barbara Mayhew's cabin, nicknamed John Brown's cave, in Nebraska City, Nebraska. Barbara's younger brother, John Henry Kagi, traveled and killed with the Reverend Brown and acted as his Secretary of War. From Nebraska City, the road could go east five hundred miles to Chicago or straight north to Canada. Either way, the hardest segment was behind the traveler.

Clarina and Dux stood in the dark near the front door of her office. Tom stood a post down the hill a bit, a shotgun at the ready. There were scouts all around using small lanterns

Dux made by hand. They had stubby wicks that burned slowly and the glass outer shells were wrapped with black fabric. The scouts could send signals by peeling back the fabric and allowing the light to break the darkness. A complex code was established that would keep everyone informed on the progress of the delivery. Clarina and Dux could see several of the scouts and were monitoring the transmissions. There were two across the river, one walking the clearing and two in the trees. Normally, there were three lights in the trees. This time, however, Lee and Luke, two of Clarina's most trustworthy helpers, seemed to be a man short. So far, it hadn't mattered. The delta was still. The slave hunters were doing their work elsewhere. Things were running smoothly.

Finally, three hours after the intrigue had commenced, Cuff emerged from the thicket at the bottom of the hill. Two runners followed, a boy and girl, both appearing to be under the age of fifteen. They met Tom first. He kept the shotgun leveled, looking into the thicket for any trouble that may come through. He looked to Cuff, who reassured him everything was fine. They hadn't been followed. Tom reached for the bag the young girl was carrying, and the group hurried up the hill to where Clarina and Dux were waiting.

The women rushed the runaways inside and settled them in the fruit cellar. It wasn't long before the lights in the trees flashed the "all clear" sign and everyone could relax.

Dux and Cuff said goodbye to the others. "We have something to attend to at home," said Dux. "We must miss the celebration this time around. I promise we will make it to the next one." Her explanation stopped there. She hugged Clarina as she finished her goodbye. "Say hello to the Odd Fellows for me. I am grateful to God for their helping hands."

Clarina answered, "I will."

Tom grabbed a jug—the special occasion jug—and asked, "Are you coming, Mother?"

She answered, "Yes, I'm on my way. Go ahead and start without me."

17.

When Charlie finally awoke, it was dark. He had come to a few times before, but between his lack of sleep over the last month and the episode in the river, his body wouldn't allow him to get up. He still felt weak but better. The sleep had helped. He took a moment to focus on his surroundings, figuring out quickly he was someplace new.

He was lying on a bed in a one-room cabin, and a fire was burning, keeping the space warm and cozy. There was a small cot across the room near the door. Shelves were nailed to the wall, there was a bookcase and what looked like a wagon filled with pots, pans and other cooking utensils. There was a pot near the fire with a large cast iron lid atop it…something was simmering, overwhelming his sense of smell. Charlie was hungry. Being dead will do that to you.

His body ached a bit, mainly in his chest, but he was able to sit up and stretch. He noticed his pants and shirt hanging above the fire, put there to dry, and they had. He reached for them, coming closer to the pot of food, and his stomach growled loudly. Suddenly, he heard movement outside, near the door. It sounded like footsteps on stairs and a porch. Someone was coming in.

He threw his clothes onto the bed, reached for a fire poker leaning against the chimney stones and prepared himself for a confrontation. A large, muscular black man entered holding a rifle and a jug of water. It was Cuff. He looked at Charlie standing against the wall, in his shorts, holding the poker. Cuff laughed and, turning to the doorway behind him, said, "He's up," then went about his business.

Behind him entered an older woman, black as well, round but solid. It was Dux. She smiled at Charlie and said, "Ah, you are feeling better, yes?" She noticed the poker and continued, "Good idea, the fire needs some attention. Give it a poke, we'll eat when the heat is right." She, too, went about her business.

Charlie rushed to put his clothes on. Cuff walked over and took the poker, paying Charlie no mind. He stoked the fire while Dux grabbed a wooden spoon and tended to the pot. She yelled and asked Charlie if he was hungry, and he nodded silently. Both Cuff and Dux, busy working, not hearing a reply, turned and looked to Charlie. Realizing his mistake, he said, "I'm sorry. Yes, ma'am, I'm very hungry."

Dux turned to Cuff and said, "It is ready now, set the table." He laid a board over a shelf and a table materialized. She invited Charlie to sit and filled three bowls.

Charlie ate quickly at first, in silence. Once the stew hit his system and he regained a bit of strength, he spoke to Dux. "You saved me. At the river, I mean. I remember you, vaguely. Thank you. And for your hospitality." He looked around the room. "I can pay you…"

Dux cut him off. "You were saved and given comfort because you are one of God's children, not for payment. You can keep your money. It buys nothing in these woods anyhow."

Cuff grunted. He didn't agree.

She corrected Cuff with a look and continued. "Eat slowly now. Too much too fast will do more harm than good. You need water too." She ordered Cuff, "Get him water." He did.

As Charlie drank, Dux introduced herself. "My name is Dorcas but people here call me Dux." Pronounced "Doo." She lived here on the delta, mostly by herself, unless Cuff was visiting. Her owner, a local man named William Walker, bought her a few years ago and since then, had allowed her to live free. He offered several times to send her north, but she refused. The area called to her and she felt God put her here to do his work. Walker, a Christian man himself, acquiesced. However, fearing her capture by slave hunters and the chance she would be shipped south, Walker kept the papers on Dux as proof of his ownership. If caught, she was as protected as any other piece of his property would be in the eyes of the law. At least on paper. And while Mr. Walker was alive.

"This man," she continued, pointing to Cuff, "is called Cuff." "He was born on a plantation in Alabama on a Friday, hence the name." Male slaves born on Fridays were given the "day of birth" name of Kufi. Cuff liked the shortened version better and took the name as his one and only. He was freed several years ago when, on his deathbed, St. Peter himself paid a visit to his owner. As Dickens' ghosts had changed poor Ebenezer, the plantation owner, too, was changed, by the most powerful of motivators. Fear. So, in return for his immortal soul, the man got rid of all his property and freed every last slave, including Cuff. Better late than never. Since then, Cuff moved from place to place. Only recently, he began staying around the Quindaro area, helping Dux fulfill her purpose. "He also pulls foolish young men from the river whenever God calls on him to do so."

The woman finished and said to Charlie, "Now you."

Charlie thanked Cuff for saving his life, Dux again too. Then, he told them about his ride from Wyandotte and his reasoning for leaping from the ferry. Dux spit at the mention of Henry Cook but seemed pleased upon hearing Charlie was acquainted with Lee and Luke. Remembering the missing scout in the tree, it all added up. She had made certain in her introduction to let the stranger know both she and Cuff were free, just in case he was not an ally. Now, it seemed the boy could be trusted. Cuff even warmed to him a bit, pouring Charlie half a cup of wine.

The three talked for an hour or so when Dux finally ended

things. She packed up the table items and told Cuff to head back to town and let the cousins know their boy will be staying in the cabin tonight.

Cuff replied, "I'm not going back to town tonight, it's too late. I'll take him home tomorrow, at daybreak."

Dux made sure Cuff understood this time. "The boy will be needing your bed tonight, so you won't have a place here anyway. By morning, there's no telling where them two will be. You will go tonight. They will be with the others for a few more hours, so you have time to make it to the meeting place. You can stay in town this evening and bring them back with you first thing."

Cuff tried to argue and Charlie tried to make it clear he didn't want to impose, but Dux was hearing none of it. She finished Cuff's directions. "And make sure you don't doddle getting back here in the morning. We have plenty of things that need doing. Hear?"

Cuff grabbed his rifle and a biscuit for the road and gave the only answer he could, "Yes, ma'am."

18.

The Independent Order of Odd Fellows, Western Territories, Lodge 13 met in the back room of the W&M Hardware Depot. The store, owned by William Walker and Reverend Mills, sold a variety of items from nails to coveralls and was centrally located within the town of Quindaro. The members of the Order included the most important leaders of the community along with like-minded folks from the surrounding area who could attend the meetings and pay the dues. Unlike most Fraternal Orders, the Odd Fellows allowed women as members under the "Beautiful Rebekah Degree," named after the biblical wife of Isaac, mother of Jacob and Esau. Lodge 13 had several women members and went a step further by bestowing membership privileges to people of color. The more the merrier.

The Order had a standing meeting, usually on the second Saturday of the month, and several smaller ad hoc gatherings as necessary. One such gathering, for the exclusive members only and usually held in secret, was the Celebration of Liberty. This meeting, more of a party, was held after the "all clear" signal was given and a runaway was moved to safety. The members would recount the night's activities and make changes to their strategy if the leadership deemed it necessary. Tonight's activities had gone as planned and resulted in two souls being a step closer to freedom. Everyone in the store's back room was pleased.

The Noble Grand, Abelard Guthrie, started the meeting as usual. "Officers, take your stations. Guardians, secure the doors."

The Inside and Outside Guardians, Lee and Luke respectively, closed and locked the doors, and Lee replied, "Noble Grand, the doors are secure."

Abe then consulted the warden, Tom Nichols. "Warden, examine all present that we may know them to be Brothers or Sisters."

Tom raised a wine-filled glass in the air, his second already, and replied, "Noble Grand, all present are Brothers!"

The room let out a cheer and the festivities began.

Tonight's group was small but mighty. Clarina as treasurer and Tom as warden were required to attend. They would have been there anyway. Lee and Luke held lower posts as door monitors but were working their way up the ladder. William Walker, half owner of the store and full owner of Dux, was there along with his business partner and town spiritual advisor, Reverend Mills.

A Jayhawker named David Sorter had just returned to town and made it to the meeting. He and his men had been gone a week or so, causing as much trouble as possible for their Missouri neighbors. They, like their counterpart Henry Cook, were heroes to their followers but reviled by those they opposed. Sorter and his second-in-command Colonel William Tough, who was also at the meeting, were men of violent means who accepted their violent natures willingly. In fact, many locals feared them as much as they feared the enemy. With good reason.

The Noble Grand was the vice president of the incorporated town of Quindaro. He was also the head of the town council and a territorial representative. He took his work seriously and was well respected in the town and territory at large. However, his greatest achievement, at least as far as the men of the area were concerned, was his marriage to the Wyandotte Indian princess after whom the town was named, Nancy Quindaro Brown. She was considered a beauty by anyone who had eyes, and for an older man like Abe to have won her hand was nothing short of a miracle. Of all his titles, that of "Nancy's husband" brought the most esteem. She was also a member of the Order but was not in attendance due to an illness in her family. A few other members milled about as well. Most gathered around the Noble Grand.

The aim of all Odd Fellows was to elevate every person to a higher noble plane. To extend aid to those in need, to war against vice in every form and to be a great moral power and influence on all of humanity. They did so by visiting the sick, burying the poor and promoting the Order's basic principles of friendship, love and truth. Finally, they were to be humble and motivated by the philosophical question of "How am I going to spend my life?" The members all held these beliefs, some more than others, naturally, but occasionally disagreed on the methods employed. Therefore, there were definite factions within Lodge 13: one led by Abe, the other by Sorter.

Clarina was one of a few who could ride the line between the two parties, so she moved freely within the room. She was talking to Lee about the night's activities, thanking him for his help and commending him and his cousin on a job well done. However, in her opinion, the area was too large for two scouts to monitor. Three was the ideal number. They should stick with that next time around.

David Sorter overheard Clarina and intervened. He chastised Lee, "You two covered the trees by yourself?" Lee shrank. "I thought we went over this, two won't cut it. If you're short a man, you get in touch with me, it's that simple. You don't take that risk, Lee. Besides, that's not a decision you make on your own!"

Clarina tried to defuse the situation, but Lee wanted to provide an explanation. "I'm sorry, Mrs. Clarina. Luke and I had a third man, but he didn't show. I apologize, ma'am." He turned to David. "I should have let you know, David, and I will next time. I'm sorry."

Clarina was satisfied but David was not. "A third man, huh? Who?" he asked.

Lee told David and Clarina about Charlie and how he and Luke had taken the new kid in. Charlie was from Boston and had been sent by the Aid Society, so they trusted him. He had become a fast friend. Lee also told them about Charlie's trip to Wyandotte and the fact that he never returned. He and Luke were worried and planned to go searching for Charlie the next morning.

David was content. "Makes sense." However, he decided to press the kid a bit, just for fun. "Did you plan on bringing him here tonight? To the meeting?"

Lee's eyes darted to the floor. He started to answer but David didn't allow it. The Jayhawk leader took over.

"Are you kidding me?" He looked at Clarina, shaking his head disapprovingly. Before he tore into Lee again, David called Luke over to join in the lesson. "You don't bring outsiders to an Order meeting! You sure as hell don't bring outsiders to an Order meeting after a night like tonight. There are secrets to be kept, boys!" David took a breath and a swig of his whiskey. "One more time, you don't make those types of decisions. I do." The cousins took their thrashings like men.

Hearing Lee's chiding, Abe approached and offered his opinion. "It's a small wonder, but David and I are in complete agreement on this matter, Leland. Your young friend needs vetting before he can come to the hall, and it must be done by me or an officer of the Order."

David, not being an elected official of the Order, shook his head and gave a huff.

Abe looked his way and continued. "I suppose Sorter's approval would carry some weight, but there are procedures and they must be followed to the letter. Is that understood, gentlemen?"

A "yes sir" came from both boys.

Being on the same side as Abe made David uncomfortable. Especially against Lee and Luke. He liked the boys and trusted their judgment more than most. If they thought the new kid was safe, he probably was. All he really wanted was to give Lee a hard time, and he did that. He quickly flipped sides and threw his arm around Lee's shoulders. "Goddamn, Abe, give the kids a break already. They apologized, what more do you want? Jesus, you just can't let anything go, can you?"

Abe turned, clearly not amused, turned and rejoined his group. He seemed to be the only one who found David's hilarity tiresome. Clarina shook her head and called David "childish" but couldn't suppress the smile that came with it.

With the business portion concluded and the mood lightened, Tom offered refills to any in need, proposing toasts as he went. Reaching Colonel Tough near the entryway, Tom stopped, hearing a pounding on the outer door. He shushed the group and they all listened intently. The pattern was correct, the secret knock executed.

Tough opened the inner door and disappeared in the space between entries. David followed closely behind. The rest of the group stayed put, not knowing how to handle something so unorthodox. Once a meeting was started, it was not to be interrupted. It wasn't long before a man walked into the room, breathing heavily. It was Cuff. He scanned the room and found the cousins, then spoke. "I pulled a fish out of the river. It says it belongs to you two."

19.

From across the street, Walter stared at the giant mahogany door of Florendo's, a restaurant in downtown Boston. He sat on a bench, waiting patiently for an old family friend to finish his dinner. He had followed the man for the better part of the day, looking for the perfect opening for a "chance" reunion. The gathering this afternoon at Rowe's Pier, near Fort Hill, for the christening of the man's new vessel was private and Walter could not gain access. He then followed the man and his troupe through the busy streets, halfway across town to the National Theatre at the corner of Portland and Traverse streets. Walter was able to procure a seat but nowhere near the boxes enjoyed by his prey. The play was a bore, a waste of time and money. Finally, the man, Calvin Ringgold, entered the restaurant across the street and had been there ever since. Walter, tired from the day's hustling and unsure when he would have another opportunity, decided now was the time. He would get his chance with Calvin if it killed him.

The Ringgolds and Pomfreys had a long history. Walter and Calvin's fathers were very close, their mothers were as well. The families would spend weekends together during the summer at a place up north they all loved. Walter and Calvin were about the same age so they spent a lot of time together swimming, boating and fishing. The kids, including Sarah and the Ringgold's three daughters, got along reasonably well, but the closeness of the parents never really translated to the next generation. They were friends but not particularly intimate.

The idea to contact Calvin popped into Walter's head a couple of days ago. He was sitting on the floor of his office, scared and defeated. The night before, someone had broken in and trashed his place. It was a mess. Mrs. Wedge suspected it was the work of a group of vagrant boys who ran in the neighborhood. She called them "trash" and pledged to contact the local police right away. Walter agreed with her so as not to cause Mrs. Wedge more anxiety, but a few things in the disaster pointed him in another direction.

First, Walter had come to an agreement with the leader of the neighborhood boys—Cooper, they called him. Twenty cents a week to "keep an eye on the place" was a fair price for both parties. Walter never told Mrs. Wedge about the covenant because she would heartily disapprove of him having dealings with the dregs of the city. Walter had dealt with worse and considered the Cooper arrangement more of a way to help the less fortunate as opposed to a simple extortion racket.

Another quick deduction Walter made had to do with the pungent smell of bourbon that filled the room. The bottle was half full the day before, but now the smelly liquid was splattered from floor to ceiling, leaving blotches of light-brown stains everywhere. If Cooper and the boys had been in here, they may have smashed the bottle. But there was no way a single drop of booze would have been left in it before they did. What seemed more likely was someone didn't appreciate the decanter and its embossed "P" for Pomfrey. Therefore, they smashed it with enough force to cover the entire room with shards of glass. There was a rage in the way it was broken, a definite, purposeful rage. Not the boys' style.

The backbreaker for Walter stood on the very edge of his desk, at the corner where Daniel gave his chilling warning before taking his leave. A single .22 caliber bullet was placed with care, defying the wreckage all around it, sending a clear message only Walter would understand. There was no doubt the Murrays were behind the ransacking, and they were ready to take the search for Charlie to the next level.

Sitting on the floor, Walter knew he needed help. He needed financial backing. He needed a respectable name. He needed someone he could trust. He needed someone like Calvin Ringgold. Seeing as Walter was no longer a part of the privileged class of Boston, getting a meeting would be next to impossible. However, if Walter could get face-to-face with Calvin, just for a minute, maybe he could appeal to his old friend's sense of nostalgia and sell him on helping Charlie deal with the Murrays. He spent the next couple of days tracking Calvin's movements and preparing his approach. It was a long shot but worth trying.

The door of the restaurant finally opened and Walter, seeing a familiar face emerge, stood up quickly. The first man through the door had been part of Calvin's group since this afternoon and, because of his long, ridiculous beard, was easily recognizable. Walter hesitated for a moment, letting the entire group exit and fill the sidewalk between the building and a row of waiting carriages. When Calvin came out, Walter's pulse quickened and he started across the street. Rounding the first carriage in the line, Walter pulled a folded newspaper from his jacket pocket and pretended to read it as he closed on the cluster of bodies. Eyeing his target over his glasses, he made a direct hit.

"Oh, pardon me, sir!" Walter feigned. He gave Calvin just enough time to recover from the collision, then began his performance. "Calvin? Is that you? Calvin Ringgold?"

Calvin hit the bait. "Walter? Pomfrey? How the hell are you, buddy?"

20.

Charlie was eating breakfast in the blue hotel. It was his first full day in Quindaro since his run-in with the river, and he was celebrating with as many goodies as he could fit on the table. Eggs, bacon, sausage, pancakes, fruit—you name it, he ordered it. And everything tasted so good, he couldn't get enough. It's funny how much more you appreciate things when you've been dead. The waitress was enthusiastic and happily kept the food coming. She thought it was nice to see a young, hungry man at work. It didn't hurt that Charlie had become a bit of a celebrity as word had spread quickly about his near-death experience. She hadn't waited on a famous person since she was back home in Ohio, so Charlie got the star treatment.

He didn't remember much about the whole dying ordeal, which he thought was for the best. The only details he had was what he picked up from Dux telling the story to Lee and Luke the next morning. The cousins were thoroughly impressed with Cuff's rescue and Dux's magic kisses. However, they were the opposite of impressed with Charlie's decision to leap from the boat. The word "jackass" was used more times than Charlie would have liked, mainly by Luke, but after all that had transpired, the description was undoubtedly accurate.

He slept like a rock in the cabin. Dux emitted a sense of warmth and comfort that Charlie desperately needed, and his body absorbed it. He woke up in the same position he had fallen asleep in, and he figured he hadn't moved in ten hours. If it weren't for the smell of biscuits and the muffled conversation from the porch, he may have never awakened. Once he did though, and after a small bite to eat, he and the cousins made their way back to town with Cuff as guide. Evidently, the area around Dux's cabin was rich with booby traps set to keep slave hunters and Missouri refuse from coming around. However, the traps didn't discriminate according to political affiliation and even Lee and Luke needed help getting around them. Cuff took the boys to the edge of the woods where they would be safe and said goodbye. He shook hands with Charlie and gave him a word of advice. "Stay out of the river."

"Will do. Thank you, Cuff. For everything," Charlie replied. Then Cuff was gone.

That night sleeping at the cousin's cabin was not as restful, but it felt good to be with the boys again. He went to sleep early and woke up the next morning with terrible hunger pangs. He dressed quickly and, noticing the cousins had already left for work, made his way to the hotel, as it was the fastest way to get a meal. He had just eaten the last piece of his second order of bacon when he heard a loud voice in the lobby area. He heard it easily as it was the first British accent to hit his ears since coming West. If the man would have been blowing a bugle, it couldn't have sounded more out of place.

The Brit was cheerful, to say the least, greeting everyone in the next room heartily and as boisterously as possible. A couple of the hotel staff left the front room quickly, ducking into the main eating area where Charlie sat, then through a back exit to the kitchen. On their way, the two runners signaled two other men sitting a few tables from Charlie. One of the seated fellows listened carefully and upon hearing the Brit, whispered, "Oh shit! Let's go," to the man with him. They shoveled as much of their remaining meal into their mouths as they could, and with cheeks like chipmunks, headed out the back through the kitchen as well.

Charlie, still chewing, took notice of the few folks still there. They were looking at him, too, all of them, and he suddenly felt quite uneasy. He made eye contact with an older woman sitting across the room and, shrugging his shoulders, silently asked her what was wrong. For a second, it looked as though she was getting ready to speak. Like she had a secret that would save Charlie from some unimaginable horror. The look frightened him. Then suddenly, she, along with everyone else, shot a quick glance toward the door, then down at their plates. Charlie looked to her one more time and she to him, but this time her look was more forlorn. Like she was looking at a ghost. She turned away a final time as if to say, "It's too late for you now," and that was it. He was left to face the unknown by himself.

"Why hello there, young man!" the British voice bellowed. "I haven't seen you around here before, have I?" Charlie turned toward the door, looking up into the man's face. He started to shake his head no but was interrupted by a loud, "No, I don't think so. I never forget a face, especially one so young and bright. Mind if I join you?"

Before Charlie could answer, the man pulled up a seat and yelled to the waitress, "Mary, I'll take some coffee and a couple eggs, please. Over medium. I want the whites cooked through. Yes? And no rush. I'll be dining with my new friend here…" He looked at Charlie, eyebrows raised.

"Charlie," said Charlie. Dammit! He should really work on an alias.

"Charlie," repeated the Brit. He leaned back in the chair, looked around the room, nodding at the other tables, and finally introduced himself. "Charlie, my name is Oliver. Oliver Henry MacCauley. Some people call me OH, others Oliver, still others Mr. MacCauley. You can call me any of these things or something else, if you come up with it. Whatever suits your fancy."

Mary brought the cup of coffee out and sat it in front of Oliver. He leaned back to allow her room and said, "Thank you, madam!" Then reached his arm across the table to shake Charlie's hand. "Please to make your acquaintance, young Charles."

Charlie took his hand and answered, "Likewise, I'm sure."

Oliver wrapped on the table with his left hand. "I'm sure, indeed."

21.

Sir Joseph Whitworth was a brilliant man. Born in Cheshire, England in 1803, he rose to prominence as an engineer, entrepreneur and inventor. Most known for devising the British Standard Whitworth system, which is an accepted standard for screw threads, Whitworth, despite being a pacifist, dabbled in, of all things, military arms improvement. In doing so, he pioneered the concept of polygonal rifling whereby a rifle barrel's normal "lands and grooves" were replaced by "hills and valleys" in a rounded polygonal pattern. He was sure the new design would improve both range and accuracy and would replace the current British-issued rifle, the Enfield, which left much to be desired during the Crimean War. In an 1856 demonstration, his Whitworth rifle clearly outperformed the Enfield, shooting farther and displaying an above-average accuracy. When equipped with a scope, it could be considered the world's first sniper rifle with a range of nearly a mile.

The man crouched in the woods below Quindaro wouldn't need the whole mile in distance, only about half that. However, he would need the power of the full range to get the projectile up the hill and into the town. He was well hidden as usual. He had crept slowly through the deep woods avoiding the guards stationed high in the hills. They were posted there because of him. They watched diligently, fearfully for him. He was the one who brought terror and death. From a distance, he kept the bustling Kansas town on edge. He had only struck twice, this time being his third, but his reputation had built quickly. He was known as The Whistler.

His job was simple. Fire as many rounds into the small town as he could, causing as much terror as possible until his position was compromised. Then he was to disappear. So far, the job had been a piece of cake, and it paid decently too. He was already positioned on the Missouri side of the river, so when he was discovered, it took at least ten minutes for anyone to get close enough to return fire. The town didn't have a weapon with that sort of range, which gave him plenty of time to fire a few more rounds and make a clean break even after he was located. If the wind was right, he could kill three or four people in that time. Easy money.

Of course, money wasn't the only reason for what he did. He had his own personal beef with the town and its people, so it felt good to get a little payback. Sorter and his band of assholes thought they could do no wrong and were given free reign, for the most part. It was fine for them to kill and maim but if anyone else did it, they were evil. He always hoped to see Sorter in the scope again one day. He would take his head off. He had a bead on him the first time he visited, but the wind blew the slug just wide of the target. The bullet, because of its unique shape, made a distinctive whistling sound as it cut the air. Therefore, Sorter, after his close call, started referring to the shooter as The Whistler. The town, like sheep, soon did the same.

The marksman liked being known. He liked being feared. He liked that when he walked through the town—and he did all the time—no one whistled. Not without being "shushed" by someone. Whistling in Quindaro was akin to summoning the devil himself, and that was his doing. His handiwork. But he wasn't Lucifer. He was more like Michael or Gabriel. Archangels doing God's work. Punishing sorry souls for their wrongdoings and bringing justice to the unjust. He brought God's wrath. He was the reckoning.

The wind died down and a window opened. He scanned the town once more, closer this time, looking to get lucky and catch Sorter meandering about. He would bring the highest payday. Nothing. He then looked for the second best-paying target, hoping against hope not to find her. She was the Indian princess. First, he hated killing women. Second, he was sure there would be a harsh punishment delivered by the universe for taking the life of such a beautiful creature. Sure, she was a catalyst for much of the violence in the area, as much if not more than Sorter. And her notion of "all men being created equal" was ignorant and unchanging. But oh God, how she sparkled! When she looked into your eyes, you were seized. Not just by the splendor of her perfect face but the power and grace of her presence. She was the very definition of beauty. And that was why she carried such a hefty price. She was dangerous on a completely different level, and that made others hate her deeply. Today, thankfully, she was staying out of sight.

He scanned quickly and picked an easy one for the first shot. The target in his scope was standing still, reading a sign posted near the hotel. He was alone, too, so there wasn't anyone close by to see him fall. A gift. If the wind held, the man's fate was sealed. The Whistler took a deep breath and let it out slowly until all the air was gone from his lungs. The pointer finger on his right hand moved just slightly and the gun kicked back against his face. But he held firm. The man in the scope fell to the ground. The shooter held his position for a moment, making sure it was clear, that he wasn't spotted. Then he reloaded.

He looked back into the scope to see the man lying on the ground, dead. Probably. Easy. Let's find another one.

22.

Breakfast at the hotel turned into lunch and then some. Initially, all Charlie could think about was how to escape from his British captor. His new friend Oliver was a relentless conversationalist who seemed content to waste the entire day talking to a man he just met. He spoke quickly, words flowing like poetry, covering several topics with expert detail. It was all Charlie could do to hold on. Oliver was hard work! But Charlie was sure there wasn't anyone like him within a thousand miles, and it wasn't long before he started to enjoy the company. Soon, he was talking as much as Oliver, if not more.

Oliver knew almost everyone in town, and he and Charlie compared notes. He thought Lee and Luke were "fine lads" and enjoyed the venison they provided the hotels. He confessed, they sometimes made him feel like a failure being as they were half his age and possessed twice his experience. Charlie bragged a bit and relayed the story of the deer hunt and his small part in it.

Charlie also talked about his time with Dux and the wonderful stew he had while he was her guest. Oliver was familiar having been a guest of Dux's himself and educated Charlie on the meal's exotic contents. "Personally, I was surprised at just how tasty racoon can be," said Oliver.

"Racoon?" asked Charlie. He didn't know he'd eaten racoon.

"An odd little beast to be sure, with its little mask and all," said Oliver. "But when cooked correctly, quite succulent, don't you agree?"

"I guess," was all Charlie could muster.

"Say," started Oliver. "You must be the sad young man everyone is talking about. The one who tried to kill himself in the river. Is that you?" he asked.

Charlie laughed. "I didn't try to kill myself, I just made a bad decision." Charlie was confused. "Who said I tried to kill myself? And how did you hear about it so fast?"

"Oh, my boy, gossip moves swiftly in these parts, as fast as the wind itself," replied Oliver. "The truth, however, can be quite sluggish," he confessed.

Charlie told Oliver the real story, including the vision he had of his mother. Oliver was surprisingly receptive and thought the encounter "utterly fascinating."

For the next couple of hours, the two shared stories and ideas as if they had known each other for years. At one point, Oliver whispered something to the hotel manager, who brought over a small bottle of wine wrapped in a white napkin. Drinking was not allowed in the hotel, but Oliver explained he and the manager had an understanding. "He understands I want a bit of wine and I understand he wants a bit of money. It's simple, really." They shared the wine and became fast friends. Oliver was impressed to meet a young man so well read and Charlie loved the stories about London. Since coming to the territory, neither had found anyone they could talk to about art, travel or other refinements. To both men, it felt like home.

When they finally decided to part, they promised to meet again for dinner, either that same night or the next. For now, Charlie's only plan was to go down the hill to the docks and mess around until the cousins finished the day's work. He had become fascinated with the workings of the ferryboats and found it relaxing to sit and watch them come and go. Eventually, he knew he would encounter Captain Webb and had already decided he would take his lumps. He wasn't looking forward to it, but he knew he needed to apologize to the captain, and the sooner the better. Maybe it would be today.

As he walked down the main avenue of town, he noticed something peculiar. For some reason, it looked like everyone on the street was hiding from something. A small group was crouched behind a carriage, looking off into the distance. Another larger group had taken shelter between two slender buildings. A man from the larger group saw Charlie and started to yell at him to come their way. And to "get down!" He had no idea what was happening but started toward them to find out.

Then *she* came out of a building across the street, and Charlie's legs froze. He didn't know who she was, but from all he had heard, all the warnings, it was clear. The lore surrounding her, all the accounts of her beauty, he now knew, he now saw with his own eyes. It was not hyperbole. If anything, the descriptions fell short. She was astounding. She was the Indian princess, Quindaro.

The combination of the wine and the woman possessed Charlie. He stood still in the middle of the road ignoring the warnings and waves from the folks taking cover around him. A strange whistling sound followed by a shattered windowpane to his left partially broke the spell. Charlie was fully restored to the present when a man appeared out of nowhere and violently tackled him.

"Dammit, boy, get down!" yelled the man. "Your ears broken or something?" he asked as he yanked Charlie behind a wooden horse trough. The hero simultaneously chastised Charlie for his stupidity while at the same time hollering orders to a group of men rushing around on horseback. He was an impressive general and a talented swearer. He also yelled instructions to the princess, who relayed the orders down the road to another group of men, who then took off to execute the plan.

"Keep your damn head down and follow me," the man instructed. "We're going right over there," he pointed, "through that door, into that building. Understand?"

Charlie nodded and followed the order. Once inside, he crept on the floor while the man took a post at the window, both pistols drawn and ready. The two waited in silence for a few minutes until two other men came to the door and yelled it was safe to come out. The gunman holstered his weapons and left the building, leaving Charlie alone on the floor.

Walking outside to the street, Charlie rubbed his hip and shrugged his shoulder, trying to relieve a bit of the residual pain left from the collision. The dust was thick from the commotion, and the wind swirling between the buildings blew it into tiny little tornados. Men on horses were still driving the animals hard up and down the hill, but it seemed the danger had passed. Folks gathered in groups around victims who lay dead or dying, trying to help as much as possible. Down the street, Charlie noticed the largest of the groups included the man who saved him and the princess. They were surrounding the body of a man who someone had covered with a sheet. He was gone. Charlie walked to them and joined the group.

David Sorter, the man who had saved Charlie's life, led the discussion. He explained that the shooter—The Whistler, he called him—had abandoned his position and disappeared as usual. Unfortunately, he had taken four souls before he left. David's men were searching the woods, but he doubted if they would find anything. Just then, a woman came running into the fold, crying and yelling the name of her husband who was beneath the sheet. She pulled it away from his face and fell into him, sobbing. The princess knelt to comfort her but was little help.

As word of the damage spread, more and more people joined the main group, and the mood quickly turned from sorrow to anger. Much of the ire was directed at David, who accepted the criticism entirely. To many, including him, it was David's duty to protect the town from these attacks, and today he had failed. Again. Finally, a local merchant yelled to David, "If we had ourselves a cannon, that son of a bitch would think twice about sitting down in them woods."

Everyone agreed wholeheartedly, David too, but he countered with, "We've tried to get more firepower, Mr. West, you know that. But the military isn't on our side, and every time we try to ship one this way, it gets hijacked." The crowd mumbled their displeasure. David continued, "Listen, I agree with you. And one of these days, me and the boys are going to get our hands on a six pounder, and it'll change the game. But for now, we'll have to make do." The crowd liked that answer even less.

David shook his head at the princess, who tried to regain order. Upon seeing her again, this time up close, Charlie wanted nothing more than to make an impression. He spoke up gallantly, "I know where there's a cannon!"

23.

David Sorter was not the type to ask for permission. He possessed an unusually good instinct for action and he normally followed it with little or no outside guidance. He occasionally talked through an idea with someone he trusted, but the final decision was always his. During the Mexican War, he followed the orders given, as a good military man should. But once discharged, Sorter vowed he would never take another order as long as he lived. And so far, he hadn't. However, he came to understand that if he was going to make a go of it here in the new territory, he would need to be seen as part of the team, so his decisions, on occasion, would have to be approved or at least agreed to.

When he heard the kid in town mention the cannon, David was very intrigued. First off, he recognized Charlie from his recent visit to Wyandotte and figured out he was probably Lee and Luke's third scout who never showed. He also figured he was the kid who tried to kill himself by jumping off Webb's ferryboat only to be saved by Cuff and Dux. The fact that Dux let him go was a good sign, as she was an excellent judge of character. Finally, although Oliver was known as a bigmouth, he rarely talked about the cannon. For the new kid to know that story already was significant.

A quick interrogation of the boy revealed what David already suspected and filled in a few details as well. The kid's name was Charlie, probably. The boy had stammered when asked, blurted out "Charlie" and then seemed upset with himself for some reason. He was an odd kid for sure. He was staying with the cousins and was the same one pulled from the river by Cuff; however, he made a point to inform David he wasn't trying to kill himself. He had met Oliver that same day and the two hit it off well enough to spend most of the morning and afternoon together. David joked, "Bet you wanted to kill yourself then!"

Charlie ignored the crack and continued his story. Over the course of the conversation, Oliver had told him the story of the cannon. Supposedly, it was donated to the town of Lawrence by some folks in Wisconsin, and Oliver was part of a group from Ohio that was helping to accompany the gift to the territory. Somewhere near the Nebraska border, the group caught wind of a pro-slavery band in the area that was planning to attack and confiscate the artillery piece. Being outgunned, Oliver and a couple men took the cannon and hid it so it wouldn't fall into the wrong hands. There was a small confrontation but since the cannon was gone, neither party saw the point of fighting, so both went their separate ways. A few months ago, the only other member of the Wisconsin and Ohio party returned home, leaving Oliver as the only person who knew where the cannon was buried.

Thus far, the kid knew what he was talking about. Just to make sure David asked, "Do you know what they called the cannon?"

Charlie answered, "Lazarus."

Correct again. David wasn't sure why Oliver would have shared this story with a stranger but there wasn't another explanation for him knowing so much. The information came from Oliver and it was legitimate. Most people, including the town council, discounted the tale, believing it to be fiction. Oliver was known to tell stories where certain facts didn't add up, and they assumed the Lazarus story was just that, a story. But David knew better. He knew the cannon was real, that it was out there ready to be found, ready to be put to work, posted at the top of the hill to square the odds. And he wanted to find it. Badly.

David had tried several times to get Oliver to help him find Lazarus, but it never ended well. Oliver didn't trust David and like Abelard, considered him one of the main reasons for the continued conflict in the area. But it seemed Oliver trusted the kid. Why else would he have shared so much so soon? Now, David planned to use that trust to get what he wanted and what the town so desperately needed. He just had to convince the council, mainly Abe, that the idea had merit.

When he told the plan to Abe, Clarina and Nancy, they had reservations. Abe and Clarina didn't believe any of the story and disregarded it right away. To them, it was risky to have David and his men gone for so long with no real prospect of a payoff. Nancy wasn't sold on the story either but trusted David's judgement more than most. If David was convinced the cannon existed, she was willing to accept it sight unseen.

After much debate, Abe made it clear where he stood. The search was a fool's errand and David should know better. Besides, Abe was in contact with the Aid Society and had been assured more resources, including able bodies, were on the way. He felt the town just needed to wait it out and chastised David's propensity for violence. Clarina didn't like the idea either but sensed the decision had already been made. She deferred to the person who would ultimately determine what would happen—Nancy.

The princess sat silent for a moment, then addressed her husband only. "Abe, the town needs the weapon and if David is willing to retrieve it, then we will let him." Abe didn't answer, knowing it was futile. He stood up and left without saying a word. He would speak his mind to his wife later, when there wasn't anyone around to witness his defeat. Nancy smiled at Clarina and said, "Don't worry about him. He'll come around."

Clarina, sure the decision had been made, asked David to fill her and Nancy in on the details.

David, not sure himself, thought it through aloud. "Oliver will never agree to find Lazarus if he knows I'm involved. The kid will have to convince him it's the right thing for the town. Then they can get a small group together, maybe Lee, Luke, Oliver, the kid…"

Nancy interjected, "Cuff."

"Cuff would be nice, he trusts Cuff," David continued. "I'm sure Oliver won't care who goes as long as it's not me. Or Tough." He paused, thinking. "If I can get them on the road, maybe up the Leavenworth Road, near Six Mile or something, Tough and I could join them there. Then Oliver won't have a choice but to let us come along."

"Six Mile? Why would you send them through Six Mile? You're going to get them killed before they even get started," said Clarina.

Nancy countered, "I'm sure David will work it out." Then to him, "Plan on leaving within the next day or two, at the latest." He nodded his consent. "Bring Lazarus back."

24.

In the Brazer Building, downtown Boston, Walter waited alone in Calvin Ringgold's massive office. The space, adorned with deep, rich mahogany paneling, filled an entire floor on the south wing and two floors on the north. Calvin's primary work area centered on a walnut desk that was larger than Walter's bed. It took up most of the single level and was surrounded by custom-made bookshelves stuffed to the gills. Rosewood furniture filled the room, paying homage to the Victorian era and Louis XVI. A spiral staircase led to a luxurious living space above, topped by an imposing hammerbeam roof. Rich patterns and leather pillows filled the bed that was used only when Calvin stayed in the city overnight. The entire floor was enclosed by giant windows stretching from floor to ceiling, most of which were cracked to let the air circulate and cool the expanse. Walter was glad they were open as it was hot today and he had been waiting a while. His appointment was for eleven but the original Simon Willard longcase clock behind Calvin's desk was ten minutes away from chiming once. Walter knew Calvin was a busy man, but this was ridiculous.

He figured he would give Calvin until the clock struck one, then he would sneak out to avoid the embarrassment. Luckily, the massive ash doors flew open and Calvin entered, followed by a clerk he employed and his house servant. Calvin walked straight to Walter, apologized with a handshake and then ordered the servant to bring drinks. Bourbon. Quickly. Pleasantries were exchanged, small talk mostly until the drinks arrived. Then Calvin held his glass in the air and offered a toast. "To the lovely Sarah. May her soul rest in peace." The men drank. Calvin offered his sympathy for Walter's loss and apologized for missing the memorial. He was out of the country, but his wife told him it was a lovely affair. Walter agreed.

Then Calvin made the statement Walter had been waiting for. "If there is anything you need, please let me know."

Walter tried to ease into it as he had practiced on the way over and a dozen times more during his wait. However, the excitement got the better of him and he pounced. "Now that you mention it, Calvin, there is something I would like to ask of you."

The news of James Murray being double-crossed by his dead wife had spread through the city like the plague. Publicly, most reacted with disdain toward Sarah for leaving her family business to an inept heir who would most assuredly lead the company to ruin. Privately, however, most of the Boston elite relished in the Murray's predicament and smelled blood in the water. The Murrays were diligent, however, and began circulating news that Charlie's shares were going to be signed over to the family trust and control would return to James in the very near future. The heir was simply on an extended vacation, healing from the pain of his mother's passing. And when he returned, the transfer would be made and it would be business as usual at Pom. Some believed the story as told. However, it was clear to Walter there was another motive for the damage control. The Murrays were getting the company ready to sell outright, to take the money and run.

However, Walter knew that James was no fool. If Charlie was gone for good, his next best move was to merge the company with another firm to dilute Charlie's shares and all but close Pom Shipping forever. If the rumors were true, this plan was already in the works. From what Walter had heard, a willing party had been approached and negotiations had begun. Consequently, the clock was ticking on the Pomfrey family business.

Calvin knew the state of things and let Walter know as much. He asked, "Do you know the Murray's potential partner?"

"I don't," answered Walter. "I'm not that high on the food chain in this city, let alone in the worldwide shipping industry. I was hoping you could find out."

"I could," Calvin said. "But I'm not sure why I would. Why do you care, Walter? I know how things were left between you and your father. You're not a part of the business anymore. Can't be, by law, if my recollection is correct."

"That's right," Walter agreed. "It's not for me, per se."

Calvin was intrigued. "Are you working for Sarah's boy? What's his name? Charles? I didn't think he wanted any part of the company."

Walter needed to be careful. He couldn't give away too much information but he needed to give Calvin something, a nugget. "I'm not sure what his plans are but I was thinking, if he had someone at the table with him, someone with capital, a fine, respectable name, maybe he would have some options. He could step away if that's what he chose or he could keep it in the family. At least it would be his choice. And who knows, maybe it would, or could, be beneficial to both parties."

Calvin pondered in silence, keeping his eyes on Walter as he did so. Finally, he broke. "I'll be honest with you, Walter, I'm not sure if this is something I want to get involved in. I've heard Sarah's boy is a bit dim. Maybe dim isn't the word—flighty, maybe? Yeah, that's it, flighty. Not to mention, if one is to believe the rumors, he's disappeared. No one knows where he is! How could I possibly think about getting into business with someone like that?"

Walter had to give a little. "He hasn't disappeared, I'm sure he could be contacted if it was necessary."

Calvin, always open to fresh gossip, leaned in and whispered, "Do you know where he is, Walter?"

"No," Walter answered. "But I'm sure if you wanted to sit down with him, he could be reached." He needed to change the subject. "Also, you would find out he's a good kid and should be given every opportunity to step up and take what's his. It's the right thing, Calvin, of that I can assure you."

Calvin paused again and the clock behind him gonged. He stood abruptly and loudly summoned his assistant. He had another meeting at one and needed to take his leave. He looked at Walter still sitting and said, "I'm not going to make any promises, Walter, but let me see what I can find out. I would rather not take on the Murrays if I don't have to, they are certainly a volatile bunch. But if things look square, I'll expect you to summon the boy and we can discuss terms." He held his hand out to Walter and they shook on it. "It was good to see you again, old friend." Calvin left the office yelling orders to his assistant the entire way.

Walter stood, letting his shoulders finally relax and his lungs fully fill with air. He downed the last bit of alcohol in the glass and smiled. There was a lot yet to do. He needed to get the numbers down, send word to Charlie about maybe coming home, definitely avoid the Murrays. But the meeting went well. As well as it could have. Maybe, just maybe, Calvin would be their redeemer.

25.

Charlie stood in W&M Hardware Depot checking off the last of the items he was tasked with gathering before the search party left to find Lazarus. He had been to several stores already on a makeshift scavenger hunt to find the supplies Oliver deemed "absolutely necessary" for their journey. The list, which included pillows, shoe polish, an umbrella, sugar and tea, among other comforts, was, in Charlie's opinion, a complete waste of time, money and most importantly, effort. Specifically, his effort. However, David Sorter had made it clear that Charlie was to do, promise or offer anything, no matter how absurd, in order to get Oliver to show him where to find the hidden cannon. Once Oliver agreed and doled out his demands, Charlie complained and showed the useless list of supplies to David but received no compassion. Only the spirited advice, "You better get to shopping, boy." So, shopping Charlie went.

He left the store with the items packed in a large burlap sack thrown over his shoulder. It wasn't that heavy, but it was bulky, and Charlie occasionally had to wrestle it to keep it under control. The hill was a nightmare. He was hot and sweaty and his hands were killing him, making his frustration grow with each step. He suddenly wondered what everyone else was doing while he did all the legwork. Hell, he was the one who had to talk Oliver into going in the first place. And that was more difficult than lugging the bag up this stupid-ass hill.

He nearly had to beg Oliver to go and then had to make promises he knew would be broken. The biggest being that

David and his men "must not be a part of our operation as they are animals and heathens!" Charlie hated lying to Oliver and felt terrible for doing so. When David was explaining the plan, Charlie had reservations and expressed as much. However, he was told to "grow a pair" and to "stick to the plan." David was a bully!

Luckily, Nancy was there too, and she helped Charlie make sense of it all. She asked him if he could put aside his personal doubts and do what was necessary to help the town. Just this one time. She knew he was capable of great things and felt the spirits had brought him to Quindaro to fulfill a purpose. This could be it. After all, the people were in danger, and what they needed most, what she needed most, was a hero. Charlie was all in.

He settled into a rhythm hauling the bag up the hill by rocking it back and forth slowly. However, it wasn't long before he ran out of steam. He put the sack down and found some shade beneath the stilted back end of a small home. From here, he could see the muddy water of the Missouri for miles in each direction. He had been up and down the river a few times now, and he could make out some of the curves that become recognizable to an experienced traveler such as himself. The wooded areas of the delta held a multitude of serious dangers but from above, they looked like the woods of a fairy tale. The tops of the nearby towns cut through as well. Wyandotte to the east, Parkville to the north. Even a few structures over in the City of Kansas were visible on such a clear day. The view was spectacular. What a shame so few seemed to notice.

After sitting a few minutes, he caught his breath and decided to get back to it. However, as he looked down the hill one last time, he noticed a commotion and a gathering of people just above the docks. He had seen this type of movement in the town before, when The Whistler struck and nearly killed him. Something was happening and it wasn't good. He stuffed the bag under the house to get it out of sight and started down the hill. This trip was much easier and didn't take half as long, so he joined the group in no time. From the back, he assessed the problem.

A man was on the ground at the center of the group. Charlie couldn't see him all that well but it seemed a couple of townsfolk were tending to him while the others circled and shouted for the doctor. Nancy appeared quickly, cutting through the crowd like a knife. David shot through next, pulling the doctor along as if the old man was weightless. He shouted orders to "get back" and "make some room," and the crowd obliged.

Nancy, kneeling next to the victim, looked to a man nearby and asked, "What happened, Andy?"

The man spoke in a thick Russian accent and explained the situation. He and a few others had spotted the wounded man floating down the river on a small raft. They attempted to make contact but the man was unresponsive. As he neared the Quindaro landing, they realized why. The man on the raft was barely conscious and bleeding from his head and stomach. Quickly, they fished him out of the river and pulled him up the hill to where he was now. Just who he was or where he came from was a mystery.

The doctor examined the stranger, concentrating first on his abdomen. The man's coat was cut open, revealing a deep and expansive wound just below his rib cage. When the doctor rolled the man onto his side for a better look, a gush of red liquid poured out and pooled in the dirt. The man moaned as he was rolled back over. David followed the doctor's eyes as he looked down the hill and traced a solid bloody line clear to the docks. The doctor looked at David and shook his head. He pulled a handkerchief from his coat pocket and wiped the thick, sticky liquid from his hands. It was clear that the man from the raft was nearly empty and as good as dead.

A wooden bucket full of water had been brought to the

scene, and Nancy pulled it close to her and the dying man. She spoke softly, "We need to clean him up."

David looked around the crowd and noticed a man standing close holding a towel. He asked for it silently then handed it to Nancy. She dipped it in the cool water and began wiping the blood from the man's face. He was still.

The doctor looked above the man's eyes where the blood originated and said, "The head wounds don't look too bad. Skin deep at best." Then, as more blood was cleared, a darker picture emerged. The doctor continued, "That's curious. Is that a letter?" He was horrified. "No. It's…it's a word."

David leaned in, grabbing the man's jaw, rotating the lifeless head to get the full story. When he did, his face flushed with anger and his teeth clenched tightly. He spoke slowly, putting the pieces together. "It's not a word." He turned and scanned the crowd behind him, searching for the subject of the letters carved so brutally on the comatose man's forehead. There, between two townsfolk, near the back of the group, he found who he was looking for. He locked eyes with Charlie, who froze when he caught David's glance.

Somewhere from the back someone yelled, "What does it say?" The murmur of the crowd grew.

David spoke quietly but they all heard. "It's not a word. It's a name." He paused for a moment, then broke the news. "It says 'Charlie.'"

26.

As the crowd dispersed, David made his way over to Charlie. The kid was understandably distraught. David wasn't good at consolation but tried to be as easy on the kid as he could. He asked, "Did you have a run-in with Cook?"

Charlie couldn't make words, he just nodded his head. The tears were coming, they were just below the surface, but so far, he had held them back. He looked terrified.

David noticed the emotions coming and looked away. If the boy started crying, he at least wanted to be respectful enough not to watch. He said, "I don't know what happened, but if Cook and his goons are looking for you, you did something right in my book. I'm sure everyone in town feels the same." He looked back at Charlie—no tears yet, so he continued. "Don't let it worry you too much, but you best be sure to take it as a lesson. Now you know what they're capable of and why me and Tough do what we do. Sometimes you have to fight fire with fire because the only way to deal with those bastards, the only thing that works, is retribution."

Charlie nodded his head in agreement but he really didn't understand the message. He just wasn't built that way. He wasn't thinking of vengeance, he was only thinking of the poor soul who paid with his life for Charlie's mistake. He looked to the group carrying the man and said, "That was my fault. I should have gone to Leavenworth. I should have seen Cook's man there. But I didn't. And now this man is going to…"

David put a hand on Charlie's shoulder and stopped him. "That was not your fault. That was Cook's doing. You remember that. Don't you dare take on that burden, understand?" Charlie didn't answer. "We're leaving tomorrow anyway, and now you know how important that cannon is to this town. We need it. You're going to help us find it and we're going to put it to use. We're going to even the odds. You're part of something now. You're with us, you're with this town. You may not have wanted to be but you're in the fight now, boy. And you can stand your ground or run on back home, it's your choice. And you'll have to decide. But not until we get back with that cannon."

27.

David left Charlie standing in the road. He knew he couldn't help the kid any more than he had already. Not now, anyway. In time, Charlie would be able to process the incident and keep it in a safe place inside him. There would be a scar for sure, but the pain he felt now would wane and become manageable. It just takes time and reflection. Life has a way of throwing you into situations that you must survive alone. If you make it out the other side, you're better off for it. This would be a test, a big test, to see just what Charlie was made of.

David had his own business to attend to at Clarina's, and he headed that way. Outside the front door stood a brawny Wyandotte Indian named Kayrahoo. He was a large man, with long coal-black hair that hung straight down, masking a portion of his face. His arms were large and dense, his hands substantial. He was an impressive man and because he usually wore a thick layer of black paint from the bridge of his nose to his hairline, he was a chilling presence. He was Nancy's second cousin and sometimes acted as her personal sentinel when she was in town. His name meant "first of many" in his native tongue, so around the whites, Nancy called him "Adam." Therefore, everyone else did too.

On the rare occasions when David and Adam spoke, they would tease each other in a way that seemed, from the outside, playful and harmless. However, there was a nastiness to their words, a realness. In truth, the jabs were fashioned from a genuine hatred that boiled just below the surface. They could control it, but just barely.

David approached the door and coldly spoke a single word

to Adam, "Move." Adam stayed put for a moment, then shifted his body ever so slightly, just enough for David to reach for the doorknob. The two men puffed up and stared at each other silently. David, noticing a weakness, spoke again. "What happened to your eye, Adam? Did somebody finally give you what you had coming?"

Adam's right eye, swollen and bruised enough for David to see it through the black war paint, was an easy target. Adam leaned closer to David, nose to nose, and through clenched teeth answered, but in Wyandotte. David stood his ground and shot back, "Say what you have to say so I can understand it, idiot. Or maybe you're afraid I'll take on the other eye…"

Nancy interrupted the hostilities from the second-story window above the door. She stuck her head out and spoke solemnly to both men. "That's enough."

David shot one last harsh look toward Adam and went in. Clarina was working at her desk in the front room and welcomed David with a nod. She stood and began packing a few items into an easily manageable stack and asked if David would be available later this evening. She wanted his opinion on a few items she planned to run in the paper while he was gone and didn't know when she would have the opportunity again. David told her he planned to stay in town tonight and they could get together once he made sure Charlie and the others were ready to leave the next morning. She thanked him and said, "Nancy is upstairs." She grabbed her stack of work and went out through the back exit, avoiding Adam stationed out front. He gave her the creeps.

David went to the staircase and started his climb. He saw Nancy at the top of the stairs and from the look on her face, he knew he was in trouble. She asked, "Why do you and Adam have to do that every time?"

"It's not me, it's him," David replied, stopping mid-way up the flight. "I don't know what his problem is." He tried to change the subject. "What happened to his eye? Did you do that?" he asked, half joking.

"No, I think he's been spending some time in Six Mile," Nancy said. "I told him to stay away from there but he doesn't always listen to me. That place is filled with pirates."

David agreed and started back up while Nancy turned and walked across the room. She stood at the open window and looked down at Adam standing guard. His hair blew in the wind and when hit by the sun, it was so dark it looked purple. "I wish you two could figure out how to get along. He is a proud man and a powerful warrior. It would take three average men to match his prowess in battle, and right now you need all the help you can get."

"It won't work," David said quietly.

"I know," said Nancy.

She stared at Adam and with both hands, pulled the creaky window shut. Below she saw a slight tilt in his head as Adam heard it. However, he didn't look up. He was a statue. She forced herself to look away from the sadness of the solitary warrior. His melancholy was not what she needed to dwell on right now. She looked out over the hillside, searching for something beautiful, something magical to change the climate in both the room and her heart. She found a patch of wild daisies in the distance, waving like white flags in the wind. They seemed to do the trick as Adam disappeared from her thoughts. A much more pressing issue now consumed her. David was leaving tomorrow and would be in peril until his return. If he returned. Every minute with him now was precious. She turned and slowly walked back across the room, unbuttoning her blouse on the way.

28.

The next morning, with their horses packed and loaded, the small band started their quest. The group included Charlie, Oliver, Lee, Luke and Cuff, who acted as both guide and de facto leader. Cuff was the obvious choice to lead the way because he knew the terrain better than the others, was fastest with a gun and possessed the instincts they would need to survive alone on the wild prairie. Just in case there was uncertainty about who should lead, before they took off, David informed Charlie and the cousins to "stay close to Cuff and do what he says, when he says it." Then to Cuff, David delivered a solitary request with a wink. It was simple. "Keep these boys alive as long as you can." Additionally, they all knew to keep quiet regarding David's involvement in the search lest Oliver find out and renege. With that, they were off.

The small village of Six Mile was to be their first obstacle. It was located on Leavenworth Road, six miles west of the city of Wyandotte, hence its name. It was small, comprised of a mere five buildings total, of which three were taverns, one was a hotel and the last a church. Or what used to be a church. It had caught fire a year or so back and no one came to the rescue. The heathens of the town watched as the pastor fought with all his might to save his tabernacle. With no help offered, resigned to his loss, he ran inside to recover some personal items just before the roof gave way and collapsed in on him. The pastor burned to nothing. His spirit, however, some say, still wanders the area but is usually only seen by those who partake of the Chinese smoke. Now, all that remained of him or his house of worship was a large stone foundation with half walls, both of which were stained forever with chalky black soot.

The other four buildings were only slightly better off but did have full walls and roofs that hid the activities inside. It was here, in Six Mile, where men from both sides of the river could come and participate in any and all behaviors, legal or otherwise. Mostly otherwise. It was a rough place and difficult to get around unscathed. David planned for the group to skirt the boundaries of the village by staying on the road, heads down. If they moved slowly, avoiding attention, they may get through without incident. However, as they neared the village, they noticed a man on horseback stationed in the middle of the road who seemed to be awaiting their arrival. There would be an incident, but to what degree, no one knew.

They approached the rider, who greeted them. "Morning," he said.

Lee spoke for the group. "Hello." Nothing else.

The rider wore a floppy hat that was a bit too big and when he spoke, he leaned his head back in order to make eye contact with Lee. He said, "I'm to collect a young man named Charlie from your group. He's to ride along with me. The rest of you will stay put." With his head tilted back, he scanned the group and found Charlie. "You Charlie?" he asked.

Lee answered, "I'll go, my name is Lee and I can speak for our group…"

The rider cut him off, repeating his instructions as if he was reciting lines of a play. "I'm to collect a young man named Charlie from your group. He's to ride along with me. You stay here." He looked to Charlie and asked again, "You Charlie?"

The group looked to Cuff who, a moment earlier, had picked up some movement in a nearby wooded area. He assumed, and rightly so, that a few more Six Mile men flanked them on the left, hidden by the trees, and if something were to happen, he and the group would be cut down before they could take cover. He whispered to Charlie, "You best go, boy."

Luke's eyes grew large and he started to protest, but Cuff shook his head. "We don't have a play here. He's got to go." To Charlie he said, "You'll be fine. Use your ears, not your mouth."

Charlie nodded and broke rank. He moved toward the rider, who met him halfway, grabbing the reins of Charlie's horse. He wrapped them around his saddle horn and started toward the buildings of Six Mile.

They came to the door of one of the taverns, and the rider opened it for Charlie to enter. Once inside, Charlie took a couple steps and turned to see the door shut behind him, his escort on the other side. He was alone now, in a dark, dank hallway that opened to a larger room a dozen feet away. He eased his way down the hall and came to the threshold of the main chamber. A few candles fought hard to illuminate the space, as the windows were covered and sealed. It smelled like stale alcohol and smoke from a fire. Also, something, a rat maybe, was dead very close by and rotting in the heat.

He peeked into the room, on high alert, and searched wall to dirty wall for anyone or anything that may want to do him harm. Finally, in the corner of the room to his left, he saw the bright red glow of a cigar draw. There was a figure there, in the dark, seated on what looked to be a throne raised off the floor. There was movement at the foot of the chair, people maybe, on the dirt ground. It was hard to tell from the doorway. The king on the throne wore a large hat with a long feather attached to it that hung far out in front of his face. In any other setting, the hat would have been comical. But here, in this room, the hat made a scary man seem even more sinister. It made Charlie shiver.

Charlie looked behind him to the door he'd entered through. He thought about making a run for it, taking his chances with whatever was waiting on the outside. If he got past his escort, he could make it back to the group. Maybe. He didn't get the chance to plan much further because the man in the chair finally made contact.

The king's voice echoed as if he were talking through a can or a bucket when he said, "Charlie, young Charlie. Come this way."

It took a moment before Charlie's legs would work. When they did, the movement was slow and guarded. He took a few steps toward the throne and when he was nearly in the middle of the room, he was told, "That's far enough."

The people on the floor were clearer now and much more disturbing. There were three or four total, mostly women, but one man for sure, in varying stages of undress. They seemed to be asleep for the most part but would squirm and moan occasionally as they rolled over each other searching for a comfortable spot. Charlie had seen addicts on the streets of Boston and it seemed these folks were of the same ilk, the poison rendering them inert.

The man on the chair was in total darkness with his face completely hidden by the hat, the feather and a type of fan he waved in front of his face. The fan swirled the smoke around him like an evil mist, and when he spoke, it made his voice quiver like an old man. He said, "Before you ask, I have friends all over the territory, even spilling across the river. They tell me things. Things I don't even have to ask, the damn words just pour out. One of them told me about you and that you would be coming my way today. I couldn't pass up the chance to meet you."

Charlie didn't answer. He heard a noise behind him and turned to check it out, then heard the king chuckle.

He said, "There's nothing to be afraid of, Charlie, you're safe here with me. There isn't a thing in the world that would harm you at this moment. You can relax. Can I get you anything?"

Charlie shook his head and said, "No, thank you. My friends and I have to be someplace, so I can't…"

The king interrupted. "There's a Territorial Magistrate's wife on the floor in front of me. I don't know what a Territorial Magistrate is or what one does. But I like the ring of it. The way it sounds, it just sounds important, wouldn't you agree?"

Charlie looked to the floor. The man pointed out the woman with his metal fan, then brought it back to his face and continued. "She's there, lying on her stomach, wearing only a vest I gave her. All the prestige of her husband's title means nothing to her." The mass of flesh on the floor repositioned with a common groan. "But she's still a member of the territorial monarchy, if you will, and that's worth something, isn't it? It's stimulating, to say the least." He paused and adjusted his hat. "She's there for the taking, Charlie. A gift to you as my honored guest. You can take your time. Relish taking the power from the powerful. It's a feeling you'll never forget."

Charlie quickly replied, "I have to join my friends and…"

"I'll send them on their way, unharmed. You can join them later," the king said.

"I can't," Charlie said. "We have a schedule to keep. I'm very sorry, sir, and much obliged of your…offer."

"Ah, a right gentleman. I haven't seen one of those here in a long while. You are very special indeed," said the king.

There was silence as the king measured Charlie in the darkness. Charlie could almost feel the man's stare touching his body, and goosebumps rose hard on his neck. He had to get out of this place, but the stare and the terror it infused in him held him firm.

Finally, the king spoke as he rubbed his chin. "You and your friends are free to pass. Today. However, it has a price. You will come see me when you return, just you. You'll be my guest and will stay as long as I need you. We have a great deal to discuss."

Charlie shook his head slowly, trying to comprehend the arrangement, but he couldn't put the pieces together. He said, "I don't understand what you could want of me, sir." He began to stammer. "I have very little to offer. I-I-I'm new here. I-I don't even know who you are, your name or anything…"

"I have no name, boy. I just am!" shouted the king. Then, his composure regained, he said, "And you have more to offer than you know." His voice lowered and with the quivering of his fan, became barely audible. "See, I have a fascination, an obsession, really, with the one thing you know more about than anyone else around here. Some of these fools on the floor have come close, but nothing compared to you. You've been there and back again and that makes me tingle." He took a deep breath, moving his head to shake the feather on his hat like a child. "My passion, my pursuit, Charlie, is death itself. And you hold her secrets. You do. My magnificent little dead boy."

29.

The sun was only a few hours old, but it was blazing already. When Charlie opened the door of the tavern and stepped outside, the light blinded him and the thick heat, filled to capacity with moisture, choked him. Since his arrival in Quindaro, he had yet to acclimate fully to the legendary humidity that accompanied the Kansas summers. He had learned to tolerate it to some degree, but it was different today. The truth was, the meeting with the man on the throne had shaken him, and his body was paying the price in waves of burning sweat. He leaned on the door with his eyes closed tight and tried to fill his lungs the best he could. Then, as if by habit, he spoke the words rooted in him by his mother for such occasions. "Get your bearings. Get. Your. Bearings." It worked. Like it always did.

He steadied himself and took in his surroundings. First, he noticed his horse tied to a tree nearby. Then, beside her, he noticed a pump marking the cap of a well. He hurried over, grabbed the cast iron handle and cranked it vigorously until the water started to surge. He stuck his head under the stream and after a second or two, the cooler, refreshing liquid from deep in the earth replaced the warm water close to the surface. He let it run on the back of his neck, then splashed it on his face and arms. The change in body temperature made him feel like a new man.

He walked over to Betty, the mare issued to him for the journey, untied her and jumped on her back. He had no idea where to rejoin the group, but he felt he needed to put some space between him and the tavern before the king changed his mind about letting his guest go free. He was sure the group wouldn't have gone far without him and if he hurried, he should be able to catch up with relative ease.

Charlie yelled to Betty to "get up," and she took off on a quick gallop back toward Leavenworth Road. When he neared the trail, he let Betty slow to a walk and turned her to the west to look for the boys. He hadn't traveled far when up ahead, he noticed several horses tied to a fence line on the side of the road. He pushed Betty forward and as he closed, he was happy to see the horses belonged to his companions. However, the joyous feeling didn't last long.

The men were missing and so were a few of the bags they had attached to their horses. It would have been a mistake to leave the horses and supplies unattended, a mistake Cuff would not have allowed. Something was wrong. Charlie scanned the area for clues, anything that would help him figure out what had happened to the group. Then, from the other side of the fence, in the distance, he heard voices. He jumped off his horse, cleared the fence with a bound and ran to the top of a small knoll to see what was on the other side.

The good news was he had found his friends and they were all still alive. The bad news was that they were in the clutches of three Six Mile men who, by the looks of it, were planning a hanging party. He closed on the group, screaming as he did. "Whoa, whoa, whoa, hold on a minute!" The captors turned to aim at Charlie but he continued undeterred. "My group and I were given free passage through here by the man in the tavern. He promised we wouldn't be harmed, we made a deal! You better go check with him before you do something you may regret."

The escort from earlier was holding Luke's travel bag, rummaging through it for any treasure it may hold. Charlie walked to him and grabbed the bag from his hands, saying, "And keep your hands off our things!"

One of the Six Mile men pulled a second pistol and rushed toward Charlie, sticking the gun an inch from his face. He said, "You don't tell us what we can nor can't do. You hear?" He snatched Luke's bag back from Charlie and continued. "You'll get in the hanging oak same as your friends here, I don't care what anyone says." He shouted to the escort to get another rope for the "loudmouth" and make it quick.

But the go-fer hesitated and protested meekly, "This one sat in the tavern. I took him there myself. And he come out same as he went in. I don't think we ought to put him in the oak."

"Oh hell," groaned the executioner. "Fine! He's free to go. The rest are going in the oak!"

Again, the escort protested. "If the whole group was given passage, I'm not sure any of them should go in the oak. Maybe we should run up to town and see…"

"Someone's going in the goddamn oak! You hear?" interrupted the leader. He looked to the third member of the gang for his endorsement but didn't get what he was searching for. Number three, who was tending the four travels who had been placed on their knees, looked to the ground instead. "Fine, then. How's this?" the leader conceded. "The black one and the old one go in the hanging oak. The other two, we bring back to town and see what we can get for them. This one," he said nodding toward Charlie, "goes free."

Oliver was indignant. He looked around and asked aloud, "Am I the 'old one'?" Of course, the outburst made matters much worse, the accent being proof to the Six Mile men that Oliver was less than human. The three agreed wholeheartedly to the settlement and moved to get the "black" and the "foreigner" strung proper.

"You can't do this!" yelled Charlie. "I have free passage!" His objections were loud and strong but did nothing to slow the hangmen from their mission.

Oliver and Cuff were hustled closer to the trunk of the tree so the physics involved in hoisting their bodies made more sense. Lee and Luke were yanked the other direction. Man number three pulled the cousins to the ground and guarded them closely, neutralizing any potential threat.

Charlie was the only member of the party left free to move about but that too soon came to an end. When he grabbed one of the men's arm to stop the rope around Cuff's neck from being pulled tighter, the man in charge knocked Charlie back with a wrap from his pistol handle.

Charlie fell to the ground with stars in his eyes. Cuff's rope was pulled tight, lifting his helpless body, his feet floating a few inches in the air. Another strong hoist and Cuff would be done for.

Suddenly, through the fog in Charlie's head, he saw two figures spring from the hedges. Before the Six Mile men could react, Colonel Tough and one of David's Jayhawkers attacked with impunity. The blitz was fierce and complete, ending with all three would-be hangmen comatose in the dirt.

Tough and his colleague untied the prisoners, paying particular attention to Cuff who assured them he was unharmed.

As the group regained their faculties, David himself emerged from behind the hedgerow. Surveying the scene, he let out a laugh. "Nice going, fellas, you lived to almost lunchtime. Hell, I figured something would have eaten and shit you out by now, I'm impressed." No one said a word. "Look here. Normally, I'd be perfectly comfortable watching you all wander into the wilderness like little babies to face certain death and destruction. However, seeing how much this trip means to the town, I can't let that happen. So here's what I'm going to do. I'm sending Tom here back to Quindaro, and Tough and me are going to join your merry band."

Oliver immediately started to object, but Charlie stopped him. "Oliver, we can't do this alone. We need the help."

Oliver's suspicion was impossible to hide. "I don't like it, not one bit."

"Would you rather have ended up in the hanging oak?" David asked. "We can leave and let these idiots finish what they started. When they wake up anyway. You want that?"

Oliver thought for a moment, then answered curtly, "No."

"Then let's get going," David ordered.

The group started for their horses. Charlie waited for Oliver to get beside him and with a nod, whispered, "It'll be fine." Oliver didn't reply.

The group, now including Colonel Tough and David as leader, mounted their horses and started west once more. Charlie was the first to break the tension. "By the way, the tree back there, the 'hanging oak', it's a sycamore, not an oak."

David looked back at the tree, then to Charlie. "You sure about that?"

"It's the only thing I've been sure of since I got here," answered Charlie.

"Huh," mumbled David. And with nothing more to say on the matter, he ended the conversation in his usual way. "Well. I'll be damned."

30.

Henry Cook stood on the bank of the Missouri River chewing a fat cigar. He was supervising a crew of nearly fifty men working twice as many mules and oxen. The recent lack of rain and a shifting of the river's main channel had exposed a steamboat that sank a couple years back. Cook and his men worked hard, battling the river and the day's heat, hoping to salvage the wreck and put the bounty it held to good use.

The boat, called the *Arabia*, sank after hitting a tree trunk concealed just below the water's surface. These giant hidden logs made trips on the Missouri River treacherous and, along with other hazards like sandbars and large rocks in the shallows, sank nearly a hundred boats a year. Most of the wrecks fell to the bottom of the river and sank deep into the muddy earth below. But occasionally, during a flood or a drought, both of which were painfully commonplace and oddly, could occur within the same year, the river would cut a new channel leaving what was once hidden visible. Scavengers like Cook's crew had to act fast in order to retrieve what was revealed before the river swallowed it up again and the opportunity was lost.

Most of the steamboats carried everyday items like clothing, shoes, dishes and such. Whiskey and other medicinal substances were popular as well. However, when a great boat like the *Arabia* was lost, rumors of riches swirled. To many, the fact that the manifests never listed gold, silver or other valuables was proof enough treasure existed. These romantics dreamt of rubies, emeralds and diamonds because, of course, whatever was not on the official record, logically, must have been part of the boat's "secret" cargo. Therefore, everything from the Holy Grail to King John the Bad's lost riches were likely somewhere in the depths of the muddy river.

Cook was a born skeptic. He never heard of anyone finding gold on a wreck and considered the treasure hunters common fools. However, he kept his view to himself. He found a man would work exponentially harder to find gold than he would to find boots or blankets, so whatever it took to drive his crew, he exploited.

The recovery of the *Arabia* was a long shot. It sat on the edge of the newly carved channel, ready to fall over at any moment. The two smokestacks stuck out of the water along with a small portion of the wheelhouse. Cook's men were running lines and chains to the stacks and other portions of the boat, tying them off to nearby trees until they were ready to pull. It was impossible to lift the boat from the river. All they hoped to do was tip it on its side away from the channel into the shallow edge. Then they could work fast to empty the goods stored below, throwing them onto the shore.

Cook was yelling orders to a group of men on the river, anchored near the boat when Blue approached. His lieutenant asked, "Do you have a minute, sir?"

"Yep," Cook answered.

Blue had just come from the town of Wyandotte. There, he met with The Whistler in order to pay him for the latest attack on Quindaro. It had gone well—four dead, two others hurt badly. Cook was happy to hear the good news.

The Whistler also shared a useful bit of information. He told Blue that David Sorter had left Quindaro with a small group and was heading somewhere up near the Nebraska line. The Whistler didn't know all the details of the trip, but the fact that Sorter was gone, probably for a week or better, left the town vulnerable.

"And Tough?" asked Cook.

"He went too," replied Blue.

"The Indian girl?" asked Cook.

"She stayed behind," answered Blue.

Cook thought a moment. The legend of a lost cannon hidden near the Nebraska border had circulated for some time. But Cook didn't buy it, and David Sorter surely wasn't the type to believe in fairy tales. Blue didn't like the cannon as a reason either and suggested to Cook that maybe Sorter was going north to meet with old Reverend John Brown. After all, he had a hideout near there, and Brown and Sorter had been close at one time.

Cook agreed the theory had merit but he wasn't completely sold. Frankly, the reason for Sorter's departure wasn't important. He was gone, that's all that mattered. Quickly, a plan started to form and he asked, "We have a shipment of rifles and shells coming, right? When are they due here?"

"Day after tomorrow, three days at the latest," replied Blue. He decided to share a strategy he'd been working on since he heard the news. "You know, I was thinking. If we had another hundred men or so, we may be able to charge up that hill. There's a chance we could march right into Quindaro proper and do a ton of damage. It may not work, but we'd have a far better time of it without Sorter and Tough around."

"I was thinking the same thing," Cook said. He yelled to the men to get off the river and get the animals secured. It was time to give the *Arabia* a yank. Then he turned back to Blue and gave his orders. "Send a man south to Joplin and tell Martin to send as many men as he can afford. We need at least eighty or ninety here by sunup Thursday. I want you personally to ride to Leavenworth and tell Harris to send what he can. Have them set up in Parkville and I'll get instructions to them real soon. Also, tell him I thought it would be a good idea to send eight or ten men out to the prairie. Maybe they can run into Sorter and his group and get the drop on them out there. They could stall them if nothing else."

He shouted a final order to the crew to pull on his mark. Then he turned to Blue and dismissed him, saying, "Nice work, son. You did good." Blue rode off, beaming with pride at his commander's approval.

The men and animals were all in place and Cook gave his signal, a single pistol shot in the air. The teams pulled with all their might, rocking the boat toward the shore. The men whipped the animals and yelled like banshees. They could almost taste the gold bars they were sure to find hidden in the hull of the wreck. As the boat neared the tipping point, a sudden snap caught Cook's attention. Then another. One by one, the chains and lines gave way and with each snap, the boat tilted back toward the river's jaws. Finally, the number of lines was less than enough to hold the boat, and it rocked slowly the other way, falling ever so gently into the deeper water.

When the smokestacks began to fill, Cook knew the battle was lost. He mourned as he lit his half-chewed cigar and let out a quiet "Shit!" The steamboat sank completely within minutes.

Shockingly, the *Arabia* would be found 132 years later, buried beneath forty-five feet of mud and silt in the middle of a Kansas cornfield.

31.

As the miles passed, David, Colonel Tough and Cuff rotated riding positions, taking turns in front, back and middle, shifting without signals or an official schedule. The conversation was light the first day and dominated by David's interrogation of Oliver concerning their route and overall direction. To David's chagrin, Oliver gave little detail. His directions were simply to set a course for the area near the Nebraska border, somewhere between the main road north out of Lawrence and the main road south from Leavenworth. David was frustrated, to say the least. By his calculations, there were nearly fifteen miles between these two roads. And even if Oliver could get them within five miles of the border, that would leave nearly a hundred square miles of search area. The group would need more to go on, by God! The only counter Oliver would offer, as each successive tantrum grew in potency, was a chuckle and his observation that David "worried too much."

They traveled the first day until sunset. Then they made camp and set a watch schedule for the few hours they planned to sleep. Early the next morning, they packed and started north again, sleepy but able. The conversation was much more interesting the second day, covering a variety of topics, from guns to girls.

By far, the most interesting topic covered Charlie's meeting with the man in the Six Mile tavern. Everyone in the group had heard stories about the mystery man, none good. He was a ruthless leader of a gang who stole and murdered to feed their addictions to opium, whiskey and adrenalin. They held no loyalties other than to the man with no name and no official title.

The fact that Charlie lived through the experience was a miracle as far as the cousins were concerned. They'd had a run-in with some of the crazies across the river in Westport and barely escaped with their scalps. Five or six of them chased Cuff once, clear down to the thick woodlands. He finally lost them by ducking into a cave he knew. The story was even more entertaining considering the men who gave chase were all naked as jaybirds.

Oliver had never heard of the man as he tried not to associate with what he called "common garbage." David however, seemed to know him more than he wanted to let on. He was vague, giving few specifics, but it was clear he and Tough had worked with the Six Mile gang at some point. Maybe more than once. There was one thing he did make clear, however. The man Charlie met may well have been "garbage," but there was nothing "common" about him at all.

The group made camp earlier the second night as the excitement and the long ride of day one had finally taken its toll. They built a fire in a small clearing, filled their stomachs and settled in for the night. The subtle crack of a twig just outside camp caught everyone's attention and then, from the trees, a man—a soldier—with an oddly relaxed gate emerged and stood near where Charlie had made his bed.

Charlie was flustered but seemed to be the only one. David had given him a pistol on the way out of Six Mile and offered only the most basic instructions. "Point this end at what you want to kill and pull this trigger. It's easy." David had offered the same weapon to Oliver, who abruptly refused to take it on the grounds that he was much too civilized. Charlie now had his gun tucked under his jacket, lying just beside him, and he wondered if he should reach for it. Something about the intruder made him uneasy.

"Evening, Lieutenant," said David. He was calm. Steady.

"Good evening, gentlemen," answered the soldier. "What are ya'll doing way out here?"

David seemed playful as he told of how they were out looking for runaways but so far had no luck. In fact, he said the group had concluded that all the runaways had truly run away, from here anyway. Or they plain decided not to run at all.

The soldier played along with a smirk. Then he looked at Cuff and asked, "What about him?"

"Oh, he wouldn't bring a bounty big enough, he eats too damn much," David explained. "Besides, he's a free man. Has papers and everything."

The soldier wondered if he could see the papers but David was sad to inform him they were left back in town. However, if need be, David would be more than happy to vouch for Cuff. "And I'll make sure he doesn't walk around looking too free," said David. "We wouldn't want to upset anyone."

The soldier had no answer for David, but it was clear he wasn't leaving. He looked down at Charlie, then to the cousins, his nerves starting to get the best of him. As he thought of what he should say next, his eyes betrayed him by darting into the woods for just a split second, inadvertently giving away the position of at least one of his cohorts.

David's gaze never left the man, and seeing the tension mount, he tried, halfheartedly anyway, to diffuse the bomb. He asked, "Is everything alright, Lieutenant?"

The man pulled his pistol and pointed it at Cuff, saying, "This one is coming with us." Around them in the woods, Charlie and the group heard the *click* of several weapons readying to attack. To Charlie, it was a sign his side was outnumbered. And surrounded. He tried to get as flat on the ground as he could and hoped a peaceful surrender would bring a similar resolution. They would have to save Cuff later.

However, to the trained fighter's ear, the clicks served

nothing more than to expose the location of the men that must be dispatched. David counted the sounds and determined they were indeed outnumbered but not by enough to change the outcome. After all, Lee and Luke never missed. Tough and Cuff would kill nearly as many in a fight as David, so the only deadwood was Oliver and Charlie. This would be easy.

David couldn't see Tough as he was behind him, but he made sure things were ready on that end of camp with the one-word question, "Tough?"

"Anytime," Tough answered.

It was decided. Things would get physical. "Then someone get things started," said David.

Cuff made the opening salvo by throwing a large knife into the intruder's neck. Blood poured from the man like it was dumped from a bucket and covered Charlie from the knees down. The woods erupted with gunfire and giant puffs of smoke as the other soldiers tried to avenge the loss of their leader. But the reactions of their targets were too quick, and the fight turned against them faster than they thought possible. David and Tough split up on instinct, blowing holes in the flanking positions in the woods. Lee and Luke opened up, allowing Cuff to hit the trees and drop into the darkness. There he became an executioner.

Charlie went for his gun, but Oliver stopped him. He grabbed Charlie and yanked him toward himself, yelling, "Run!" as he did so. Charlie didn't want to leave but Oliver took off and left him no choice but to follow. They ran hard and fast through the trees while crouching as low as they could. With each shot, Oliver altered his route to put as much distance between him and Charlie and the fight that was raging. Oliver surprisingly ran like a deer and made good time. He pressed Charlie to stay close and drove him by saying "Faster!" every few steps. Branches bent in Oliver's path and whipped at Charlie in the wake. Some of the cuts were deep and would certainly hurt. Later.

They came to a stream with a steep cliff wall on the other side; in the dark, they were unable to find a way up or around. Oliver scrambled for a hiding place and found a fallen maple leaning against a smaller oak. The two trees together were big enough for both men to duck behind. The shots still echoed through the forest but seemed to be getting farther away, so the pair took a moment to catch their breath. Their chests heaved as they leaned over, trying to be as quiet as possible while gasping for air.

Upset and angry, Oliver whispered loudly to Charlie, "Do you see? Do you see now why I don't trust Sorter? This mayhem is what follows him. The man is a violent animal, a beast! I swear, he's going to get us killed!"

Charlie didn't want to discuss David's involvement right now and tried to appease Oliver. "I know, I know," he said. "Oliver, we can talk about that later." Charlie paused, listening. The gunshots had stopped. "Right now, we need to figure out how to make our way back to the others."

Oliver didn't like the idea of backtracking since they had no way of knowing who won the battle. He and Charlie very well may be walking right back into the grip of the wicked soldiers. He thought it better to wait until morning, then find a way out of the forest.

Charlie ignored Oliver's plan to wait. He didn't know anything about the soldiers, their training or their pluck. But he would have bet all he had that David's team won the fight. He stepped away from the hiding place with a "Shh!" and looked around. There was a hill nearby and Charlie slowly, quietly made his way to higher ground. Oliver started to say something and Charlie turned and gave him a louder "Shh!" Turning back toward the hill, he almost ran into the tip of a pistol barrel aimed just below his left eye. A soldier was there in the dark, and he had Charlie dead to rights.

Charlie's face flushed, and he tasted a splash of bile as it hit the back of his tongue. His mind went blank, and he couldn't find his voice. He had been here before, alive but just barely. He heard the shot, or rather felt the sonic wave hit his chest, but he slept through it. He was only brought out of his stupor by the stinging in his eyes from the blood splatter that burned like salt. The soldier was gone suddenly and David was there. He touched Charlie's shoulder and waited until his color returned. Then he quietly asked, "Where's Oliver?"

Oliver stepped out from behind the trees and walked behind Charlie. He put his arm around him and wiped some of the blood from his face. "This is your fault," he said to David.

David didn't blink. "I've saved your ass twice now. I'm starting to wonder if it's worth it." He asked Charlie if he was able to travel and was assured he could. "Good," David said. "We have to get back. Luke's hurt."

32.

Walter had slept in his office the night before, working through the evening to finish a project for one of his clients. The payday for the job would be nice, but it needed to be complete before he was able to bill for it. He pushed himself hard through the fatigue and boredom of the work because frankly, he could use all the cash he could get his hands on right now. Calvin had not made contact yet but it had only been a week or so since their meeting. In Walter's experience, bad news traveled quickly. He held out hope that Calvin was just extremely busy and no news could truly be considered good news. In the meantime, Walter prepared as much as he could for the potential partnership.

The large couch he kept in his office was old and worn but offered more comfort than most beds. When the law office upstairs secured an extremely significant retainer, they decided to replace the furnishings in the office to keep up appearances. To sell the used furniture would be in bad form considering their recent ascension on the social strata, therefore they offered Walter the opportunity to take their hand-me-downs. He accepted only the couch, not wanting to look needy himself, and it became the nicest item in his otherwise basic office. He slept on it often, mostly to nap in the afternoon, and considered it one of his luckiest breaks.

It was early and he was awake but not up. Mrs. Wedge opened the office door and placed a mug of coffee and the newspaper on his desk. He stretched and yawned to wake up his bones and muscles in order to grab the coffee with the least amount of back and shoulder pain possible.

"Morning, Mr. Pomfrey," greeted Mrs. Wedge on her way out.

The front of today's paper told about the *Pennsylvania*, a steamship that exploded near Memphis, Tennessee, killing a few hundred passengers. It seemed the engineer was not at his post and was seen shortly before the explosion "in the company of some women." Whatever that meant. It happened just a week ago yesterday and already the paper had cause, blame and reaction. Bad news indeed travels fast.

There was also the daily update of the Senate race in Illinois where the newly organized Republican Party was making waves. Their candidate, a Springfield attorney named Abraham Lincoln, had given what was being called the "House Divide" speech to great fanfare. The fight there, though still verbal in nature, was heating up.

Like many of his fellow Bostonians, Walter favored Lincoln over Stephen Douglas, the architect of the pro-slavery Kansas-Nebraska Act. But not everyone saw things the way Walter did. He recognized the rhetoric and the escalating violence as sure signs that war was coming. He was also sure it would spread over the entire country once it began. Kansas Territory was the blueprint.

He was nearly finished with his coffee and craving a second cup when he heard a commotion in the receiving area outside his office. Mrs. Wedge was arguing with someone, which wasn't that uncommon. But the other voice seemed to belong to another woman, and that was strange. The door to his office cracked open, then shut again. Then open and shut again. There seemed to be a struggle, and the door was paying the price. The last time it opened, he heard Mrs. Wedge raise her voice explaining that Mr. Pomfrey was out. The second voice, however, was even louder and called through the gap in the door. "Walter, are you in there?" It was Cara. And Walter was always in for Cara.

He rushed to the door and diffused the situation the best he could. He thanked Mrs. Wedge for her diligence, then dismissed her. She stepped away in a huff, and Walter was sure he would pay for her hurt pride for the rest of the day. At the very least. He invited Cara into his office, where she skipped the formalities and jumped right into the reason for her visit.

One of her colleagues at the Aid Society had informed her that his office had been broken into and vandalized. When her friend relayed the details of the intrusion, he expressed how thankful he was that nothing of value had been taken. However, he would need Cara's help to rebuild the information kits they had put together for the towns in the West they were currently populating. Oddly, he deduced that only three folders were missing. One was for a town in Ohio being used as a supply depot. Another for a small burb in Nebraska. The last missing folder was for Quindaro.

"Do you have any idea who did the deed?" asked Walter.

"No," replied Cara. "Daniel asked about my work, but I squashed the conversation."

"Good for you," added Walter.

She continued. "But you know as well as I do, Walter, Daniel is clever. And resilient. Just because I was a dead end doesn't mean his search would stop. Moreover, if the Murrays had an inkling that the Society had anything to do with Charlie's disappearance, my colleague would be a plausible next suspect."

The news was disturbing, to be sure. The Murrays may be on the trail, and that could jeopardize everything. But Walter, the consummate worrywart, had thought about this scenario and planned for it. He thanked Cara for her concern and for coming to him so quickly. This would give him time to make arrangements and have Charlie leave Quindaro for safer pastures. He was thinking San Francisco.

"I have a friend in California," he began. "I was hoping I wouldn't have to send Charlie that far but if I have to, I will. I would rather not tell you everything, for your own protection of course. But rest assured," he boasted, "I have things under control, so you don't have..."

Surprisingly, Cara wasn't impressed with Walter's foresight and cut him off in the middle of his thought. She hadn't told him everything.

"Stop, Walter," she said. "The break-in occurred while my friend was away on business. A neighbor noticed the door ajar and reported it to the authorities the next day. He only learned of the breach when he returned and saw his door boarded up and a notice not to enter the premises unless accompanied by the sheriff. Once he was able to get in and figure out what was missing, he contacted me to help replace the lost information."

"How long was he away on business?" Walter asked.

"Two weeks," she answered.

Walter started to panic. "Then when was the break-in?"

"The report is dated the second. Eleven days ago," she answered.

Walter did the math in his head, but Cara didn't wait for him to get the result she already knew. "If they broke in eleven days ago and sent investigators west, they could have people in all three towns by now. There's no time to send a warning. Charlie is on his own."

33.

The *Otis Webb* hit the dock at Quindaro with a thud. Captain Webb shouted orders to his crew to tie up while Lee and Luke's fill-ins helped from shore. They secured the thick hemp lines and the boat sat motionless as if on land. Webb stayed in the wheelhouse while the passengers grabbed their luggage and lined up to go ashore. Some were hauling large trunks, others only small duffels. Nevertheless, they all protected their belongings as if they held all their worldly possessions, which they probably did.

Lee's replacement was doing a great job welcoming the newly arrived to town. He was polite, like Lee, and seemed content with the role he was playing. The kid doing Luke's job was struggling. He couldn't lift one of the large trunks and nearly dropped an elderly woman's hatbox in the river. Webb shook his head in disgust, then yelled to his crew to stop what they were doing and help the "dimwit" get the luggage unloaded. He couldn't wait for the cousins to get back to town.

There were eight passengers getting off in Quindaro, but Webb was particularly interested in four of them. They were all men, from out East most likely, and Irish for sure. They had one large bag between them, and the biggest guy in the group was put in charge of its care. The smallest and what seemed like the youngest was clearly in charge. He paid the fare and seemed to be making the decisions for the whole group. He wore a fancy shawl-collar vest that looked expensive but was a bit dirty from his travels. Webb guessed it was the nicest thing the kid owned, and he probably never took it off. The bowler hat on his head was older and broken in but respectable in its day and was clearly a sign of status when compared to the others' flat tweed headgear.

The leader of the group spoke in a thick Irish accent that was, at times, difficult to understand. When he had tried to tell the captain the group wanted to go to Quindaro, Webb was sure he misspoke. Or that he didn't understand what the man had said. Either way, this group didn't belong in Quindaro, that was for sure. Some Irish were in the area already but usually stayed on the Missouri side in Westport, the Town of Kansas or Independence. They rarely crossed over to Kansas Territory and they sure as hell didn't go to Quindaro. If that's where these guys wanted to go, they were up to something.

Of course, Webb, like many in America, didn't trust the Irish or any of the ethnic groups that were beginning to overrun the larger cities back east. The fact that most Irish were of the Catholic faith made them doubly dangerous because everyone knew Catholics pledged allegiance to the church over the state. In response, Protestant gangs like the Plug Uglies in Baltimore cracked Irish and Italian heads almost on a daily basis. Webb certainly didn't enjoy or condone the violence directed toward these people. In fact, on many occasions, even women and children were beaten severely—or to death. And that was right cowardly. However, the social structure was rigid and these groups needed to be shown their rightful place. And that was one rung above the common slave, a promotion earned by the whiteness of their skin and nothing more.

The captain kept a close watch on the men as the boat went upriver. They were quiet and stayed in a huddle for most of the trip. Once docked, Webb kept tabs on them the best he could, thinking he may be able to find out what business they had in Quindaro. He noticed the leader stopped on his way to shore and was conversing with one of the deckhands and Luke's replacement. Webb's man turned to the wheelhouse and made a gesture for the captain to come down. The man was asking questions the deckhand couldn't or wouldn't answer. And the deckhand was doing what he was told, following one of Webb's cardinal rules. "Keep your mouth shut until you know for sure what you say won't get someone killed."

Webb approached the young man in the bowler hat, and after a rather friendly greeting, found out just what the strangers were after. The story was that the group of men were looking for a friend they grew up with who they thought may have come west to Quindaro. It seemed the missing man's aunt had passed and he was needed at home to settle the estate. The man they were looking for was named Charlie. He was tallish with a rather normal build, light-brown hair, nice as could be. And quiet too, probably kept to himself for the most part. The Irishman reached into his pocket and pulled out a shiny three-dollar coin. He handed it to Webb with a wink and said he would appreciate any help the captain could offer. It was important they found their friend as soon as possible as the business back home was urgent.

The coin went into Webb's pocket while he rubbed his chin, feigning the difficult work entailed in probing his aged memory banks. "I can't say as I recall anyone like that around here. I wish I could help."

The young Irishman glanced at Webb's pocket where the coin had disappeared, not sure if he had gotten his money's worth. Webb noticed, and with a slight pat on the man's shoulder, explained, "The cost to find out if someone knows something is the same as it is to find out if that same person knows nothing."

The Irishman shrugged. "I guess so." Then, since he figured he had already paid the price for a couple more questions, he asked about the town's hotels and the grub situation.

To these inquiries, Webb was more than helpful. He told them the hotels had a great deal of turnover and they probably wouldn't be much help regarding the missing friend either. And since they were usually booked to capacity, the men may have a better go of it across the river. He recommended Westport. Then, returning the Irishman's wink to him, said there was a lot more "opportunity" to be had across the river too, if that helped.

As for food, Webb pointed them toward the Russian vendor halfway up the hill. "His name is Andrey but folks that know him call him Andy. You should call him Andrey until told otherwise. His stew is famous around these parts. You'll enjoy it."

The Irishman thanked Webb, and he and his men were off. The captain climbed to the wheelhouse and immediately pulled the line to blow the ferryboat's air whistle. Three short bursts followed by a long tug. Then the same pattern again. Finally, he pulled four times in a row. Now everyone within earshot of his warning would know there were strangers in town. Four, in fact. And the way this town could clam up, those poor Irish bastards would be lucky to get directions to the nearest outhouse.

34.

Chris Kelley was awakened by a slight rap on the door of his hotel room. The noise brought him around slowly and for a moment, he wasn't sure where he was. His eyes opened to the chair in the corner, where he saw his bowler sitting just to the side of the dusty windowpane, and his whereabouts came back to him. He remembered coming into the room and tossing the hat there, then sitting on the edge of the bed, near the foot. He had a while before he was to meet his men downstairs for dinner and decided to stretch out on the soft goose-down comforter. He rubbed his itchy eyes hard with his knuckles until stars flashed on his eyelids. It felt good to shut his eyes finally, so he kept them that way, thinking he could give them some rest for a moment. Obviously, a moment was too long. Sleep quickly took him, and he probably would have slept through the night if not for the knock at the door. Last week's traveling had taken a heavy toll.

The hotel he found was surprisingly quaint and exceedingly cheap compared to the New York digs he was accustomed to. When he and his men arrived, a polite couple, the proprietors themselves, greeted them from behind a large, shabbily carved front desk. The hotel management informed him, as the captain had warned, that the hotel was at full occupancy. However, there was an empty floor in the basement that stayed cool year-round and would get them out of the elements. The place also had a restaurant that would open in an hour, dinner would be served then. Chicken and dumplings, thankfully. Turns out the helpful captain was a bit of a jokester and the Russian stew recommendation was his playful way of hazing the newly arrived.

Chris and his companions were hardly above sleeping on the floor and in fact, had slept in worse conditions. Much worse. But tonight they wanted beds, and Chris wasn't taking no for an answer. Fortunately, as is usually the case, money solved the problem. And a delightfully small amount at that. They would have paid three times as much for a room half the size in New York. Therefore, when he and the hotel owners settled on an amount, Chris was more than satisfied. His group had to wait in the foyer while a couple of rooms were "vacated," and they got to enjoy the magnificent show the evicted patrons put on as they were hurried from the premises. Nowhere on Broadway could they have taken in the swearing and theatrics presented for less than ten dollars. And to get it included in the price of a room was unheard of.

He and his men had made zero progress in finding the trail of this "Charlie" character. They decided to get a room and try again tomorrow. The folks he met while climbing the hill, which never seemed to end, were extremely well mannered and welcoming. They listened to every question he asked about his missing friend and wanted to help in any way they could. However, no one did. In fact, not a single person had seen or heard of a man named Charlie or anyone who fit the physical description given. And a few of them answered so quickly that it seemed to Chris they would have blurted out the same "Sorry, I can't help you" no matter what name or description he asked about. It felt eerily like being in the Five Points neighborhood where he lived, only more polite. Whether they knew anything or not, no one was talking.

Chris respected the code of silence because he and his lived by it as well. You learn early on to keep your mouth shut about certain things and you absolutely would never give information to a stranger. Or a cop. But sometimes, the silence can tell you just what you need to know if you read between the lines. Chris' intuition told him the denials from the townspeople came too fast, and he had a hunch the kid was here. Or was at one time. Either way, he had to find the trail no matter how cold and then finish the job he was hired to do.

He looked again at the hat in the corner and thought about putting it on to answer the door. He was sure his hair was a mess and made him look even more worn than he really was. But he figured it was probably one of his men coming to check on him and they didn't give a shit how he looked, so he let the hat sit. He hated it anyway and all it represented. He stood up and made his way to the door, stretching his neck to loosen the kinks. When his hand touched the knob and turned it, the door smashed open, shoving him back onto the bed. A large Indian man put a giant hand over Chris' mouth and stuck a shiny blade to his neck. The attack was quick and silent. And since they fell onto the bed, there was no reason to believe any of his men heard the commotion from their room on the floor below. He was at the Indian's mercy.

Chris looked into his attacker's blacked-out eyes and saw an intensity that scared him. His life had been threatened numerous times, but this guy was different.

The Indian lowered his head slowly until it was next to Chris' ear. "Quiet," he whispered menacingly.

Chris obeyed. If the goal was murder, he'd be dead by now. Something else was afoot.

He heard the door shut quietly and footsteps come toward the bed. He couldn't see who it was because the large man was blocking his view. But he didn't have to wait long to find out it was a woman when she spoke to him gently, calmly. Like they were meeting for the first time at a Sunday social. "If my cousin allows you to sit up, you must agree to stay quiet. If not, he'll cut out your tongue."

Chris nodded his agreement. There was no doubt the threat was sincere. The weight of the man lifted and Chris was able to breathe deeply again. He sat up on the edge of the bed and checked his neck for blood. There was none. He looked to the woman and his breath was lost again. He had never seen anything more beautiful in his life, he was sure of it. He tried to speak but nothing came out, and he was surprised to find his hand had begun to smooth his wild hair. He wished he could put on his hat.

She introduced herself as Nancy and welcomed him to town. Some welcome. She asked his name and from then on, addressed him with it. The word "Chris" coming across her lips was a gift from above and he found himself begging, yearning for her to say it after every sentence. She used it frequently, like she knew the power it wielded, but he didn't mind the supremacy she abused. He loved it.

She walked to the chair in the corner, picked up his hat and hung it on the bedpost. She took a seat, then explained, as he suspected, that the town was tipped off when he arrived. Their proverbial lips were sealed. "Questions are a dangerous business and could be considered confrontations in Quindaro," she said. "You should be aware that you made enemies today on your way up the hill. That happens fast around here." She also hinted that if a man named Charlie was currently in town or had been to town and was accepted by the locals, he would now have friends. Powerful friends who would protect him from outsiders wishing to do him harm. "The town accepts strays quickly, too."

Chris' judgement was right again. Charlie was here. Her threat was all the corroboration he needed.

Nancy then explained she would allow Chris and his men to stay for three days, as the hotel needed the income. They were free to move about town if they wanted, but the inquisition was over. Any more questions about a lost boy would end badly for the visitors. Then, in three days, her cousin Adam, the painted warrior, would return with reinforcements and the hospitality would be replaced by hostility. She stood and returned his hat to the chair. Then she walked to him and asked, "Do you understand the agreement?"

Since he had recently regained his ability to speak, he replied, "Yes." Then, since it had been determined he would live through the meeting, he tested the waters with a little flirtation. "And thank you for the kind welcome, my lady. I'll never forget it."

She smiled with her whole face and it shot lightning bolts through him. She leaned close to him and whispered, "Neither will I."

At dinner that evening, Chris couldn't keep the broad smile from his face. He replayed the scene in his room again and again, skipping the assault and jumping right to her. It was all etched in his memory: her voice, her hair, the sound her clothes made when she walked. His senses were still overwhelmed. He didn't remember saying much to her until the end, when his mind cleared, but he would the next time they met. There was a connection. As real as he had ever felt.

His companions noticed his demeanor and traded stares with each other trying to figure out what was wrong with their leader. Finally, one spoke up. "What's with the shitty grin? It's giving us all the creeps."

"Can't a man just be happy without getting the third degree?" asked Chris.

His man thought a moment and answered, "No. He can't."

Chris smiled even bigger than before and answered the only way he knew how. "Mind your own fucking business, Tommy." Everyone laughed.

He planned to tell the men what happened to him and the rules they had to abide by while in town, but he didn't feel like doing it tonight. There would be pushback and he would have to answer too many questions. Hell, right now, he wasn't sure how the meeting changed the mission, but he had three days to figure it out. All he knew for sure was that he had been in the west for only one evening and just like the story books told, he had already been attacked by Indians. Beautiful Indians.

35.

The midday sun beat everyone and everything without mercy or favor. Charlie and the group moved slowly over the rough terrain, saving their horses from the heat as best they could. Luckily, their route north was escorted by a rather determined creek that cut back and forth and offered a cool crossing every other mile or so. The horses would take a pause when their feet hit the mud of the watershed and the men allowed it, taking the opportunity to fill their hats with water to splash over their heads. The trees growing near the creek helped too, their shade offering a break from the sun that the open prairie lacked. Often, these oases held secret stashes of wild strawberries that were great snacks and huge patches of sour grass that helped to ward off thirst. When they found these gifts, the group ate all they could.

David deliberately planned a slow pace for the day but warned the others they would travel clear to nightfall. No one objected. However, after the firefight the night before, certain accommodations would have to be made for Luke. A single shot from one of the soldiers had blown through his left forearm and, on the way out, nicked his thigh on the same side. After a quick and extremely painful cauterization, his attending surgeon, Cuff, gave him a clean bill of health, stating, "He will live." He would need help and consideration for the rest of the journey, and the group took turns attending to his needs and comfort.

David rode next to Charlie in the middle of the pack on a beautiful horse he called Saint Joan. She was gray and spotted, like Cook's ride, and elegant in every way. She happened to be one of the few topics David enjoyed discussing, so Charlie used her to start a conversation with the man who had saved his life at least three times. "She's beautiful. Where does everyone get those horses with the spotted coat?"

David's reply was curt at first but softened the more he talked about Joan. He explained that not "everyone" has a horse like this. Very few had them, in fact. And around here, they're almost unheard of. As far as David knew, he and Henry Cook rode the only two within a hundred miles. Cook was one of David's commanding officers during the war with Mexico. He was a prick then, by the way, maybe more so now, if that was possible. The men of the unit were issued these dapple-gray horses and most grew accustomed to it, mainly because of what they stood for. They used the horses as a symbol of power and unity. And they filled every Mexican soldier they came across with the primal fear usually reserved only for bears and lightning. Even after the war ended, those who could afford it rode a gray because nothing else seemed to fit. It was part of them and always would be.

However, truth be told—and David had no issue spilling it—the grays themselves were not that different from any other horse. The spots were simply a way to estimate the age of the animal, as the pattern was merely a byproduct of the hair whitening over time. When these grays got old, their coats would be completely white and no one would ever know what they used to look like. To ride the grays was more of a habit than anything else, but it made David feel better about himself, so he stuck with them. The superstitious fools like Henry Cook found a deeper meaning or a certain spirituality about the whole thing, but not David. Those ideas were for the oblivious who had time to waste. Like the churchgoers and Voodoo practitioners. Joan was a thing of beauty and did as she was told. That was about all there was to it.

It was hard to fully believe the explanation from David, as the sense of pride he had in Joan could not be concealed no matter how hard he tried. Charlie knew the gray horse and what it stood for still resonated with David and probably everyone he rode with while in Mexico. Looking back on his encounter with Cook, Charlie recalled the man had an aura about him that was undeniable. He ruled from the saddle that day, even from the shoreline, as if he and the horse were one creature, one monster, striking fear in both his enemy and, as was Charlie's case, his prey. There was no doubt Cook still believed in the message his gray sent those around him. And although David denied it, he had the same glow about him when paired with Joan. And the two were just as fearsome, just as monstrous, even to Charlie, who was technically on the same side.

They had ridden for hours in the heat, covering a fair amount of ground, when they finally came to the edge of a wide valley. The land below sprawled out for miles in each direction and the vast divide would take a day to cross. At least. The walls weren't steep, just lengthy, which was helpful and would certainly make for a safer descent. Especially for the injured Luke. The elevated perch where they stood offered a view of the entire area, and they were able to plan their path through before getting to the valley floor below. It could have been worse for sure. Nevertheless, the size and distance, especially after the day's ride, depressed the whole group. They didn't have enough left today to take on this obstruction.

David was the first to show his frustration. He sighed heavily, removed his hat and slowly rolled his head around, stretching his stiff neck. He asked Oliver if they were crossing this abyss or if he had other plans. He was sure Oliver wouldn't give a straight answer, so his question had a whiny tone to it that sounded odd coming from a man of his nature.

Oliver, however, gave the answer they were all waiting for. "You can quit crying, we're here." He aimed his right arm at a large tree on the prairie's deck, opposite from where they were. He touched his thumbs together and rotated his wrists, making measurements that only he understood.

David was unimpressed and mumbled, "Are you serious," under his breath.

Oliver gave a quick "Shh!" then settled on an area. He pointed to an outcrop of rocks at the bottom of the valley and said, "Right down there."

The men descended the valley wall and rode to the position Oliver pinpointed from above. It was rocky, with crevices here and there, some big enough for a man to stand up in. The glacier that cut the valley millions of years ago had chewed the ground as it moved and exposed the large, solid rock below. The wind and rain since then had fine-tuned the caverns and created the perfect hiding places that would last for eternity. Or at least until the next ice age.

Oliver got off his horse and started searching the area. He walked from stone to stone, rubbing his hand over them, feeling for something familiar. Finally, on a giant twenty-ton boulder lurched on its side, he found what he was looking for. There were markings on the rock, symbols cut shallow, hurriedly. He moved his hand over the carvings and whispered, "I told you I'd come back."

When Oliver turned to face the group, Charlie was the first to notice something was different. Oliver looked confused, lost. His eyes were blinking quickly like he was trying to focus but his glasses held the wrong prescription. He shook his head as if trying to make sense of his surroundings, trying to figure out where he was. When he finally looked over the top of the rims, he appeared to regain his focus on the men around him. He locked eyes with Charlie, who felt the cold stare of a stranger, an enemy, even. It was disturbing.

Oliver tore the glasses from his face and leapt toward the man closest to him—Luke. He cussed and yelled at the top of his lungs about how he planned to kill them all and make them pay for what they did. He grabbed at the rifle strapped to the side of Luke's horse but struggled with the knot holding it in place.

David screamed at Luke to fight for the gun and make sure Oliver didn't get it. He pushed Joan through the tight spaces trying to get close enough to help, but it was slow going. The men and horses were packed into a small opening that didn't allow for much movement. Luke would have to fight on his own until David could close the gap. Oliver pulled at the barrel and Luke the butt. The men yanked on the rifle, each doing what he could to get the upper hand. The bullet wound Luke received the night before began to bleed through the bandages as Oliver delivered blow after blow to the perceived weak spot of his opponent. This Oliver fought dirty, and Luke wouldn't be able to hold him off much longer.

David knew he had to make a move. He jumped from his horse onto a boulder and then raced across the tops of the rocks until he was right above Oliver. He pulled his pistol, reached down and smashed it into Oliver's head, knocking him to the ground, unconscious.

Charlie got down and ran to his friend, baffled by what had just occurred. Something was wrong, different. And it seemed only David understood the joke. He yelled to Cuff to throw him a blanket then propped it under Oliver's head, trying to comfort him as he lay within the rocks. He grabbed the canteen from his horse and sat next to his injured friend, waiting to give him a drink when he came to. He looked up toward David standing over them and finally asked, "What the hell was that all about? That wasn't the Oliver I know."

Luke agreed. "You know, I think he would have killed us all if he would have got that rifle."

Lee was rewrapping his cousin's arm with clean bandaging cloth. He didn't want to ask the next question, but someone had to. "And his accent, where did it go? When he was yelling, he didn't sound like a Brit anymore. How's that possible?"

The group looked to David. He didn't answer. Instead, he jumped down to the ground and peered into the cavern Oliver found. The cannon was inside as promised. He tried to change the subject. "We need to get this thing loaded and figure out how we're going to get through these rocks with it."

Charlie and the cousins weren't having it. "You know what happened, don't you?" Charlie asked quietly.

Again, David didn't answer. Finally, he looked at Tough, who gave him a nod. He needed to come clean.

"Oliver will be fine and should be back to normal when he wakes up. He usually is, anyway. Luke, you're right. If he would have gotten his hands on that rifle, he would've killed a few of us for sure. Nice job fighting for it, hurt and all. I'm proud of you." He paused, not knowing how to explain the last part. "And his British accent went away because he's not from England. He's from Ohio. Like me." He took a deep breath. "He's my brother."

36.

The docks of Wyandotte were bustling. Three ferryboats were parked and unloading while several more waited their turn. The Missouri river was dynamic, with goods and people arriving daily, and the towns located on its shores were reaping the benefits. Especially Wyandotte. Because it was located where the Kansas River met the Missouri, it was the jumping-off point for those heading into Kansas Territory or those traveling north along the border. A wait to offload here was normal, but today was worse than usual. Henry Cook was the cause.

His much-anticipated weapons shipment had arrived and his excitement was bubbling. He directed the offload from the dock, issuing orders to both the ferry crew and the men on shore. Blue helped once the items hit land and moved them to the staging area nearby. Earlier in the week, Cook had contracted with Stan to use his facilities to receive, inventory and sort his inbound hoard. Now, Stan's entire property was crammed with boxes, bags and containers of all sizes. Cook's remaining crew worked like ants counting allotments for distribution to each division under his command. The items were meticulously tallied and so far, only one crate of shells seemed to be missing. Considering the size of the shipment, that was a miracle.

It had been a long time since something this size had shown up in Wyandotte, and Stan was impressed. And a little concerned. Sure, the pay was good, but the amount of firepower coming off the boat was ominous, and it gave him pause. Something big was about to happen, he was sure of it.

He hated taking sides, as it was bad for business. However, the balance of power that had worked so well in the past was clearly gone now. Sorter and his bunch would be outgunned, out-bulleted and out-shelled by a long shot. That was also bad for business since the nice, even, semi-fair fight that had been going on worked well for Stan and the folks of Wyandotte. However uncomfortable it felt to meddle, something would have to be done to sustain the traditional arrangement.

From a distance, Stan watched Cook and Blue work the men. They were efficient but not rushed, much to the dismay of the cued ferryboats. The waiting captains and crews were visibly frustrated since they would likely run behind for the rest of the day. A few snide comments echoed off the water but they didn't last long once Cook was identified as the culprit. After all, keeping to a schedule wasn't worth getting shot. So, one by one, they settled in and embraced the wait.

Stan was waiting too. He wanted to find out what Cook planned to do with all this equipment, but that was hardly a question he could come right out and ask. He figured once the work at the dock was complete, Cook would pow-wow with Blue to make sure everything was running smoothly on this end. There was a good chance that at the same time, Cook would give Blue his marching orders as well. Stan wanted to be there when that happened. When he saw the leader of the Ruffians mount his horse and ride toward the staging area, he hustled through the stacks and piles to get as close to Blue as he could.

A large crate marked "US Rifle Co." gave Stan the cover he needed to eavesdrop on the two men. Blue tended to mumble when he spoke, so it was tough to hear him completely. Even with his good ear, Stan could only pick out a few words here and there. However, Cook's voice radiated and echoed like a man shouting into a cave. That, coupled with his excitement, elevated his voice. Stan and everyone within twenty feet of Cook heard every word as clear as day.

From what Stan could gather, the little town of Quindaro was in serious trouble. Over the last few days, the entirety of Cook's forces had been summoned to the area and were awaiting orders. By dusk the next day, Cook wanted them in place at the base of the Quindaro hill, hidden as much as possible in the thick trees. Once he decided on which side of the hill to make his charge, he would divide the troops accordingly. His cannons would open first to get the rats scattering. Then once he felt the town's knees weaken, the men would start their climb and the bloodbath would begin. He was relatively confident he had the manpower to overwhelm his enemy. After the delivery today, he was more than certain he had the firepower as well. But just to be sure, he had taken precautions.

He had reinforcements, on loan, coming from southern Missouri; these men would guard his rear lines and join the fight if need be. Their exact arrival time was still up in the air but Cook had a notion the heavy lifting would be over by then anyway. If they were here in time, great. But he wasn't going to wait for them to make his move. He also had a group of men, mostly off-duty soldiers, coming down from Leavenworth. They would set up camp just north along the river in Parkville and wait for Cook's signal. Then they would continue south and help with the final squeeze. That left Quindaro's only possible retreat west on Leavenworth Road, straight into the jaws of Six Mile. No doubt, the animals there would smell the blood and take full advantage of the smorgasbord as it passed.

Cook calculated some would make it out and probably beat a path to Lawrence. But he could live with that considering the town left behind would be blown off the hill and into the muddy river below. He was sure—as sure as one can be when warfare is involved—that if they delivered the blows properly and according to his design, the victory would be absolute. More than that, the defeat on the other side would be too much for the town to come back from.

After hearing the details, Stan was as convinced as Cook of

the validity of the plan. He slipped away just as the crate of rifles was lifted behind him and made his way onto the street to think. He wasn't sure what to do with the information but he needed to do something, and quick. The clock was ticking on the town of Quindaro. And just as surely, the status quo of Wyandotte. Sorter and his crew would need every second they could get to figure out how to absorb the impact of Cook's attack. He doubted they could make much of a stand, but maybe if they had enough time, some of the innocents could make a run for it. The women and children could be spared at least, and it wouldn't be a total loss.

Speaking of children, he suddenly noticed a couple of them standing on the sidewalk across the street. As luck would have it, the young boy was exactly who Stan needed right now. Maybe it was a sign! He looked to the sky and shrugged his understanding to the Almighty. The old man hustled to meet the kids and nearly lost a toe to a passing buggy. He closed on them quickly and put one arm around Billy Cody's shoulder and the other around Polly Welborn's. Together, the three hustled between two buildings where Stan could say his piece.

The old man greeted the two kids as fast as he could, asking about their parents and siblings and found everyone satisfactory. He knelt on one knee to be eye to eye with Billy and told the boy to listen carefully to what he was about to hear, as Stan only had time to relay the information once. Then he spilled the news of the attack. The boy's face turned white, as did the girl's, and she grabbed his shaky hand to steady them both.

Stan had only one measure of comfort to offer and he used it as he finished his speech. "Just find Sorter. Tell him what I told you. Every bit of it. He'll know what to do."

It provided little relief because the boy replied, "Mr. Sorter is gone. Has been for a few days. No one knows when he'll come back…"

"Dammit!" whispered Stan. "Sorry, girlie," he said to Polly, embarrassed for the swear that popped out in front of the young girl. He was out of time and had to get back to the store, so he sent the kids to the only other option he could think of. "Go now, over to Quindaro. Find Mrs. Brown and let her know what I just told you. She'll take it from there." That's all he could think to do. He sent them on their way with a pat on the head and said, "Hurry, boy. As fast as you can."

"Yes, sir," replied Billy. He and Polly climbed up onto his horse and took off towards the town.

Stan slowly walked back across the street and it all made sense. Cook didn't have the balls to challenge someone holding the high ground. Unless he knew he had an edge. The amount of ammo was a plus, but not enough to make a charge that steep. He must already know what Billy relayed. Sorter was gone. The town was vulnerable. That could mean only one thing. Quindaro has a traitor.

37.

Walter wrote a letter to Charlie warning him of the potential pursuers. If Cara's information was correct and the break-in gave the Murrays a list of towns to search, Charlie could already be in serious danger. Walter needed the letter to be on its way quickly, today if possible. He sealed the envelope and, on the back, marked the lower right corner with three stars. The code he and Charlie had established before the getaway was simple but effective. So far, anyway. They agreed to mark their correspondence with stars so each would know the letter was bona fide. They would also increase the number of stars to indicate the importance of that particular letter. The three stars on this envelope was the most either had scrawled. So far, anyway. Finally, Walter had a friend, Peter, who lived a few blocks away and would send and receive the letters under his address, just in case the Murrays decided to intercept Walter's mail. The friend was sympathetic to Walter's situation, agreed to help and had been quite accommodating. So far, anyway.

He shoved the envelope into his breast pocket and grabbed his cane. He didn't like the way he looked carrying it because he thought it made him look older, feeble, even. But he made sure to always have it with him now just in case. Better safe than sorry.

Peter's office was in the same building that Walter's father used to lease when he started the family business many years ago. It was a short walk from Walter's office in distance, but with the heavy city foot and carriage traffic, the time it took to make the trip could be weighty. He'd lived in the city most of his life, and knew how to navigate the busy streets. He could weave in and out, barely touching shoulders with those he squeezed past, and could make it to where he wanted to go faster than most. However, as is the case with all of God's creatures, age had caught up with him. The graceful maneuvering he had when he was younger, along with most other aspects of his life, had depreciated. He could still see the dangers coming at him—kids running, thieves fleeing, dogs growling—but his body just couldn't get out of the way as quickly as it used to. Therefore, a bruise here or there after trips through crowds was more common now. And as he reached the office building, he rubbed his forearm where a nice purple mark would surely appear in the next couple of hours. Damn kids!

The doorknocker was brass and heavy and made a huge clank when Walter slammed it. Peter's man answered and invited Walter into the foyer to wait. The adjacent room, the parlor where Walter had visited with Peter on many occasions, usually sat open and inviting. Today, though, the door was shut and excited voices from inside poured out of the gap between the bottom of the door and the solid oak floor, echoing throughout the home. There was a party in progress, and it was a doozy. The door swung open and Peter emerged holding a full glass of brown spirits and smelling as though he used the same spirits with which to bathe. He made Walter's eyes water.

Peter greeted Walter with a hug of all things, shaking him wildly and spilling a swallow or two onto the wall behind them. He held onto Walter's shoulder for balance and apologized for the damnedest case of the hiccups a body ever had to endure. Walter said he didn't mind and pulled the envelope from his pocket, trying to make quick work of the exchange and leave as soon as he could. Unfortunately, it didn't work.

Peter was a sincere man and honest, for the most part. Walter liked him, everyone did. But he was a merciless drunk. And when he attached to someone, he was hard to escape.

He invited Walter to join the festivities. "Franklin is in town! We're celebrating Nathaniel's birthday. He was born on July fourth, you know. That must have some meaning, wouldn't you think? But he's not here, Nathaniel, he's in France. Or Europe. I mean, England. Hell, who knows!"

The "Franklin" was Franklin Pierce, the former president. He and Peter were close friends, having grown up very near one another in New Hampshire. Pierce was from Hillsborough, Peter from the next town over, Deering. They attended the same school as children, along with "Nathaniel", the writer Nathaniel Hawthorne, and had been thick as thieves since. So much so that after the election of 1852, Peter lived and worked in Washington and served on several ad hoc committees throughout Pierce's single term. Unsurprisingly, he was able to affect absolutely nothing, positively or negatively, in the entire four-year span.

Walter was not a fan of the former president and declined the invitation. Politely. He again pressed the issue of the letter, but Peter's mind was raging. "You must stay, Walter. I have breakfast coming, a bubble and squeak. Mrs. Rundell's recipe, right out of the book. It is fabulous! Should be ready any moment."

Clearly, Peter and the president had been at it for a while, since breakfast was to be served at nearly four in the afternoon. They had obviously lost track of the time. Again, Walter declined, envelope in hand.

Peter drew close and spoke softly, slurring. "Walter, I know you don't appreciate Franklin. And I understand. I do. If you met him, you would see he's not the monster he's made out to be." He turned and looked to the open door. He wheeled back around, appearing dizzy, and held a finger up to Walter's face. "And you should give him latitude. He's had a difficult go of it."

Pierce and his wife had lost all their children. The last one, eleven-year-old Benjamin, was killed just weeks after his election while traveling from Boston. Tragically, an axel on the train they were riding broke and caused their car to roll down an embankment near Andover. Franklin and his wife Jane survived with bumps and bruises. Young Bennie, however, was crushed to death and his body nearly decapitated. The sight of the child in such a state devastated both parents. They were ruined. For good.

Walter could only agree. That was the best course for the moment. The truth was Walter didn't like Pierce even before he became president. He was a weak senator and what's worse, a doughface. To be a northerner with southern sympathies was akin to being a traitor. Walter and the rest of the abolitionist crowd knew Pierce would sell them out to the slave owners in the south; hell, that's why it took forty-nine ballots for the man to win the party's nomination. No one wanted him to be president. He wasn't qualified. Besides that, he had been a drunk for years. He and Peter both. There must have been something in the New Hampshire water. Therefore, to blame his ineptness, or his drunkenness for that matter, on the crash was like deciding to skip the first twelve chapters of *The Scarlet Letter*. The narrative was incomplete.

Peter finally noticed the envelope in Walter's hand and snatched it quickly, shouting, "Ah! another letter. I'll get right on it." He yelled to his man, who appeared out of nowhere, then instructed him to get the package to the post office "post haste!" The play on words tickled him deeply. Before his man could make a break for it, Peter grabbed him by the jacket and pulled him near. "If this letter isn't posted this very day, you will be skinned alive and fed to the dogs who roam the streets downtown. Is that clear?"

His servant bowed, gave Walter a deadpan smile and began the errand immediately.

With the front door open, Walter saw his chance to run

too. He thanked Peter for his help and grabbed the knob but couldn't quite break free.

Peter grabbed his shoulder and, in a whisper like before, he asked, "Have you had any luck with your business quandary? I hear the Murrays are on a rampage, looking for the lost heir. I figured that might have something to do with you and me. And our letters." He attempted a wink but failed.

Walter eased toward the door, straddling the threshold, almost free. What's the harm in sharing? His friend wouldn't remember this conversation anyway. "Still looking for financing, but I have a lead. Already met with an old family friend and it looks promising." He stopped a second, withholding the name. Then came out with it. "Calvin Ringgold."

Peter exploded. "That's why I love you, old man, so much grit! My God, I'd love to see the look on James Murray's face when you rip his crutch from him." He held up his glass and toasted Walter with a giant swig. "Ringgold! You give it to the bastards, Walter."

Walter could have gotten away as Peter went on and on, but something felt off. He needed clarification. "Peter, Peter! Stop please. What did you mean? You said 'crutch.' I don't understand what that means."

With the question, his drunken friend's mania suddenly subsided. Peter emptied his glass with one gulp and placed it on top of a nearby hutch. With both hands, he cradled Walter's face and spoke solemnly. "You poor fool. You weren't being heroic, you simply didn't know."

Peter couldn't hide the pain, the empathy he felt for his friend. His eyes were filled with a cold sadness that Walter didn't understand. It was uncomfortable; for some reason, embarrassing. Nevertheless, Walter couldn't look away. Not until he understood. He had a notion but he needed to hear it.

"They are partners, Walter. The Murrays and Ringgold.

Have been for some time," said Peter, crushing his dear friend. "Calvin is not your salvation, he is your destruction."

Peter cradled Walter and silently led him into the parlor. "Mr. President. Honored gentlemen. This is Walter Pomfrey, an old friend. He needs a drink." He got one.

38.

The wind had shifted and was now coming from the east, a fair indicator weather was on the way. With the energy provided by the heat of the day, if storms did come, they would likely be severe. The dark, mile-high clouds were visible on the horizon and seemed to be closing in quickly, forcing Charlie and the group to move fast. David promised he would explain the news he dropped on them soon enough. But he wanted to get the cannon pulled up the valley wall and get under cover before all hell broke loose. He tasked the cousins with constructing some sort of cradleboard to help move Oliver until he came to. He hoped they could attach it to the cannon so the dead weight of both the gun and Oliver would travel easier. The work was nearly done when David pointed to a cottonwood grove about a half mile away from the valley lip. That's where he wanted to be when the rain came, and everyone consented without a word.

Cuff was the first to arrive under the thick canopy. He saw a few low limbs from one of the younger trees and decided to hang a couple blankets to impede what rain made its way through the higher leaves. The group could make a stand there and wait out the weather. It would also provide cover to help keep Oliver comfortable and dry. He dismounted and with a nod, called Lee to duty. Once the makeshift shelter was secure, the group settled in, awaiting the promised explanation. And the thunderstorm.

The cotton shed was thick, ankle-high in places, and it swirled eerily in the strong wind gusts. The men sat on the soft ground and looked to David like kids waiting for their teacher to share the lesson. David's unusually strong constitution was gone and he struggled to begin. He apologized for not telling them sooner but the secret was something he only shared with his closest confidants. He looked at Tough as an example. He tried to start again, to tell his brother's story but couldn't. He shook his head, looking to the ground to hide his eyes. Seeing his service was necessary, David's best man took over.

"It's a long story, so pay attention," Tough began. "You know how I feel about repeating myself." He began.

"Oliver's real name is Alexander Sorter and he's David's older brother. By ten years or so. They grew up in Ohio." They are the sons of a minister-farmer who, along with his pacifist wife, raised all his children, the two girls included, to be sturdy and smart. Both men left home to fight in the war with Mexico but only David came back right after. Alex re-upped and went to California with his regiment. It was there where his troubles started.

Under the command of Nathanial Lyon, Alex was present at what became known as the Bloody Island Massacre. His regiment, on the hunt for two Pomo Indian men who had allegedly committed murder, came upon a settlement of mostly old men, women and children. Lyon decided to punish the village and ordered every Pomo killed. And most were. A couple hundred, at least. Alex, however, refused the kill order and was promptly arrested. While detained he was beaten, taunted and finally informed he would hang for insubordination the following afternoon.

"That evening, he decided to make a run for it," continued Tough. "He overpowered two guards on his way out of camp, killing the first one out of necessity. After breaking free, he considered himself 'discharged' and decided he was done with military life. Technically, he's still a fugitive."

Rather than seeking safety back home, Alex stayed in California. "Just what he did there and with whom he did it exactly is unknown," said Tough. David heard rumors over the years that his brother rode for a stint with Joaquin Murrieta, the famous Mexican outlaw. He also heard stories putting Alex with Harry Love, the Ranger whose job it was to track and kill Murrieta. Both stories had flaws. Alex was white so he probably wouldn't have been welcome with the outlaw Murrieta. And his experience with Lyons at Clear Lake had soured him on any and all organized military work.

"Whatever the real story, whatever happened to him there, one thing is clear," warned Tough. "Alex was transformed. And when he returned to Ohio, he was an experienced and efficient killer. The best I've ever seen."

That wasn't to say he was cold and unfeeling when it came to human life. It was quite the opposite, in fact. He followed his father's footsteps by joining the church and became a fervent abolitionist in the mold of Reverend John Brown. He feared God and tried to do his work daily. However, like Brown, when provoked or cornered, Alex was a force of nature. He was fast, lightning fast. And as accurate with a pistol as anyone could be. It was scary what Alex could do with a weapon—any weapon, really. Even scarier once his mind was made up that action was necessary. Then, there was no stop. No halt. No quarter. He finished his fights like a lion, bloody and victorious. It wasn't long before news of his prowess spread and his reputation led to a proposal from the Society.

Three years ago, Alex accepted an offer to accompany a group of abolitionists to Kansas Territory and protect them from any harm they may encounter. Feeling it was his duty, he took the job, asking only for the cost of travel and ammunition. The territory was a battleground where men like him could make a real difference. What's more, news that his old commander Nathaniel Lyon was now stationed at Fort Riley, Kansas made the offer even more appealing. He dreamt of settling that score. So, he was all in.

The main reason for the trip was to deliver a cannon to the Free-Staters, who were having trouble keeping up in the arms race. It was a gift from the state of Wisconsin and a godsend. They planned to deliver it to the town of Lawrence and dispatch it from there as needed. At a public ceremony to consecrate the trip and give thanks for the battles the gun would help win, the travelers christened it Lazarus. Then they hit the trail.

They stopped here and there for water and supplies. Mostly small towns, homesteads and farms. Then, near the border of the Nebraska Territory, the story got fuzzy. From what David had been able to piece together, it seems a local farmer tipped off the group about possible trouble. A party of pro-slavery men was stalking the area. They knew about the cannon being shipped and planned to confiscate it before it could be delivered. Rather than risk losing the cannon to the enemy, Alex and the others decided to stash it somewhere safe and take their chances with the hostiles. It was a good thing they did because the two groups met up later that evening.

First, there was talk, then a skirmish, then a full-blown gunfight. Alex's side was outnumbered but held their own for a bit. It was in vain. There were just too many to fight. Finally, a truce was proposed and accepted. However, when Alex's group refused to reveal the cannon's hiding place, the truce was forfeited. They were killed one by one, with Alex being the last standing. He was beaten, stabbed and finally shot in the chest and left for dead. Luckily, the farmer who helped them earlier watched the fight from a distance. When the pro-slavery forces left, he searched the group for survivors and found one, barely holding on. The man took Alex back to his home where he and his wife tended to the many wounds. It took three days for Alex to awaken. When he finally did, he used the name Oliver. And spoke with an accent.

After a few weeks with no word from his brother, David retraced the settlers' route, ending at the farmhouse where

Alex was rehabilitated. The farmer gave his account, telling David the only survivor was a British man who, after his recovery, joined another wagon train heading for Kansas. David needed to know what happened to his brother so he went after him, arriving first in Lawrence. There, he learned the surviving Brit migrated to Quindaro shortly after his arrival. David followed.

"David found Alex his second day in town," said Tough. "Initially, he thought his brother was teasing him or something. Then, when the charade continued, David figured Alex was hiding from something or someone, and he played along. Finally, one day when they were alone, and Alex still didn't break character, David got pissed." He grabbed Alex and shook him, screaming at his brother to "snap out of it" and "quit fucking around." But it didn't help. It only scared Alex—now Oliver—and turned him against David Sorter. For good.

The people at the hotel broke up the melee and sent David packing. The next day, when he approached Oliver to try again, he found the situation unchanged. The day after that, the same. David was confused and overwhelmed. He wrote his family that all was well and that he and his brother had decided to stay in the newly organized town of Quindaro, Kansas for the time being. He also wrote to his friend from his cavalry days, Colonel Tough, asking him to "report for duty." He did so, gladly.

"Ever since, David has watched over Oliver," Tough explained. "Usually from afar." As the sectional fighting intensified, David joined in with vigor. He fought for his family's convictions but also, to take revenge for those who took his brother away. For that, he would fight to the death. "We all will," Tough concluded.

David nodded his appreciation to his friend. He picked up where Tough left off. "I don't remember the last time I saw Alex. I've seen a flash every now and then but nothing like today." He stopped a moment, noting the arrival of the rain. He looked at Charlie specifically. "If he's Oliver when he wakes up, I'll be disappointed. Again. I want my brother back." He looked at Tough and Cuff with his last bit of advice. "If he's Alex when he wakes up, watch out."

39.

News of the impending attack didn't surprise Nancy. It was a good move for Cook, bold. She respected it. She thanked Billie and Polly for the information and within a matter of seconds had instructions for both. She sent Polly to Clarina's to sound the alarm. The town needed to prepare and Clarina was best suited to lead the charge. Then she told Billie to gather supplies and get ready for a trip onto the prairie. She told him Adam would ride along and the two of them were to bring David and the group back as soon as possible. Adam contested the order, assured his services were better utilized in town, protecting Nancy. She casually overruled his opinion and sent him and Billie on their way.

The town was hard at work, boarding up windows, building barricades and digging trenches. They had the high ground, which was advantageous. However, Cook had the numbers and the weaponry. When the fighting started, it would take everything the town had to survive. Nancy was doing her best to ensure that survival. She had the final two cases of "Beecher's Bibles" laid out in the road. She doled out each rifle personally, making sure the recipient was proficient enough with the weapon to do damage. Luckily, the vast majority of folks in town were more than capable. They readily accepted the weapons and dutifully took a post.

Clarina worked with Abe to get as many noncombatants as possible away from the coming cataclysm. They sent the children, along with chaperones, into the forests west of town. There were shallow cave systems in the hills that could provide refuge. Temporarily, anyhow. If the town fell to the attackers, the guardians were instructed to make a run for Lawrence, taking care to go around Six Mile rather than through. The elderly and any women who were unable to fight or make a run for it were stashed in cellars and crawlspaces throughout the town. Armed guards would watch over these hideouts for as long as they were able. It wasn't ideal but it was the only option available.

Further up the hill, Chris Kelley and his three men walked out of the hotel. They stared in awe at the mania of the preparations and between gulps of coffee, commented on the energetic nature of the small town. The people running here and there, the shouts, the sounds of hammering and digging. It was spectacularly bizarre. Like they were watching a traveling circus. If they had heard someone yell "Hey, Rube," the rallying cry of carnies in distress, they wouldn't have been surprised in the least. Their curiosity reached its peak when a group of women ran by carrying rifles and shouting about finding more ammunition. That was something you didn't see every day. They stood in confused silence until Chris finally said, "I got to find out what the hell is going on here."

He stepped into the street to find answers. Two men approached, but Chris let them pass without inquiry. They were a couple of David's Jayhawkers, serious men. Chris recognized the species and thought it best not to start a conversation with trained aggressors. He would find a more sensible target. A round, older woman suddenly appeared from around the corner of the hotel, and Chris stopped her. He took off his hat and addressed her politely. "Ma'am? There's quite a hubbub in town today. May I ask the cause?"

The woman was surprised how anyone in town could still be ignorant to the impending attack. She educated him on Cook and his intentions, even pointing out the mass of men assembling in the woods at the base of the hill. Chris' men crept up behind him, trying to get the story themselves by following the woman's finger as she pointed. Noticing they were associates, her tone sharpened. She was suddenly altogether indignant that four able-bodied men, had skirted any and all responsibility to the town and its citizenry. She looked around for help and pointed down the street at Nancy, telling them to see her at once to find out how they could help. Then she stormed off.

Chris couldn't have been happier. Seeing Nancy was just what he needed.

A group of townspeople surrounded Nancy, Abe and Clarina as they strategized with a few of David's men. Nancy saw the Irishmen approaching and motioned for room to be made for Chris to join the discussion. Sheepishly, he took a place with his men behind him. He listened as the people around him spoke but had a difficult time processing the information. He was more concerned with filling his eyes with the beautiful princess. She looked back at him just often enough to keep his heart racing.

Reverend Mills addressed Chris first. "Do you men need rifles? We have enough to go around. Nancy will get you set up."

Chris' trance was temporarily broken. He started to answer, "No, sir..."

"It's Reverend," Mills interrupted.

"Apologies. No, Reverend," Chris said. "This isn't our fight."

There was a collective laugh, everyone appeared in on the joke except the Irish. And Nancy. She didn't laugh either, her stare now cutting through Chris.

Another man explained to the strangers that there would be no escape now. The fact that Chris and his men were even on the hill was akin to signing their death warrant. It was guilt by association. Cook's design was the same for everyone here —death.

"I guess we'll have to make a run for it," said Chris. Again, he was rebuked with laughter, more raucous than before.

Clarina weighed in this time. "I'm afraid there's no place to run," she assured him. "The trap has been set."

Chris turned to look at his men. They weren't the type to scare easily, but the news made them anxious. One shook his head "no." He didn't want any part of this.

Across the crowd, Nancy looked to Abe. He knew what needed to happen. He nodded his approval to his wife and gave her the space she required. He dispersed the crowd, instructing them to finish the tasks assigned and return in an hour to obtain fresh orders. He walked toward the Hardware Depot, where he and the other town leaders were to meet shortly. As he turned off the main street, he glanced back at Nancy. She was holding the Irishman's hand, standing close, very close. The strangers would join the fight. His wife would make sure of that.

40.

Adam and Billie rode through the night. Adam led the way, tracking any and all footpaths trending north. He knew the trail would be old, a few days at least, so he chose to disregard any fresh tracks. That narrowed his focus, but it was still a struggle. Luckily, he and the boy found a promising trail early. Though it disappeared now and again, he chose to maintain the same general direction. He tracked on instinct and so far, this felt right.

It was nice to ride with Billie. He could be quiet when necessary and followed instructions. He did ask questions, several, in fact. Initially, more than Adam cared to answer. However, the more he asked, the more Adam came to realize they weren't questions to challenge judgement. Or a ploy to show how much the young white boy already knew. Billie was genuinely inquisitive and aimed to learn anything the more experienced tracker was willing to impart. Before long, Adam was sharing his suspicions with the boy and explaining his actions in more detail than he ever thought he would. To a non-Indian, anyway. Surprisingly, he enjoyed the role of educator. And the boy was an excellent student. Billie had won him over.

This was to be expected, as Billie Cody was not like other twelve-year-olds. He was fearless. And plucky as a crow. The last few years had been hard on his family but it shaped him into the man he would become. His mother was still in the area, along with his sisters. His father, though, died last year. When the older Cody, Isaac, made the mistake of giving an impassioned antislavery speech in Leavenworth, a spectator promptly stabbed him twice for his troubles. Although he lived another three years, he never fully recovered. His death was a result of complications caused by the long-ago attack. Billie never forgave the pro-slavery contingent and held a grudge the rest of his days.

He was forced to become the man of the house and where most would shrivel, Billie thrived. At eleven, he took a job on a wagon train and traveled clear to Utah during the Mormon uprising. There, he killed for the first time. But not a Mormon —an Indian. Back home, he worked for the freighting company Majors and Russell, delivering messages to and from the telegraph office. Majors and Russell would add a third partner, Waddell, to become the largest shipping company in the West and create the Pony Express. Billie would help in that endeavor as well.

The boy was special and everyone around him knew it. It was palpable. It was the reason Stan trusted him to deliver the news of the attack to Nancy. It was the reason Nancy trusted him to find David. It was the reason Polly Welborn, despite being four years his senior, followed him everywhere he went. And it was the reason a hardened Indian brave like Adam showed him any regard whatsoever.

The two riders stopped at a pond to water their horses and cool themselves. The ground sloped upward from where they stood and Billie asked to ride ahead to the hilltop to see what lay beyond. Adam didn't like the idea and nixed it right away. He looked to the west and pointed so the boy understood. They would travel that way, rather than north up the hill. His intuition was telling him the track had shifted and their heading would change accordingly.

Billie disagreed but stayed quiet nonetheless. He was still learning, after all.

They began again, walking their horses to let them rest. They traveled to a point where the hill was nearly out of sight and the ground began to flatten. Suddenly, the humming sounds of the prairie ceased as a gunshot in the distance echoed around them. They both searched, trying to pinpoint the origin of the shot. Billie found it first and pointed to the top of the hill. "It's Cuff!" he yelled. He jumped on his horse, gave a holler and pushed his pony upward.

Cuff was concerned to see Billie and Adam so far out on the prairie. His worry was substantiated once Billie shared the town's dire predicament. The rest of the group was behind Cuff, probably an hour, maybe less. He told Billie and Adam to follow him, they needed to get to David quickly.

It took less than twenty minutes to find the others and again, Billie shared the news. David cursed. A lot. Then he thought. Then cursed some more. He hated to make the suggestion but couldn't think of a better solution. "We have to split up," he started. "I'll stay with the cannon, get it there as fast as I can. It's hooked to me already. Besides, Joan is the only one I trust not to die pulling the goddamn thing. The rest, you all have to get back. Nancy will need every gun she can get."

Oliver, who finally woke up near daybreak, didn't agree. "I'm not leaving you alone with Lazarus," he said. "It's not a one-man job anyway. Even if that man thinks he's supernatural. I'll stay back and help."

Charlie spoke up. "I will too." He wasn't about to leave Oliver alone with David.

"Jesus Christ," spat David. "Fine, you two stay with me if that's what you want. Neither of you will be worth a shit in the fight anyway."

"You and Joan may need the help. It's not a bad idea," said Tough. "We can travel faster with fewer men, may be there by sundown. If we push it."

David agreed. He asked Billie, "How was Six Mile when you came through?"

"It was jumping. We went around," Billie replied.

More bad news. David told Tough to get to Quindaro no matter what. Leavenworth Road through Six Mile would be best. If they had to go around, do it. But do it fast.

Tough understood. He wanted to set a quick pace to start, and he ordered the others to fasten their supplies securely. Also, Adam and Billie would need fresh rides, so theirs were swapped with Oliver's and Charlie's. He barked orders and in no time, the band was ready to ride for town. Tough rode to David and the friends shook hands. "Hurry back," said Tough. "I'll try not kill them all before you get there."

"Will do," said David. Before he let go of Tough's hand, David gave one more order. Quietly. "Tell her I'm on my way."

"Will do," answered Tough.

41.

The Missouri bushwhackers camped on the delta. One by one, item by item, Henry Cook and Blue checked off the list of preparations necessary to commence the assault on the town of Quindaro. Commands had been set and ammunition shuffled. Men were still arriving by the hour and as they did, Cook or Blue apportioned them accordingly. Currently, Cook was working on the most important aspect of the design, namely, the placement of his guns. He had a total of seven cannons and howitzers at his disposal. And he knew this would be plenty if positioned correctly. As he dispatched the guns across the forest, he was careful to consider the range and potential damage, making sure to maximize the work done by each gun. He asked for and listened to Blue's input, but ultimately made the final decision himself. After all, it was too important to leave to an underling.

He used his two twelve-pound Napoleons as bookends. Then he filled in the clearings between with three six-pounders and a couple three-inch howitzers. He planned to stock each position with enough shot, shell, case and canister to fire for hours, in case it took that long before the infantry could charge. He wanted to rotate the type of projectile with each volley to make it harder for the enemy to count the batteries and plan counterattacks. Finally, he planned to pick the first target of each gun personally. The first shots, the first casualties would be his choice.

The limbers and caissons moved back and forth, delivering the goods and supplies the army would need. Food and ammo were everywhere and the men helped themselves while they waited for orders.

Happy sat quietly near a bushel of apples, not ready yet to take his post at the front. The young woman who shadowed his every move was there as well, spending every minute possible with the man she adored. They shared an apple and half a loaf of bread, him looking at the battleground, her staring at him. When Cook approached, Happy stood up and dismissed the young girl with a word, "Scat." She took off a rope necklace and put it around his neck. He ignored it. She turned and ran away, weeping like a child.

Cook felt uncomfortable breaking up the goodbye. There was no rush for the girl to leave so soon, they had some time to kill yet. He tried to reassure the boy and called out to him. "There's time, son. If you need to go after her."

But he got the usual answer from the odd duck. Silence. Happy stuffed another apple into his pants pocket and tucked the rope around his neck into his shirt. Then he walked away to take his position. He was part of the group located at the base of the hill, the tip of the spear. He was just the type Cook wanted to reach the town first. A berserker if there ever was one.

The girl's mournful farewell was understandable. Cook's goodbye to his wife this morning was painful as hell. He also had a sister with whom he traded letters weekly. The siblings were very close as children and despite the distance now between them, remained so. He was still unsure of the relationship between Happy and the girl, but it really didn't matter. Love is love, loss is loss and pain is pain. These things translate to everyone. He said a short prayer that his loss would be light when all this was settled.

Behind him, a teamster snapped the trance with a shout requesting passage. Cook turned to see four horses pulling a wagon, trying to get past him on the narrow path. The leader moved to the side and apologized. He asked where the wagon was going and approved. "Carry on," he ordered.

Making sure he was out of the way, Cook pulled a brass spyglass from his waistband. He looked up the hill, scanning the town and found his target. The sawmill. Quindaro had the second largest mill in the territory with the capability to mill sixteen board feet of lumber a day. It was the model of efficiency and enabled the town to meet the demand necessary to nourish its rapid growth. Cook, like everyone who respects competency, admired the mill and its workings. Its success, consequently, was the very reason it would have to fall, and early in the fight. It would be one of the first targets on principle, if nothing else.

But first, he needed the mill to give him a sign. His informant, The Whistler himself, was to make sure both Sorter was still wandering the prairie and the Indian princess was in town. When these two particulars were confirmed, a red bandana would hang in the mill's upper floor window. Then and only then would the guns open up.

So far, the window was empty. Which was fine. There was still work to do, precautions to take. He could use a few more hours to get things in order, so no rush. Besides, his men were getting antsy, which always proved valuable. The more time they sat waiting, the more the ire grew. The potential energy built. Just a little longer and the men would be more than ready. His wolves would be foaming at the mouth.

42.

The Quindaro sawmill was located on the western edge of the hill, purposely built on the flattest piece of land the town had to offer. The normal work inside came to an abrupt stop the day before due to the declared state of emergency. Outside, however, several teams of mules and horses worked diligently to prepare a surprise for Cook and his charging masses. Chris Kelley, after a short discussion with Nancy, had been persuaded to help the town make a stand. No surprise there. Now, he and one of his men helped Nancy set a trap that could possibly help the town survive the assault.

Her idea was simple and ingenious. She wanted to move the large log pile fifty feet to the east and chock it there until Cook's men charged. Then the twenty or thirty solid core timbers would be cut loose to roll down the hill, crushing everyone and everything unlucky enough to be in the way. Buildings within the town would surely be lost, but the price was worth it. In fact, as the structures gave way, they themselves would become projectiles and would add to the devastation farther down the hill. It probably wouldn't end the fight, but it would buy the town time. If nothing else, the logs would make an impression. And the second wave of Cook's men wouldn't charge the hill with the same vigor as the first. Marching over dead bodies tends to make a man question his doctrine.

Chris thought the plan was brilliant, which only helped reinforce his affection for the princess. Her beauty was undeniable. That, coupled with a wickedly strategic mind, formed the type of perfection Chris had never witnessed. His brother would hire this girl in a second. Probably put her in charge of an entire neighborhood, maybe more. He would be impressed, no doubt about that.

Chris' brother, Thomas, was the leader of an Irish gang back home in New York. He took command after Chris' other brother, Richard, was killed by a rival organization. Thomas' first act as boss was to hunt down his brother's murderers and return the favor. Which he did. Four Protestant dogs paid the price. Afterwards, Thomas presented his younger brother Chris with the martyred brother's bowler hat. Chris reluctantly accepted and wore it ever since.

It was a nice hat. Fashionable. Expensive. But Chris hated it. Because he hated Richard.

Thomas was a first-rate thug for sure. Nevertheless, he ran his territory fairly, with as much honor as a killer could ever muster. The murder-for-hire racket that brought Chris to Kansas was a small part of the operation. Prostitution, drugs and gambling were its bread and butter. Ventures with few victims. But Thomas also dabbled in legitimate operations in the hopes of one day advancing the social position of the detested Irish in their new homeland. He was a terrible man, sure, but respectable.

Richard, however, was a cruel bastard. He murdered, maimed, and his favorite, raped as if he were possessed by the devil. And he was proud of himself, bragging constantly about every deplorable act. He was a fiend. An animal. As far as Chris was concerned, his brother's demise was well deserved. The job of the universe is to dispatch monsters like Richard to another realm. To protect us all. And although it was labored in the delivery, the universe, by way of the Protestant bullies, did its duty. The anger Chris was supposed to feel from the loss simply wasn't there. The reprisal by Thomas was wasted energy. Richard belonged in hell, so that's where he went. It was as simple as that.

Chris wore the bowler as a sign of status within the organization. It was expected. He didn't like it but he lived with it. It was his cross to bear. However, one issue with the hat he couldn't take for long was the smell. Despite several washes in the last year or so, when it was hot and muggy, the hat had a distinct smell. It was spicy, pungent. It was the smell of blood and body odor. It smelled like Richard. And every time a whiff of his brother filled his nose, an impulse took over and the hat was tossed as far away as he could throw it. The air in Kansas was filled with water and since arriving in town, the smell permeated the hat like never before. He couldn't take it one more second.

Nancy saw the hat fly by her. She turned to see Chris sitting on a log, rubbing his hair with both hands, caked in sweat and dust. She grabbed a water bucket and walked toward him, yelling for everyone to take a break. Her legs ached, her hands too. A quick rest would do them all good. She sat beside Chris and handed him a water-filled ladle that he took and poured over his head. The water did its job, cooling him and erasing the smell from his memory. Her timing was perfect as well.

The two discussed the trap and were happy with their progress. Surprisingly, the restacking of the logs was going much faster than anticipated. The Irishman helping Chris approached and sat alongside them. He was a rough fellow and offered a few suggestions to Nancy that would perhaps make the trap more vicious. "Set the pile on fire before you let it go," he said. "That'll show them. Fire is always a good idea." He also shared his input on the town's overall defense, impressing her with his tactical skills.

The man, Bryan, looked to the top of the mill and pointed out a platform adjacent to the open window. "Someone could do real damage from there," he said with a thick accent. He tested the wind with his finger and looked down the hill toward the coming threat. "It's high up, looks stable. Wind at your back, shooting downhill. It doesn't get any better. One man up there could kill twenty down here." He asked Nancy if the town was in possession of any long-range rifles.

She shook her head, unfortunately no. Only the Sharps rifles already distributed. But she gave a warning. "There's at least one on the other side. He's killed before, from a very long distance." She pointed down the hill into the woods. She showed the Irishmen two of the hiding spots The Whistler used and how he terrorized the town from afar. She assumed the sniper would join the fight but had no answer for him. Not yet, anyway.

Bryan was impressed with The Whistler's shot. It was longer than he'd ever seen. And uphill. "He's very good," he commented.

As much as it pained her to say so, Nancy had to agree. The shooter was fantastic. It was difficult not to respect the talent. "We call him The Whistler," she said. She began to explain the reason, but Bryan didn't need it.

"Because of the sound the bullet makes cutting through the air. It whistles, yes?" Bryan interjected. Nancy nodded in agreement, impressed again by the Irishman. "The fellow uses a Whitworth. That's the only gun that could do the work."

Chris wished aloud that they had a couple Whitworths right now. It would even the odds considerably.

Bryan agreed. It had been a long time since he'd shot the rifle, but he remembered it well. It was indeed a killing machine. Strong. Accurate. Impeccable range. For Bryan, there was only one thing wrong with shooting a Whitworth. Getting used to the black eyes.

Nancy stopped cold. "Black eye?" she asked.

Bryan explained. "The Whitworth is very powerful but also extremely light. So it kicks like a fucker. It you have a scope attached, which there's no reason not to since it's for sniping, the eyepiece gives you a nice clean shiner. As if you were punched by a baby. If you're not careful, she'll knock you on your ass." He looked at Chris and the two men shared a good laugh.

Nancy didn't laugh though. She was angry and hurt. She tried to hide her feelings but it was a lost cause. The disappointment was evident and she had to get away. Now. She asked Chris to finish the trap and come find her when it was complete. He was confused but acquiesced. As she stormed away, a solitary tear escaped her stony eyes. And she couldn't help but speak aloud. "Why, Adam? Why?"

43.

Scribbled on a piece of paper were thirteen surnames of prominent Boston families for whom Walter had worked, either presently or in the past. There wasn't a single name on the list that could be considered a friend. Acquaintance, maybe. But just barely. They were long shots, last resorts. But with Calvin Ringgold off the table, that's all Walter had left.

His desk was a mess. The temper tantrum he threw last night was childish, but it felt good at the time. Something about flinging papers and heaving books and such was freeing. He would clean up after himself of course, but that could wait. For now, he would sit in the chaos and pout.

The bottle of whiskey had taken a beating over the last few hours and a lonely quarter remained, at best. Childish behavior was the soup du jour. Between drinks, Walter would ponder the next name on the list, thinking of an approach, an opening. Time after time, he came up empty, scratching each name off as the list shrank. His pen carved the last few possibilities so ferociously he almost tore through the paper. It was useless. After all, how do you ask someone, a stranger basically, to risk piles of money to save a family business they care nothing about? It wasn't possible. And he was a fool for trying.

For the first time in his life, Walter had regret. Things would have been much different had he been more sensible. If he would have chosen the responsible path rather than the frivolous, he would have run Pom Shipping like a king and the Murrays would have stayed on the docks where their kind belongs. He could have taken care of his sister and her child, Charlie. None of this would have ever happened. It was entirely his fault.

The year Walter finished his studies, he returned home anxious to begin his life. He wanted nothing more than to enter the family business, learn everything from the ground up so that one day, he could be like his father. He loved and respected the older Pomfrey, almost to the unhealthy point of idolatry. His father loved him as well; in fact, he was so proud of the boy he bragged constantly to anyone who would listen. Fortunately, his wealth ensured that someone was always willing to sit and hear about the great Walter Pomfrey and his future conquests. The boy's legend spread quickly and the opinions became unanimous. With these men leading the way, Pom Shipping would surely take over the world.

But first, Walter's father had a surprise for him. As a reward for a job well done, the older Pomfrey gave his son the irreplaceable gift of time. Six months, in fact, to do whatever the boy could dream. There was a ship leaving the very next morning, bound for the Keys of Florida where a cabin awaited Walter, and he could use it for however long he wished. Right on the beach. It was paradise. What's more, Walter was given a note of passage that would allow him to board any of the family ships and travel wherever in the world he chose. There were accounts set up to fund the adventure so money would never be an issue. It was a grand statement of his father's admiration, and Walter was thrilled, to say the least. The next six months promised to be magical.

Unfortunately, the trip was a disaster. On his second day in the Keys, tragedy struck. Walter fell in love. It was immediate, complete and permanent. He and the woman, Elizabeth, upon first sight, realized neither could ever survive without the other and declared their love. They lived together, traveled together and grew closer every day. At the end of the six months, Walter returned to Boston with his fiancé, excited to share the news of his travels and his newfound passion, Liz. To his chagrin, his family, especially his father, condemned the engagement and forbid Walter from legalizing the affair. Liz, to put it simply, was not of the ilk required to marry into a family like the Pomfreys.

Walter was devastated. There were words, angry words that could never be retracted because they cut too deep. Both sides dug in and refused to budge. Finally, Walter's father ended the argument with an ultimatum. Liz or the business. Walter was free to choose, but the choice would stick. Forever. Attorneys would see to that.

Walter stiffened, staring into his father's eyes for what would sadly be the last time. And with cold content, he rebuked the old man. He would keep Liz. And his father could shove the business up his self-righteous ass. That was that.

It got worse. Walter and Liz moved into a small place downtown, both looked for work and found it. They would start fresh, the two of them against the world. When the cold moved in, they discussed moving back to the Keys near her family. Sadly, they waited too long to leave. Two short weeks later, an influenza epidemic hit Boston. Liz got sick and died with the first wave of victims. Walter's father, after changing his will and virtually cutting his son from the Pomfrey tree altogether, caught the same strand and died soon after. Walter was alone, broken and penniless.

For months, he was a ghost. He drank—a lot. It never seemed to help with his spiritual struggle, it only added exponentially to his physical pain in the form of hangovers. So, the drinking lessened. Sarah looked in on him, bringing food and cleaning his place. Sometimes, she held him silently while he wept in her arms. She was his savior. His only champion. Sarah revived her brother from the dead, and he would be forever grateful.

As time passed, he mended his relationship with his mother, who tried to have the family papers adjusted to include Walter once more. His father, however, had been far too thorough. Walter was cut out completely, forever barred from owning a single share of the company or working one minute for pay. Once again, his father's work was to be respected. Walter opened his shop soon after and worked to build his own name, which he did. Slowly, he grew accustomed to the snickers in town. To most, his choice of love over money was pure foolishness, and he would forever be the man who gave up his family's fortune for three months of marital bliss. It was an authentic Greek tragedy. But he never once thought he made the wrong choice. Until today.

Calvin and the Murrays were going to conduct their business, and there wasn't a damn thing Walter could do about it. To bring Charlie back would be a death sentence for the boy, and the company would be splintered anyway. He needed a new plan but his brain was fried. He needed time to think but it was running short. Hell, he was down to the last hope of the buffoon. The miracle. A hurricane. Or an earthquake. A flood. Maybe a fire…

Wait. A crazy idea started to form. The building that houses the corporate offices of Ringgold & Associates was next door to the only firm in Boston large enough to handle a deal the size of a Pom Shipping merger. Right across the street was Liberty Finance Company, the bank that handled both Walter's account as well as the Murrays'. What would happen if these three buildings were temporarily unable to conduct business? Something small would work. Buy Walter a week or two. But God forbid, if something terrible were to happen, it could take months to put everything back in order. Maybe a full year. Was it the booze again or was this a viable option? Walter couldn't tell. But he owed it to Charlie and himself to look into it. Funny, he just happened to know an arsonist who once told him, "Fire is always a good idea."

44.

    For Charlie, the first few miles alone with Oliver and David were awkward, to say the least. Talk, when there was any, was small. And only occurred when Charlie could be used as an intermediary. He was clearly the only bond between the two rivals, but he still felt like a third wheel. They were brothers, after all, blood. And it seemed impossible to Charlie that something inside of Oliver didn't know the truth.

    Slowly, however, the situation improved. Mile six was a little better than mile five. Mile seven a little better still. And so on. The two men were never going to be chums, but they at least addressed each other more often and occasionally appeared right civil.

    The first sign of a truce came when David decided it best to change course. Rather than continue due south which would take more time, he wanted to cut a diagonal route, moving southeasterly on a straighter trajectory toward town. The risk of encountering pro-slavery forces would certainly increase as they neared civilization. But if they were going to have any chance at all of reaching Quindaro before it was leveled, this risk must be taken. Surprisingly, rather than Oliver's normal suspicion and lengthy examination of David's true motives, the Brit simply replied, "Sir! Yes, sir!" and gave an overexaggerated salute. David sneered. He didn't like the new cheerio attitude either. But he didn't say anything rude or threaten to shoot anyone. And that was progress.

    Ahead, the creek crossed their path and David called for a break. The horses badly needed water and rest. Especially St. Joan. She pulled the cannon full-time while Oliver and Charlie's horses were rotated in, taking turns pulling the other half of the load. Joan was stronger than the other two horses and was used to the work. But she was drained. It was partially her fault since she constantly tried to outwork the other horses, pulling the load off balance enough to prove she was supplying more strength. David chastised her when he noticed the uneven load, but that was more of a brag. She was a proud beast and David loved it.

The sun was high but on the backside of its peak. David eyed the shadows to tell time and the weariness showed on his face. As he let Joan drink, he smoothed her neck, thanking her for the work. Her boldness was inspiring, to be sure. However, it was all for naught. David calculated the distance and time in his mind and came to an unfortunate conclusion. His scowl told the story.

Charlie understood. "We're not going to make it, are we?" he asked. "We'll kill the horses if we push any harder."

David nodded. There was silence as the three men let the reality sink in.

Oliver spoke, his empathy too much to contain. He tried to console David first, with what he thought the leader would deem the "bright side." Tough and the boys would make it to town. Probably. Moreover, they were just the type of violent assets needed right now, and they would be utilized fully. Despite the darkness, the town had life yet.

David nodded again. He looked to the horizon and in a moment of weakness, his thoughts escaped. "I'm not worried about Tough. She's..." He caught himself.

Oliver used the most reassuring voice he could. "I'm sure the Indian princess will take the proper precautions," he said. "She's an incredibly resourceful lady."

David patted Joan again and agreed, only offering a quiet, "Yep."

Charlie was confused. "Indian princess?" he asked.

David looked at Oliver, shaking his head. A silent appreciation for the Brit's big mouth.

Neither David's chastising nor Charlie's inquisition changed Oliver's manner in the least. His explanation was clear-cut. The relationship between the Jayhawker and the princess was the worst-kept secret in the territory. Charlie's ignorance was due to his newness in town. Or he was blind as a bat. He finished with a jab to David. "The notion that you and Nancy are pulling the wool over anyone's eyes is purely the result of your own conceit." Oliver had a good laugh.

Charlie had a million questions. When did it start? Does Abe know? How in the hell could David catch such a beauty?

David's only reply was, "It's complicated."

"I bet it is," Charlie mocked.

He started in again but David stopped him quickly. "Listen!" he yelled. "Did you hear that?" They stopped talking and strained to hear what caught David's attention.

Then in the distance, not far away, they heard it. A whistle. Two notes of a triple-chime steamboat whistle, to be exact. They froze and waited. Guessing. Hoping. Then, almost as if Gabriel himself were performing, the third full-throated chord sounded, and David flashed back to life.

"That's a steamboat, fellas," he said, thinking out loud. "Blowing all three chimes, so it's leaving a port."

Oliver tried to put the pieces together. "What port could it be?" he asked.

"Leavenworth. It can't be anything but," answered David. He looked in the direction of the sound. "We must be closer than I thought." His mind was racing, suddenly rejuvenated. The idea came in a flash and was brilliant. "Hope you guys brought some cash. We're taking the ferry to town."

45.

Billie was right. Six Mile was lively. Evidently, word of the impending attack had already traveled up Leavenworth Road, and the scoundrels were prepared. Men patrolled the road like spiders spinning webs. There was drink and smoke aplenty, the wheels being greased for the fun. They waited with malice and a surprising patience for any poor soul choosing to flee from the sacking of the town. They looked hungry and mean. God himself would have a hard time saving anyone who happened down the road today.

Colonel Tough led the group close enough to see what he was dealing with but still far enough away to make a run for it if necessary. They hid behind trees and silently assessed the danger that lay ahead. It took Cuff less than a minute to make his judgement. He turned away, whispering, "Not possible. We go around."

Lee and Luke nodded their agreement. The farther they could get away from here the better. They followed Cuff to the horses. Adam shot Tough a smile and headed back as well. He seemed happier with the situation than he should. No wonder David hated that guy.

That left Billie and Tough. The boy spoke quietly, "It doesn't look good, Colonel. I think Cuff may be right. But I'll do whatever you say."

The kid's bravery was impressive. "Let's go," Tough said. He grabbed Billie by the arm and led him back to the rest of the men.

They arrived just in time to see Adam charging away, heading south to go around the trouble. "Where's he going?" asked Tough.

"He said we're on our own," Lee answered.

"Figures," spat Tough. He grabbed the reins of his horse and quickly told the group his intentions. He was riding into the mouth of the beast, alone. He spoke over their objections, nearly yelling by the end of his diatribe. He knew what he was doing. They needed to trust him and stay put. He would come back for them shortly. Then, before anyone had the chance to change his mind, he took off.

The group watched him speed away. As Tough neared the road, three Six Mile sentries met him and stopped his progress. He spoke to them, pointing toward town. After a moment, the guards took positions around their new prisoner and led him away.

There was nothing to do but wait. Luke was the only man to speak, but he spoke for everyone. "This is a bad idea."

46.

The docks of Boston Harbor were dangerous. To some, it seemed everything from the boats and cranes to the unions themselves were only in existence to kill or maim. The work was hard and taxed the human body to its limits. Some lost extremities. Others suffered broken bones or skulls. And these were the lucky ones. A death a week was commonplace from the work alone. Even more chilling, the gangs and vagrants added to the body count every evening, leaving their victims to be found by the rising sun. Union and civic leaders struggled to get a grip on the violence as morale lowered daily. It was so bad at one point, a crew was hired to sweep the area of carcasses every morning before the full-time workers arrived. Happily, this did the trick. Turns out, the workers didn't mind the killings. They just didn't want to have to clean up the mess.

Walter remembered the docks fondly. He played there as a child. When his mother would allow, he marched behind his father down the salt-covered planks, greeting the men who would help build the family business. He watched his father's every move and listened to every lesson. He learned how to shake hands firmly, make conversation and show consideration. In time, he recognized his father not only had employees, he had friends.

As Walter grew, he too made friends with several of the workers by abiding by his father's codes. Respect the men and they will respect you. Work hard for the men and they will work hard for you. This was a groundbreaking philosophy at the time, but Walter witnessed the proof of its viability firsthand. The men respected his father and worked harder for him than any other outfit. This, Walter believed, as much as anything else, made Pom Shipping a success.

Walter met Eddie Tots when they were both teenagers. Edward Tottle, or Tots for short, started working on the docks as a young boy. He also worked on boats and had been around the world twice by the time he was seventeen. He and Walter hit it off quickly as boys and although their paths rarely crossed now, each still considered the other a true friend. And a friend like Tots was just what Walter needed.

After working a lifetime in and around the harbor, Tots had risen to become a leader of both the laborers and the seaman alike. He was one of the more prominent union organizers in the area as well as a famous union buster. The role he took month to month depended solely on who was signing his checks. He had very few loyalties to either side, and he often changed without sentiment or trepidation. The shop owners and union bosses who paid for his services didn't much care for his wishy-washy ways. However, the men worshipped him and would follow his every move and command. And with that kind of power, he could do whatever he chose.

Walter walked toward the shabby building his friend used as an office, which was built right on the water with wooden docks and walkways surrounding it. The walls on every side were covered in deep rust from years of the seawater's gradual assault. The doors and windows stuck and were barely useable. The roof was high and holey. It looked a mess. But the shack was sturdy, built to last by Tots himself what seemed like a hundred years ago. And it served its purpose well despite appearances.

A large, burly man with a crooked nose, a cut under one eye and purple and yellow knuckles on his right hand greeted Walter at the door. After asking the nature of the visit, the giant handed Walter a piece of paper and told him to write his name on it. A young boy, maybe around ten years old, took the paper to a door on the other side of the warehouse where another man, not nearly as big as the one guarding the front door, read the name, looked Walter up and down, then turned and disappeared. Walter, after watching the formalities curiously, looked back to the door attendant.

"Sit down and wait," said the doorman in a raspy, tired voice. So Walter sat.

It only took a second before the mysterious door across the room opened and Tots emerged. "Walter Pomfrey, you old bastard!" he yelled. "Get over here!"

Walter flashed a subtle look of superiority at the giant. He gave the same look to the kid and the other doorman as he followed Tots into the private room. Once there, he was offered a drink, which he took, and the two friends quickly caught up.

When the talk finally turned to Sarah, Walter's demeanor changed and Tots, like any good friend, spotted it. Largely because Walter felt no need to hide his sentiments. This wasn't like the meeting with Calvin where Walter had to be on his toes. He didn't need take it slow or wait until the moment was right to make his move. It wasn't necessary with Tots. His old friend didn't need to be played and would see right through it anyway. With that in mind, Walter didn't hold back. He began, "I need help, Tots."

"You name it, Walter," Tots replied.

"No," Walter stopped him. "Not this time. It's not that simple. I need real help. And I want you to be sure, positive, this is something you want to be a part of. You don't owe me anything, understand? And I can pay or whatever… But I need your expertise. And I don't want you to help me just because you're my friend."

Tots thought a moment. It was true, he didn't owe Walter anything. Their relationship was never based on favors or deeds, there wasn't an outstanding debt on either side. Rather, the friendship was based on respect. The respect Walter showed him when, as the owner's son, he never had to. And the respect Tots had for the man who gave up everything in his life without looking back or letting that choice ruin him.

The decision was easy for Tots. "What do you have in mind?"

Walter quickly, quietly laid out the plan he had to stall the Murrays' business transaction. He wanted a few wagons—three, maybe four. He also needed one trustworthy man who could keep his mouth shut. Finally, ten barrels of something that would burn like hell. Walter knew where he wanted the materials, how to get things going and the ideal time. He just needed someone to help put it together.

"Like I said, I can pay…" Walter said. But Tots cut him off with a raised finger. He needed a moment to think.

This was a big move for Walter, and Tots wanted to digest the severity of the commitment. Sure, Tots had done worse. For money. A lot of money. Work like this was expensive because it was usually worth it to someone. However, he'd never undertaken a job like this for someone with whom he was so closely aligned. And certainly, never for anyone he personally rooted for. This was as new to him as it was for Walter. But again, his choice was easy. He would help Walter with this task at no charge, with no questions asked.

"Tonight," said Tots. "Dusk. My warehouse on Tremont Street, do you know where that is?"

Walter nodded that he did.

"I'll have a man there for you. And the goods," said Tots. "It's a good plan, Walter. And it might just work. I wish you luck."

"Thank you, Tots," said Walter gratefully. "What do I owe you? I'll bring the cash tonight and give it to your man."

Tots laughed out loud. "Oh, you silly old man! Your money is no good to me. You can keep that shit in your mattress. Besides, if your plan goes south, you'll need that cash to get the fuck out of town."

47.

In an abandoned barn, a hundred yards from the Leavenworth landing, David and his two crusaders assessed the situation. It was dire for sure, seeing as they were short on time, still thirty miles from home and stuck in a town hostile to their political leanings. Besides that, David was a known enemy. If he were seen and recognized, it would undoubtedly cause a shitstorm far too massive for escape. They could run, sure, but they would have to leave Lazarus behind, and that was out of the question. Therefore, until they were sure of their next move, David would have to stay out of sight.

There wasn't a tangible plan per se, just the broad, risky design to steal a large boat that none of them was capable of operating. To Charlie and Oliver, it was barely plausible. "A near crazy scheme conceived by a near crazier man," was how Oliver described it. However, when David asked for a better idea, there was nothing but silence. Proof in his mind that his idea was the best. And until something else came up, they were going with it.

The ferryboat they heard from the prairie was going upriver, north to Weston, Atchison or St. Joe. The smoke from her stacks diffusing into the air above the trees was the only remnant visible from the barn. A northbound ferry did them no good. They needed one pointing the other way. David watched the men working near the landing, loading and unloading goods on boats still parked, readying for departure. A few of the transports pointed south, but none of them seemed ready to make a move. David looked downriver, his mind still churning, looking for an edge. He thought aloud that maybe they should sneak farther south, if they could…

"Hey!" Charlie interrupted. "It's Webb. Look!" He pointed to the landing and sure enough, there sat the *Otis Webb*.

"Sure is," David said. His mind was still downstream.

Unexpectedly, Charlie opened the barn door and started toward the landing. He ignored the demands from David and Oliver to get back inside and instead, turned to them with confidence and the solitary instruction. "Be ready."

Webb didn't see Charlie until he was on the planks of the dock, and the surprise floored him. He hadn't seen the boy since he jumped from his boat a few weeks back. He heard the kid had survived the leap, thanks to Cuff, which was good news. Nevertheless, the captain was still pissed. He had prepared a speech that he practiced and memorized for the next time he bumped into Charlie. The kid had an ass-chewing coming, but now wasn't the time. Webb looked at one of the boatmen the very moment he noticed Charlie. The man snapped his fingers at two other workers and the three of them closed on the approaching stranger. Charlie was quickly surrounded.

The questions came fast and furious. Name? Business? Destination? Webb tried to think of a way to help, but he couldn't. He had nothing. The kid was in deep now. God, he was stupid!

But to his delight, Charlie spoke up and took charge. He said his name was Boyd something-or-other. He was in town to meet with a man named Harris about a job. Cook sent him. Now he was trying to get back to Westport to gather his belongings so he could get back by tomorrow when the work starts. The kid was relaxed. He was becoming a better liar. It was about time.

Webb stood still, waiting. Hoping. He finally took a breath when the leader of the crew dismissed the other two men. The story worked. The worker gave Charlie the price of the trip, warned him about "goings-on" south of here, then went back to his business.

With the workers still within earshot, Charlie continued the ruse. "Do you have time to take me south, Captain? I need to get there as fast as possible." Webb didn't like where this was going. "I have a couple of friends that'll be along soon, they need to get there too." Charlie turned toward the barn, showing Webb the hiding place.

Oliver waved big from the doorway, happy to see the friendly captain. David angrily pulled him back into the barn.

Webb saw the two men hiding. All he could do was roll his eyes and mumble, "Jesus Christ." He shook his head at Charlie in disgust.

Charlie continued his plea. "We just need a break, Captain. We have something with us that could be very useful to some folks south of here. But we have no way of moving it." Webb shook his head again but Charlie pressed. "We need someone to help us. We're trying to do the right thing here. You should too."

Webb was torn. The simple answer was "no," and that came first. "I'm not planning to go south today, young man. Didn't you hear the fellow there?" He pointed at the worker, still meandering about. "Today is not the day to be south of here, understand? Something bad is happening. It's best to stay clear of it, and that's what I plan to do." He looked at Charlie, trying to counsel him. He finished quieter, using the kid's words against him. "You should too."

Charlie wasn't giving up. "You're the only option, Captain. The only hope. For us and our friends."

"Nope," the captain replied.

"I'll pay you double," Charlie said.

"Nope," the captain replied again.

"Triple!" shouted Charlie as Webb started to walk away.

The boatmen took notice and came closer, enjoying the argument, hoping they would get lucky and it would get physical.

"NO!" yelled the captain over his shoulder.

"Five times fare, you coward!" Charlie shouted again.

"Go to hell, boy!" yelled Webb.

The boatmen were lucky and got just what they wanted. Only it wasn't the captain and the kid in the fight. Instead, a shadowy blur knocked the lead man out cold with one punch. Another worker was hit hard too, but in the gut. It doubled him over, knocking the breath from his lungs. He remained conscious a half second longer, just until the blow to the side of his head landed. Then he joined his leader in dreamland.

A third man, clutching a knife, made his move toward the attacker. He was stonewalled, however, by a board that was slammed into his face by none other than Captain Webb himself. It was all over in a matter of seconds. The area around Webb's boat was clear and a window to make a getaway opened.

"Good to see you, Webb," David said. He turned and gave Oliver the signal to bring Lazarus up to be loaded.

The captain looked at the man he walloped, lying still at his feet. "I wish I could say the same to you, David," he bit back.

David worked with Charlie and Oliver, moving crates and boxes out of the way, making room for the cannon to come through. He had Charlie secure the ramp onto the boat as Oliver steadied Joan. She hated the water. Since there was no way of knowing what kind of trouble they were floating into, the horses weren't coming on the boat. Joan would lead the others home after helping with the final loading. David tied the bridles and stirrups tightly to ensure nothing draped from the saddles that could become tangled in the woods. Then he told Webb to get aboard and prepare to launch.

"I'm not taking you anywhere, Sorter. Especially south. I already told the kid," Webb said. He was pleading now.

David kept working, unmoved. "That's fine," he said. "You don't have to go anywhere. You can stay here and apologize to your friend there when he wakes up in a couple minutes. I don't give a shit. But your boat is leaving and we're taking it. With or without you."

Webb had no choice. He could push the kid around easily but the Jayhawker was another matter. He cussed all the way to the wheelhouse. Goddamn Sorter!

48.

"Get down," ordered Cuff. He grabbed his rifle and knelt behind a tree, leaning around it and taking aim at one of the five men riding behind Tough. They were just out of range, so he waited. Lee, Luke and Billie took cover with pistols pulled, waiting as well for Cuff to kick it off. They all tensed, scared but ready. When Tough and his pursuers neared, Cuff's finger smoothed the trigger. Only a moment more and the funny-looking man with the long beard dies. Cuff counted down in his mind, three…two…

Wait. He relaxed his finger. The man with the beard rode beside Tough and handed him a bottle of something. Tough accepted it, took a pull and gave it back. Something wasn't right. "Hold up," Cuff instructed.

Tough rode to a stop at the edge of the wooded area where he left the others earlier in the day. The men riding behind him stopped as well. He yelled for Cuff to gather his things, they were leaving. Cuff, still unsure, crept to the edge of the trees, rifle still poised to kill. Tough saw him and diffused the bomb. "It's all right, Cuff. They're coming with us."

The group mounted up and joined Tough and his new army in the clearing, just off the road. The cousins, who never needed words to communicate, shared a confused glance. For Tough to go into Six Mile alone and live was impressive. For him to emerge with five armed soldiers under his command was a marvel. How did he do it? What the hell was going on? It was baffling. But neither had the guts to put these questions to Tough.

"Who are these guys, Colonel?" asked Billie. His inquisition, more attributed to his immaturity than pure guts, was the question on everyone's mind. The cousins shushed him but waited for the answer just the same.

Tough answered quick and clean. "Reinforcements, Billie. Now let's get going."

The colonel turned his ride and kicked hard, spurring him deep to force the pace. The Six Mile men filed in behind him, followed by the still-confused original ensemble. The group of ten traveled swiftly up and down the hills of Leavenworth Road, most of the time at a full gallop. Trees whizzed by and swarms of gnats were dashed by the passing whirlwind. The dust cloud left in their wake stretched a mile behind, nearly to the tiny pond on the Welborn property. The men repositioned within the group, finding their place and timing while bonding with each other. They were all fast learners. And by the time they reached Quindaro, they looked like a genuine military unit. They made a grand entrance.

Nancy greeted the men, specifically looking for David. And Adam. Seeing neither, she went to Tough for answers. He filled her in on David's whereabouts and the reasoning behind the decision to leave him, Oliver and Charlie. She wasn't thrilled but understood. David wanted as many men as possible in town, in the fight. The sooner the better. It was probably the right move, but she missed him desperately.

Tough could see her disappointment and consoled her the best he could. He grabbed her hands in his. "He's on the way, it's just going to take some time. And you and I both know he's going to be just fine. He'll make it. If anyone can, it's David."

It was little comfort. "Hopefully he gets here before we're all dead," she said half-jokingly. She needed to change the subject.

Nancy explained to Tough how the town's defenses were set. As usual, her strategies were spot-on and impressive. The town was fortunate to have her. There were still things that needed attention, however—a few buildings needed to be reinforced and they were faced with an ammunition shortage. Her main concern was the back passage on the south side of town that she, so far, had been unable to protect adequately. She feared they were still vulnerable there.

Tough dug right in. He split the men into groups and sent them here and there to handle this and that. He and Cuff would investigate the south passage and meet back up with Nancy to discuss their findings. If a solution existed, they would find it.

As he turned to leave, Nancy stopped him. "Where's Adam?" she asked.

Tough explained how Adam ditched the group near Six Mile and that he should have been back long ago. "I have more important things to handle right now but know this. Next time I see Adam, he'll answer for his actions."

Nancy watched Tough leave. He and Cuff were great assets, she was glad they were here. And the Six Mile recruits would come in handy as well. Hopefully, they wouldn't cause too much suspicion. The news of Adam's desertion was disappointing but expected. She knew him now, his makeup. And the colonel was right, Adam would pay. But it wouldn't be Tough who would collect. She planned to do that on her own.

49.

Walter was at home, lying on the floor. It wasn't very comfortable, but it was cool. His head was on a pillow pulled from the couch. His jacket and shoes were near the door where he dropped them the moment he entered the house. He was trying to relax. There was no way he would be able to fall asleep now, his mind was racing too fast. Nevertheless, he at least wanted to rest his body and his eyes for what may be a long evening of activities.

His meeting with Tots went well. He knew it would. He tried to convince himself this was good news and that he should be overjoyed someone was finally willing to help. However, it was a tough sell. He was never good at self-deception. In fact, a few blocks from home, he noticed his left hand was shaking. He tried wringing it a few times, even rolling his shoulder up and down to get the blood flowing smoothly. It didn't help. He jerked his arm again, more violently this time, but only managed to cause a loud pop in his elbow that now ached some. He was a mess and he knew why.

How hard is it to be a criminal? Jesus Christ! The world is full of thieves and murderers who seem to live happy lives, content with their wicked deeds. How do they do it? Walter hadn't even done anything yet and the guilt was eating him alive. His brain ached. And his body was turning on him one appendage at a time. If he felt this bad now, what would he have to go through once the plan was carried out? There was a very real possibility his entire body would call it quits all at once and he would simply drop dead in the street. He wasn't cut out for this type of thing.

But he had no other choice. Charlie needed him. Walter was all the boy had left in the world. He was the savior, the protector. And despite the fear he felt now and the self-loathing that would surely follow, he was resolved to meet with the man Tots sent. Then the two of them would take action against those who deserved it. Yeah. Maybe that's what he needed to focus on. The Murrays were terrible people and...

There was a light knock on his door. Walter heard it but didn't move. The second knock came shortly after and it brought him around. Maybe he had dozed for a second. What did that mean? Maybe he was more of a criminal than he thought. After all, what kind of man can sleep at a time like this? A criminal, that's who. At the least, a man capable of one criminal act...

The knock was louder the third time, more annoyed. Walter snatched a pistol from his desk, tucked it behind his back and went to the door. He opened it slightly and through the crack, saw Cara standing on the stoop. What the hell?

"What are you doing here?" Walter asked.

"Can I come in?" she asked.

Walter opened the door and Cara entered. He walked to the desk and replaced the pistol, making sure she saw his preparedness. It would be good for her to see what his life had devolved into. He then walked to the stove and started to boil a pot for coffee but didn't offer her a thing. That would serve her right as well.

It had been a long time since she'd visited Walter's home, and she was taking stock. From the hall, she peeked into the adjacent rooms curiously, measuring the dust, judging the layout. She always liked Walter's taste in things and although his place needed a good cleaning, she approved of the overall feel. Truthfully, not much had changed since she put her spin on the place months ago. And as petty as it seemed, even to her, she found it quite gratifying that her personal style was still well represented.

While Walter worked on the coffee, Cara began. "Tots came to see me," she said.

Walter stopped working, surprised and confused. This is how people are caught! The crime has yet to be committed and already, rumors are swirling.

"He's concerned," continued Cara.

Walter listened as she described the meeting at her house. Tots did not, nor would not, tell her the details of Walter's proposal. However, it was made clear to her there was a significant amount of danger involved. And the targets, again undisclosed, were serious folks who could be expected to retaliate rapidly and forcefully. Tots feared Walter was opening a box of wildcats. And that particular lifestyle, while snug for men the likes of Tots, was not as comforting to the faint of heart. More than that, Tots worried for Walter's soul. He hated to see a good man break bad without fully understanding the costs.

Walter didn't know how to reply, so he deflected. "I'm surprised you would stoop to speak to Tots at all, considering…" He let his words fall off.

Tots' mother, Cara's aunt, who became pregnant before she was married, was forced from her childhood home a half century ago. That branch of the family tree nearly withered from existence. Today, only Tots remained above water. And with his twelve children, he hoped to singlehandedly start a new narrative.

Cara was unimpressed with Walter's juvenile ploy. "Tots has an aversion to me and my family, that's certain. And I don't blame him one bit." She had spoken to Walter about this several times before but now, it was getting old. "As I've told you, none of the family issues are my concern. Nor my responsibility. I wasn't even born yet when the split occurred so if

Tots has hard feelings, that's his problem." She moved to the kitchen door, trapping Walter in a corner. "I'm a healthy, able person who only fights battles I have a stake in. You may take a lesson from that."

Walter only grunted.

Cara seemed to shift gears, trying to erase the snide exchange they just had. She needed Walter to hear her advice, Tots' advice. She struck a more gentile tone when she continued. "The plan sounds dangerous. The people you're picking a fight with, no secret by the way, are above your weight class. They are far too powerful for you, Walter. If you expect any sort of positive outcome, you're fooling yourself. This fight, if you choose to start it, will surely only end one way. The company will be gone and you will be dead. You need to come to your senses before it's too late."

She continued, talking faster as her mind revealed the argument. "Besides, Walter, this isn't even your fight. Why should you risk your life for a company you can never have a stake in? It's foolishness! And Charlie is a grown man, or at least he should start acting like one. He should be able to take care of his own concerns. You can't take it on yourself and he shouldn't expect you to do so."

He stopped her, shouting, "You don't know what you're talking about, Cara!"

"Oh please, Walter. Who knows you better than I do?" she asked.

"You don't understand," mumbled Walter. His head shook in disgust. She used to understand, but no longer.

She recognized his anger, how it shut him down. She had seen it before, of course, many times. However, she knew the antidote all too well. She reached for him and took his hands. She lowered her voice and spoke with as much calm as she could muster. "Explain it to me then, Walter."

God she was good! It took all he had not to buckle and collapse into her arms. He wanted to fall into her and let the tears run, but he couldn't. He would never escape her again. And he mustn't give her the satisfaction.

Nevertheless, he felt he needed to provide an explanation for his actions, not only to her but also to Tots. And himself. He described the bond he felt with Charlie, the bond of family. The tie to the kid was all Walter had and all he would ever have. He needed to protect that, to fight for it against all the Murrays of the world who would work to shatter it and leave the pieces separate for eternity.

"The truth?" he asked. "No, I'm not excited about this evening's prospects, but a man has to fight sometimes, Cara, even when he's not that good at it. Tonight, it's my turn at the front of the line."

Cara nodded her head slowly, gently. "I understand," she said softly.

Walter objected. "How can you? You still have everything. A name. A business. Respect and status. You're still whole. There is no way you could know how it feels to have nothing."

She stopped him this time, still speaking softly so as not to provoke another outburst. She knew it lay just below the surface, and she knew the way to keep it steady.

"I don't need any of those things," she said softly. "Or want them. Those are not the things that define me. You of all people should know that."

He knew.

Moreover, she remembered when status didn't matter to Walter either. She asked him if he remembered the very moment he knew he was going to give up his stake in the Pomfrey business. "That moment," she said, "was you at your best. You knew what you wanted and went after it, riches and future be damned. And as strange as it sounds, even though the choice of love wasn't mine or directed at me, that man, Walter, is all I ever wanted. He is all I've ever loved."

Walter's eyes fluttered, his blood rushed and he nearly tipped over. His mouth started to move but she wasn't finished.

"Your life isn't over, Walter, not by a long shot. There's still time for you to love, to live, to explore." She paused. "You gave your heart away once before and you could do it again. This time, I want it."

Walter was silent. She looked into his eyes and delivered the last of her declaration. "I'm leaving this evening, going to see a friend. In Europe. I'll be gone six months, maybe longer. I feel like if I don't leave now, I'll suffocate. I want you to come with me." She paused so it could settle in. "Don't bother packing or bringing anything, I'll have someone take care of your things while we're gone. And we can buy all new clothes when we get where we're going."

Walter didn't answer. He just stared back at her in wonder. Cara gazed into him, trying to get a read on his thoughts. She always could before, but not now. Maybe things had changed more than she knew. She hoped against it with all of her being. But the long silence allowed the doubt to build, and Cara panicked. She had to get out of here before he made his decision. Before he had the chance to say no. "If you are willing, be at my family's ramp at 9:30. If not…"

She kissed his cheek and escaped into the street.

50.

The *Otis Webb*'s engines revved as the captain found the main channel. Due to the hasty departure, several ropes were dragging in its wake, and Charlie was ordered to coil them back aboard. The cord wasn't that long, but once wet, it was heavy. After the lines were secured and Charlie reported for his next order, his arms were on fire and his shirt was drenched with sweat and river water.

David wielded a crowbar, tearing the lids from crates he and the others had procured from the Leavenworth pier. They stole a few cases that appeared to be shells, extra ammunition and a barrel of powder. So far, most of it was unusable. The bulk of the shells were for a twelve-pounder and the bullets were for infantry rifles. Neither of which were part of the group's arsenal. Fortunately, the last two crates searched yielded the score David hoped they would. Each box held a dozen six-pound shells, "Lazarus food," he called them. He vocalized his delight with nearly as many expletives as shells found.

There were ten shots hidden with the cannon, packed loosely in three satchels and fastened to the base. They were old and had been exposed to the elements. Their usefulness was uncertain. No one wanted to talk about the fact that the shells could be duds but everyone was thinking it. Obviously, that would be disastrous. Therefore, the additional twenty-four rounds, newly packed in clean cedar boxes, helped quell the earlier fear. They would never need both cases. Chances were good they themselves would be shot or sunk long before they could send that many volleys. They had enough supply to be a nuisance and to allow for a few misses. Right now, that was their best hope.

The wet ropes secured the cannon to the boat deck. Boxes, stacked on all sides, offered cover from any rifle or pistol fire they may draw. The ammo and black powder were pulled close to Lazarus for quicker, easier loading, the powder barrel itself protected soundly against untimely detonation. David gave Charlie a beginner's course on cannonry and they were set. They had all but turned the *Webb* into a battleship.

There was a problem though, and it wasn't until David had the deck in order that he noticed. They were moving slowly. Faster than the river, but nowhere near as fast as the boat was capable of moving. Something was wrong. "We need to go faster than this," David yelled toward the wheelhouse. He calculated they were going ten, maybe twelve miles per hour. He wanted more. They would need more to close the distance. He needed Webb to fix it.

The captain stepped out, leaving the wheel for Oliver to handle. He descended a few rungs of the rusty, whitewashed ladder and stopped, hanging in midair. From there, he yelled his reply. "We're too heavy to go faster. We never off-loaded in Leavenworth so we're still hauling the extra weight," he explained. "The motor is working as hard as it can but unless the weight changes, we're at maximum speed right now."

"I'll take care of that," said David. He called Charlie to grab a side of a crate and the two of them slid it to the edge. "Ready, push," said David and the first box of unserviceable rifle shells hit the muddy river and sank from sight. They quickly grabbed the second crate of bullets to jettison and over it went.

Webb, seeing David's solution, pointed out another cause for concern. "Be careful what you get rid of, we still have to pass Parkville. The old boy I was just talking to upriver says there's a horde camped there, waiting for a call south to fight.

And they're getting a bit jumpy. They see that cannon, they're going to want to take it. Or sink me for having it. So don't throw out all of your hiding places, you're going to need some of them."

"Oh hell," David grumbled. He forgot all about passing the small Missouri town. He and Charlie would have to improvise.

David called Oliver down from the captain's roost, explaining they would need all the muscle they could get. David pointed out boxes he deemed harmless to the engine's potency—the lighter goods like shirts, shoes and blankets. They would be allowed to stay and act as building blocks in their fortification. All the other crates, bags, boxes and cases were to be fed to the catfish. Dishes, the wrong-sized cannon loads, even the whiskey and corn mash were judged too heavy, and were discarded.

Slowly, pound by pound, with each small load lost, the overall weight fell. The wind hitting their faces intensified and the water splashing up the sides packed a harder punch. The *Otis Webb* was shedding pounds and moving faster.

The captain watched from above as the three men shifted the cargo from side to side and from deck to oblivion. Some items floated in the river and chased them south. Others sank immediately like stones. Still others gave chase until the river punctured their bowels and sealed the items' fate. Bubbles would show the final resting spot, but not for long. Once the air was choked out, the river covered its tracks and it was as if nothing ever entered there. The delivery tickets for all the items sat in a stack on Webb's dash, a pile of paper now as worthless as the trash at the bottom of the river. Easy come, easy go.

The first river marker for the port of Parkville appeared. Time was running out. The captain banged on his window to get the others' attention. He pointed to the marker and held up both hands with his fingers stretched. "Ten minutes," he mouthed. David gave a thumbs-up in reply. They would be ready. They had better be.

51.

An eerie calm hung inside the Quindaro mill. All the action, still proceeding at a hectic pace, was outside of its walls. The sounds of the town—yells, crashes and such—blew through the structure's two large, open barn-style doors. The entrance, normally where massive hazelnut and oak logs entered in rough form, now let in the humid wind carrying ghostly echoes of the goings-on in town. The walls, no match for the openings, were unable to hold the resonance. So the sounds, like bumblebees, would bluster in the building a moment, then exit where the hewn material was usually sent away. The high metal roof vibrated with the stronger gusts and drowned the room with clatter. Somehow, the space was noisy and discreet at the same time.

Nancy walked in through the exit, her straight black hair blown horizontal as she crossed the threshold. Across the vast room, closer to the entrance, Adam was working. He had the mill's pulley system aligned with the tallest open window facing east. The rope snaked around his feet as his hands desperately tied knots. He removed a red bandana from his back pocket, tied it securely to one end of the lead line and then began to feed both through the wheels. When he was sure of his engineering, he started to pull one end of the rope with all his might. As he did, the red signal began to rise.

"You will need to line it up better if you want it to show through the window," Nancy yelled from across the room. "You missed it by a foot."

Adam turned around to find the voice, his heart nearly jumping from his chest. He'd thought of a lie, a good one too.

But then he saw her. He'd seen that look on her face before. He was already in the snare, caught to the knee. The lie was a waste of time.

"When I raise this signal," said Adam, "your tiny town will die. And every person here." He tried to make it sound like a threat.

"Then serve your master, Kayrahoo," she shot back.

At a side door between the two warriors, Chris entered the mill. Since agreeing to lend his assistance to the town, he had kept one eye on Nancy at all times. He saw her enter the back of the building and despite having no particular intentions, decided to follow. Sensing the mounting hostility, he decided to make his presence known to her and Adam. Although she ignored him, he felt confident she knew he was there. Probably. Either way, if she needed help, he would gladly provide it. She would just have to give the order.

The signal was lowered back down and the pulley position adjusted. Adam noticed Chris in the side doorway and began to fume. His words hissed as he addressed Nancy and allowed years of frustration to pour from his mouth.

"I have no master," he said. "This is me and only me. The warrior." He let her know that he was making choices for his own future since she, along with most of his people, had turned their backs on him and the old ways. He was alone now and making the best of it. He was finally going to create a world of his own. One without her. Her and her white men.

He shot a look at Chris, still standing in the doorway, and spit in his direction to clear the taste. Adam continued, softer now, between gritted teeth. "I was a fool to ever think you were or would ever be a part of me. Or with me in any way. You have been the treasure I have sought my entire life, since we were children. But you never looked at me like that, as a man. Only a spear or club, never a mate. Never anything more…"

Nancy had heard enough. She interrupted his tirade, speaking to him like a child, closing the distance between them. "You are so stupid, Adam." Of course, she knew his feelings, how for years his heart yearned to possess her. "However, Adam, you were never worthy, not a single day in your life. You could never be the type of man I would accept, you simply lack the talent. And the resolve. Your insides are too soggy, too tender to be a match with me. Your traitorous actions prove that beyond a doubt."

"I never wanted to betray you," Adam insisted. "Or our people. This town? Absolutely! You could never understand how it feels because you are an insider, sadly, admitted only for your beauty." His voice became more nasty, hurtful. "Only to be passed around, handled by the gluttonous." He asked her pointedly, "How can I betray a group I was never allowed to join?" It wasn't possible. "My conscience is clear."

Nancy was closer now, yards away, near enough for Adam to feel her presence. And as usual, he softened. The actions he had taken as The Whistler were crude but necessary. Again, he stressed the fact that initially, his motives were pure. A new life justly earned. And when the work started, that new life included her. It still could.

There was a payment waiting for him in Westport. It was substantial. Enough to take him west or east, wherever he wanted. Cook had assured him passage out of Quindaro as well, through the forest toward Wyandotte. After he raised the signal, he was free to go. And he would never return. Adam paused, waiting for the courage to swell for his final proposal. He whispered to her quietly, begging, "Come with me."

Nancy was revolted and it showed in a flash, just a millisecond, running like a current through her face. Chris thought he saw it. Adam missed it completely. "I'm not coming with you, Adam," she stated plainly. "After you send your signal, you can slink out through the back like a snail."

Adam started to speak but Nancy confiscated the opening.

"Raise your rag, Kayrahoo!" she screamed, her voice full and strong. "Do you think I fear what is coming? That I am afraid of any fight you would bring? Let the battle start today, right now." She was fierce. "You and Cook are fools to think the taking of this town will be easy. The work required to win this ground is more than your backs can heave. Yes, many will die today, but many are willing. And they will wield more power as ghostly hookies than they ever could as living, breathing beasts."

Adam shook his head woefully. "The invaders have enough firepower to kill everyone in this town several times over," he informed her. "They will erase all memory of every living thing in sight. Even their souls will cease to exist. There is no way for you to escape when it starts, either. I am your last option, your last chance for survival."

Nancy was unmoved. She assured Adam his concern for her was in vain. "The blood that spills and soaks this ground today will beckon thousands of others just like us. Fighters, like wolves to the wounded, to come and take our place on the field. They will come willingly, ready to continue the struggle against your allies who would own other humans as if it were a divine right to do so. They will fight harder, dig in deeper than those before them ever had. Their roots will sink farther into the dark, rich soil and will never be removed, not even by God himself.

"But this I can promise, Adam," Nancy continued. "Blood will flow like the river on both sides. You and yours will feel the loss and know you have fought when it is over." Her sermon complete, she gave her final order. "So, raise your rag and fulfill your purpose. Let it begin today."

Tears dripped from the warrior's eyes, causing the black paint to run clear down his neck. The last thing in the world he wanted was for the princess to be erased. But her stubbornness was legendary and unwavering. She would surely die today as Cook's major prize. And he could not change that outcome. He slowly pulled the rope again, the red bandana climbing in the air, higher and higher, nearing the window. He stared at her as his arms sealed her fate, wanting to show his strength but unable. The sorrow had taken him. His lifelong dream in ruin.

From the side door, Chris waited for Nancy to stop the rogue warrior. His eyes darted back and forth, from the signal rising to the princess. As the distance between the two grew, he was sure she would change her mind. A mere look in Chris' direction would be enough, his pistol would end the madness. But she never once looked away from Adam. She never blinked.

The sunlight hit the red of the cloth and the rag glowed. Adam and Chris looked to the sky, waiting for whatever was to follow. Nancy's eyes still bore into Adam, content with the movement of the chess piece. Suddenly, in the distance, the sound of the first cannon shot made its way up the hill. It beat the actual projectile by more than a second, but its message was clear. The attack had begun.

Above their heads, the sound of the opening shell whizzed by, clearing the mill then striking a warehouse two plots over. The explosion was massive as the wooden exterior crumbled and caught fire. Screams of terror whooshed into the space, telling the wretched story of those unfortunate enough to have chosen shelter in the first target. Townsfolk ran to the rescue, salvaging what they could and working to contain the fire. The first shot hurt but was absorbed.

Then another boom climbed the hill, followed by another, and another. The shelling was furious, hitting near and far, raining metal and fire throughout the town. Adam was sobbing when he finally looked back at Nancy. He couldn't save her now even if she wanted him to. She was lost, forever. "I warned you, Quindaro," he said.

"Yes, you did, cousin. Another frailty of yours," she said. She pulled a pistol from her waistband and took aim. "I give no warnings," she declared. Then she emptied the gun into Adam's chest.

Chris was frozen, stunned by the abrupt ending of the confrontation. All he could do was await instructions.

Standing over the body, she reloaded her pistol and put it away. The pulley system hung above her, the bandana waving in the breeze. She would leave it there as the fight raged, a reminder to herself that she brought the battle. It was her choice to begin. It gave her strength. And she would need it. The town would need it. Dispatching Adam, her blood, wasn't easy but it was necessary. To win the fight, it would take everyone binding together to become more than themselves. It was the very meaning of the town's name, her name, Quindaro. "A band of sticks." Strength in numbers. Adam chose to be separate so he paid the price of isolation. He knew where those decisions would take him. It was, after all, the Wyandotte way.

As her ancestors flooded her mind, inspiration struck and she decided to leave Cook a sign of her own. One of a more foreboding nature. She grabbed the rope and walked to the front entrance. She picked up an iron hook used to move smaller tree trunks within the mill and threw it over her shoulder. As she moved the equipment across the room to begin her artistry, she yelled for Chris. "Bring me the body."

52.

Tots' Tremont Street warehouse was located near the Common, on roughly the same block as King's Chapel where the last bell cast by Paul Revere himself had hung since 1814. Where School Street crossed Tremont was five or six miles from Walter's home, normally much too far of a journey to take on by foot. However, this evening was different for many reasons.

First, Walter was unsure of the direction he planned to take tonight. If things turned dark, he would prefer not to have a witness able to testify to his being in the vicinity. Since everyone knew carriage drivers were gossips of the first order, he figured it best not to commission a potential tattletale. There was a chance he would walk away from Tots and the destruction, but he couldn't be sure, so he erred on the safe side. To travel and show up alone was the best move.

Next, Cara's personal bombshell still rattled him to his bones. He was amazed that despite his inane, infantile behavior, Cara still considered him worthy. The fact that she spoke to him at all was a marvel, let alone express any sort of feeling of love or devotion. When the words left her mouth and entered his ears, he was flabbergasted like never before. He thought his heart was working overtime contemplating arson; hell, that was nothing. Cara nearly killed him by the time she finished. Looking back, he probably should have said something before she left. She seemed upset. But his mind wouldn't fire, and his body froze. Hopefully he didn't blow it.

After all, she was exactly what he wanted as well, maybe more than anything. Maybe. He wasn't sure. Charlie and the company still pulled at him, an unbroken sense of duty to blood, to history and to self. Sure, it sounded easy to let it all go. To start anew with Cara or someone like her, forget about the past, the Murrays and even his nephew. But it wasn't easy. In fact, it wasn't possible. He tried to imagine himself without worry, without the spectacle or responsibility. That just wasn't him. Was it? The answer wasn't there. Not yet, anyway. That was another reason the long walk made sense, it would give him time to choose the right path for himself. A path he hadn't considered in a long time.

The quarrels inside Walter's mind made the trek seem much shorter. He fought himself from one end of Tremont to the other, round after round, with each one ending in a draw. The pros, when stacked on one another, seemed exactly equal to the cons. Maybe not equal, but too close to call one way or another. He argued for and against Charlie. For and against Cara. Then there was the little matter of Daniel Murray's carnal knowledge of the woman he would potentially run away with. That made his skin crawl. So much so, he began to notice others noticing him. No doubt, those who saw the old man walking, talking aloud to no one other than himself, pegged him a maniac. He needed to be more discreet, to blend. Like a criminal.

Unfortunately, his time was up. Tots' warehouse, a small brick building with a single dock and two boarded-up windows, appeared out of nowhere. The sun was just beginning to sink into the night. However, this time of year, the process was slow, the darkness still a safe distance away. The real action wouldn't start for a while. Walter put his hand on the doorknob, then paused a moment as his thoughts settled. He was as ready as he would ever be, so he opened the door and walked inside.

The taller building just to the west threw its shadow over Tots' shorter structure, making the room darken already. A few lanterns provided light, but not much, seeing as they were pushed back near the walls, presumably to separate them from the incendiary devices littering the place. Surprisingly, Tots was there along with two men, a few wagons, several barrels and a barren of mules. The place smelled like manure and kerosene, making it difficult to breath.

When Tots saw Walter, he sent his helpers back to work and welcomed his friend with a bear hug. Noticing the confused look on Walter's face, Tots explained his presence. "It's been a while since I've gotten down in the dirt firsthand. And if I were ever going to do so again, tonight would certainly be the occasion for it." For Walter's sake. Before his friend could object, Tots grabbed his arm and shuffled him around the room, boastfully showing him the setup. Tots beamed with pride, confident they had the tools to bring about the desired outcome. Everything was in fine order. It should be fun!

Walter endorsed all he saw and expressed his appreciation. He was delighted and assured Tots he was ready for the evening's plot. His smile however, appeared forced and awkward. His face was white and dripping with sweat. The distress he felt was apparent, and Tots took notice. A few steps away from where the two men stood, one of the mules emptied his bowels onto the hard dirt floor. It sounded like twenty pounds of shit being dropped from the roof. It pushed Walter's body over the edge.

When he heaved, the vomit flew like a bolt halfway up the nearby wall. Walter doubled over before the next wave hit and splashed the remaining contents of his stomach onto one of the wagon's wheels. Steadying himself, he propped one arm against the side of a large wooden barrel while spitting the excess saliva from his mouth. A moment later, still bent over, a final dry heave ended the eruption. Walter took several deep breaths as the episode passed. The cold sweat seemed to help his body recover, and the sparkles in his eyes faded as quickly as they came. He needed a moment, but he would be fine.

Tots lightly patted his friend's back, offering some comfort. Behind him, his two helpers peeked from their work, hoping the order to clean the wall and floor wouldn't come. It didn't. Instead, Tots sent one to fetch a glass of water and the other a wet rag. He leaned down to check Walter's face and asked gently, "Are you alright, Walt?"

Walter didn't hear the question. He blurted out his only thought, his final decision. "I can't go through with this tonight, Eddie. I'm sorry."

The men returned with the provisions and handed them to their boss. Tots pointed to a chair in the corner and one of the men retrieved it in an instant. They helped Walter take a seat, then were dismissed to continue their work. Tots knelt down, handing the water to Walter and placing the wet rag around the back of his friend's neck. Walter slowly sipped from the cup while Tots spoke.

"I'm sorry too, Walt. I'm sorry I went to Cara," he said. "I didn't mean to be a rat. I just wanted to make sure you knew what you were getting into. Honestly, I didn't like this plan for you from the start, so you're probably making the right choice."

"Yeah," said Walter. "I don't know about that. But I don't think this," he continued, pointing around the room, "is the answer I'm looking for. My damn body can't take it."

"I understand, Walt," said Tots. His friend needed another option, so he gave it to him. "You know? She gave me paperwork to get her family slip prepared. Somebody is leaving tonight. Gonna be gone a while too."

Walter nodded. "I know," he said. "I was invited." The two men sat silently, waiting for Walter to finish his thought. "I think I'm going to go."

"That sounds like a good idea, Walt," said Tots. "Good luck with that."

Tots' support was reassuring. However, leaving Charlie on his own still hurt, badly. Moreover, leaving the company unprotected would take the rest of Walter's days to forget. Nevertheless, the choice had been made and he needed to see it through. It was right for him in every way.

Walter stood up to leave. There were things to settle before his departure so he best get to it. He thanked Tots for everything and again, offered to pay for the services. Tots refused. They shook hands and hugged, not sure if they would ever see each other again. They were old men, after all, getting older every day. And no one lives forever.

"Take care of yourself, Eddie," Walter said.

"You too, Walt," replied Tots. But he didn't let go of Walter's hand just yet. Tots leaned in close, his cold gray eyes arresting Walter and his movements. There was more to say. "Walter, I've never forgotten how well you treated me all those years ago. Hell, to this day. Your friendship, next to my wife and children, is one of the things I value most in my life. You are a true friend, a brother. And I would do anything, anything at all, you ever need. All you have to do is ask."

Tots looked over his shoulder at the two men working. "These are two of the most trustworthy gentlemen I employ," he assured Walter. "They know how to keep secrets and have in the past. Several, in fact." He paused, not wanting to push too hard. "It's a shame to be all dressed up for a party just to have it canceled," said Tots. "You're leaving tonight, old friend, for who knows how long. If you would like to ask for one last favor, you should do it now."

53.

"Where were you aiming? At the two-story?" Cook asked as he looked through his spyglass at the damage caused by the twelve-pounder stationed nearest him. The building at the top of the hill was on fire and would fail soon. However, it was the wrong building. "I told you I wanted the little white building, the store there, see it? That was where you were to aim. Did you miss the mark or did you aim at the wrong place?"

The crew leader chastised his men as they loaded the next shell. He, too, was indignant, embarrassed by the miss. Ultimately, it was his slipup, but he decided to share the blame as a way of self-preservation.

Cook wasn't impressed and shut down the act with a sharp stare. He held out his hand, stopping the ranking member where he stood pleading for clarification. The crew were either aiming at the two-story, the wrong target. Or they missed the white building by sixty yards or more. Either way, Cook was pissed and severely disappointed with the result.

After stumbling with his words for a minute, the crew leader finally confessed. "It was a miss, sir. The angle was wrong, the damn hill is steeper than we expected. It won't happen again."

"That's a fact," Cook replied, pointing his finger directly at the man. The sarcasm was thick. He yelled for Blue, who rode up quickly after the summons. Cook, wanting to check that he wasn't being unreasonable, laid out his grievances. Blue listened intently, nodding his head in agreement throughout the entire tirade. Finally, Cook asked, "Do we have replacements?"

"Yes, sir," Blue answered. "The Ozark trash made it up. They have two cannon crews we can use."

"Fantastic!" yelled Cook. "Swap 'em out."

As Cook peered back up the hill, Blue ran off the bungling crew and sent for the replacements. The first building hit was nearly gone now and even if it was the wrong target, Cook had to admit, it was a good start. The hardware store, where the Odd Fellows met, needed to feel the pain next. And it would, or the fresh Ozark crew would pay dearly. The mill was an important target as well. It was a symbol of Quindaro's efficiency, their promise and drive. When it fell, and it would soon, the town would suffer a major blow to their morale. For now though, it would have to wait. At least until The Whistler got clear of the danger zone.

Blue helped aim the twelve-pounder for the second shot. Cook added his two cents as well. When the angle was finally settled, the spyglass zeroed in on the small white building. Cook would see it fall this time if it killed him. He yelled behind him, "Fire when ready." And offered a little more sarcasm for good measure. "Let's try to hit the right target this time, shall we? Oh, and stay clear of the sawmill. It'll be next but..."

His gaze wandered to the mill for just a second when something caught his eye. A figure, a body, hung in the doorway, at least ten feet off the ground. It was bloody. An Indian. The lifeless body had been scalped, the throat sliced open too. A hook stuck from the chest, suspending in air The Whistler himself. There was no doubt it was the work of the princess, her own signal to Cook showing the penalty for sedition. She made a mess of the poor son of a bitch. What a shame.

"Damnation," he said aloud. "Well, I guess you can go ahead and hit the mill whenever you're ready, no reason to wait now." The second shot left the barrel and the W&M Hardware Depot buckled. Cook was thrilled! While the third shot was loaded, Cook called to Blue one more time. "The package in Westport? The one we left for the Indian? Send someone to pick it up, bring it back here to me. He ain't going to need it."

54.

Parkville's English Landing had been a steamship berth since the 1830s. The man who platted the town itself, George Shepherd Park, did so formally in 1844 after purchasing a ninety-nine-year lease on the property near the river. The deed extended into the nearby limestone bluffs where he also built his home, a store, a church and a hotel known as "Old Number One." Before coming to Missouri, Park had lived in Vermont, was born there, in fact, had fought for Texas independence and was one of a handful of survivors of Santa Anna's Goliad Massacre.

Park arrived in the area in 1836 and at one time or another, had been a teacher, a preacher, and a newspaper owner. Despite being a slave owner, he filled his paper, *The Industrial Luminary*, with editorials against the spread of slavery to the Kansas side of the river. In return, his neighbors stormed the paper's office and tossed his printing press into the muddy Missouri. Since then, Park and his wife seemed to travel outside of the area much more often.

He was lucky to be traveling again today as his town had been overrun. At least a hundred men, called south from Leavenworth to cover Cook's northern flank, had set up camp in and around the landing, spilling into the town's nearby park. They were a rowdy bunch, mostly off-duty soldiers who weren't good at sitting and waiting for orders. They were itching to fight and would soon, even if it was with each other. There had been several localized brawls already, and pistol shots echoed off the nearby quarry walls every few minutes or so. Luckily, all the whiskey in town had been drunk, the fever had risen just about as high as it could. For now.

The *Otis Webb* was running full throttle by the time it came upon Parkville and the detachment. Webb tried to maneuver the boat as far to the right shore as he could to get as much room between the men and the boat as possible. As he neared, he could see them tossing bottles, rocks, anything really, into the river, and he knew his boat would make an amusing moving target. When they figured out he wasn't stopping, their intrigue would surely manifest itself in violent frenzies, and his boat would take the brunt of it. Therefore, he needed to keep his speed up and get past quickly to minimize the potential damage the *Webb* may receive.

David was hidden well, deep in the lighter crates kept on board to hide Lazarus. Oliver rode up top with Webb while Charlie pretended to work the deck. The captain advised the boy to stay near the boxes as much as he could, to duck and cover if someone decided to take a shot at him, for fun or otherwise. Charlie heeded the warning and "swept" the deck while meandering in and out of the box maze.

David peeked through a small opening in the hideout, judging the situation on shore. There were fewer men than he imagined but they seemed a wilder sort. Personally, he preferred fighters to numbers, and it seemed Cook had prepared well. But David wasn't planning to fight these men, so none of that mattered much. All he needed was to get past Parkville in one piece and from where he sat, that should be easy enough.

He watched Charlie doing his act and giggled. The boy looked funny pushing a broom, like he'd never done it before. Ever. He looked scared too, but that was understandable. He'd been through a lot. David got his attention and tried to make light of things. "I bet this is the last thing you ever thought you'd be doing," he said with a laugh. "If we make it out of here today," he finished, pointing to the Parkville masses with his thumb, "you'll have them lining up to kill you too."

"Great, that's what I need," Charlie answered. "More assholes wanting to kill me."

David laughed.

Charlie continued, his ire growing. He spoke to David without looking at him so no one on shore noticed. "Honestly! First my brothers. Then Cook and his bushwhackers. Then you, probably. The Six Mile lunatic, the town of Leavenworth… God, no. I never thought I would be here, you're right about that."

The list was impressive, even to David. "Brothers?" he asked.

Charlie thought about holding his tongue. *What's the use? I'm probably going to die today anyway.* "My stepbrothers want to kill me. That's why I came out here. To Kansas. It's a long story."

"Doesn't seem that long to me," replied David. "Your brothers want to kill you so you left town. End of story. I get it."

"*Step*brothers," Charlie corrected.

"Whatever," said David. He continued, certifying the list. "I can't speak for your *step*brothers but Cook and his boys will certainly try to kill you the next time they see you. No doubt about that. Leavenworth is off limits from now on, maybe Parkville too, depending on what happens in the next few minutes. As for me," David pledged, "I promise to never try to kill you again. On purpose anyway."

Charlie returned the sarcasm. "Thanks, Mr. Sorter, for not killing me on purpose. How can I ever repay you?" For a moment, Charlie felt more at ease. It was hard not to feel that way when talking with David, as his fearlessness had a way of rubbing off on folks. Especially the young and impressionable. When Charlie snuck a peek at the awaiting trouble, his tension started returning. He retraced the steps of the conversation, working backwards to when he was calm and tried to get that feeling again. He tried to find his bearings. In doing so, he recalled that David had omitted a person from the "Charlie's Potential Murderers" list—the Six Mile man. He used the weirdo to rekindle the talk.

"You didn't mention the man with the feather in his hat back in Six Mile," said Charlie.

"I don't think you have much to worry about there," David said. "If Nana wanted you dead, you'd be dead."

"Nana?" Charlie asked.

"No one knows his real name," answered David. "Hell, everyone calls him something different. The black folk sometimes call him Legba, like the Voodoo man. Because he has 'powers' and such. Some in Quindaro call him the Scarecrow. I've even heard some call him Gabriel for some reason. Neither name has any particular meaning, I think people just want to call him something that sounds spooky. It's all a bit ridiculous to me."

"Where does 'Nana' come from?" Charlie asked.

David peeked around a crate to see how long he had until they reached Parkville. The story would have to be quick. "The Indians call him 'Nanabozho,'" David answered, "after their trickster deity."

Nana was the central character of many Indian myths and legends. Usually portrayed as a rabbit, Nanabozho fought everything from the wind and rain to sea monsters and ghosts. He was also a shapeshifter and in one particular story, took the form of a tree to avenge the death of his cousin. In doing so, he also succeeded in destroying the entire world. The story was a lesson meant to teach the harm a vengeful heart could cause. However, David found the ending especially satisfying. "Vengeance to the point of ending all life," he said reflectively. "He's speaking my language."

David reiterated that Charlie would more than likely come out unscathed if he were to visit Six Mile again. However, it would be prudent to bring a friend. And to let someone know when to expect his return. People tended to disappear in the tavern for long periods of time. Some never left.

"Look on the bright side," David said. "You can cross at least one person off your list."

The tightness returned to Charlie's shoulders, recalling the promise he made to visit Nana after the mission was complete. And despite the hot sun beating his skin, he noticed goosebumps running up his arm, confirmation his body didn't believe a word of David's endorsement.

"Yeah," replied Charlie. "Maybe I'll get lucky and get shot today. Then I won't have to worry about any of them."

Just then, a high-pitched *ping* sounded off above them. Charlie hit the deck and David laid flat on the boards. They both looked to the wheelhouse where Webb and Oliver had taken cover as well. From the bank, the hoots and hollers of the men bounced off the water and mixed with the revving engine. It sounded like a barn dance gone awry. The potshots flying over the bow and the stacks sent paint chips flying when they hit, accompanied by loud cheers. The misses cut the air with a whiz and generated equally vociferous boos and jeers. Luckily, the frisky bunch wasn't aware of the enemy on board. The target practice was less about doing harm and more about giving the crew a fright.

As the boat pushed on, the men lost interest and the forays tapered off. Soon, David and the crew knew they would make it. "Boy, Cook's got his hands full with that bunch, don't he?" David snickered.

Charlie answered with a sigh.

Next stop, Quindaro.

55.

Thus far, Cook's attack on Quindaro had been by cannon shot only. And it was relentless. The air in town was heavy and smoke-filled, with fires burning near and far. The hill shook like an earthquake. Each rumble caused damage as shot after shot reached town and left a mark. Nancy had arranged to ride out the initial bombardment in trenches and fortifications built out of sight and range. The preparations to this point had paid off, as most of the town hid under cover, somewhat sheltered from the air raid. Long-range rifles sounded off as well, from down the hill, far away. Luckily, the shooters weren't half as skilled as The Whistler had been, so none of the snipers had hit their mark. Yet. There had been a few injuries, none severe though. And only a couple of deaths from the initial explosions. The town still had good numbers, plenty of fighters. However, the buildings and other structures aboveground and in the open were being thrashed one by one. Pretty soon, nothing would be left standing and any cover would all but disappear.

Behind a grain storage warehouse, Tough and the Jayhawkers took cover, sharing information and adjusting their defenses. Nancy and Chris ran toward them, bent over as they went, trying to become smaller targets. In a nearby trough, Nancy dipped her hands in the warm water, washing Adam's already dried blood from the creases and nails. As she did so, she yelled over her shoulder for Tough to give her a status update.

He complied, stopping a moment in the middle of his report to remove a small piece of Adam from Nancy's cheek.

"Scalp?" questioned Tough, as he flicked it aside.

"I'll tell you about it later," Nancy replied. "What else do you have?"

Tough related the situation as he knew it and Nancy thanked him. The two leaders discussed their options and quickly came to a consensus. They needed two men to oversee the log stack near the mill. Because the booby trap was such an important aspect of the town's resistance, it was imperative they have someone trustworthy manage the operation. Nancy was resolute. One of the men would be Chris. Tough yielded to her ruling and it was done. Before the Irishman ran away, Nancy grabbed his hand and silently thanked him for his assistance earlier. His insides detonated.

Next, Nancy sent a couple of men to the hotel, looking to plunder anything they could before it was hit and lost. It was a miracle Cook hadn't smashed it by now, the men would need to hurry. The hotel's lifespan was growing shorter by the minute. Before the next order could be delivered, Clarina approached. She needed help fighting a fire that looked to be spreading to the sounder structures. It had to be stopped. Nancy altered her course and sent three men with Clarina to tackle the blaze. Once it was under control, they were instructed to find Tough and follow his direction.

Clarina led the men away, leaving Nancy and Tough alone. They stood looking down the hill with growing concern as Cook's men amassed at the edge of the woods. Nancy felt confident the main road up the hill, the steeper north ledge, would be protected, at least from the first charge. The log pile would see to that. However, the south passage, the flatter approach, was still vulnerable. After inspection, Tough and Cuff had spied an assembly there, smaller but able. A mean-looking bunch. They had rolled to the south earlier in the day and sat waiting to pounce. The townsfolk, dug into the trenches, had the high ground. But the numbers on that side of town probably would not be enough to capitalize on the advantage of the terrain. If Cook decided to direct an offensive from there, he would find a vulnerable flank. It would be catastrophic.

"Do you think we can hold from the south?" Nancy asked.

Tough knew what she meant. She was asking if he could hold the hill. Him, Cuff and a handful of help. He'd been running scenarios since he got back to town and none of them ended well. If Cook came that way, the hill would fall and so would the town. Any plan to stop it was folly. But Nancy knew that already. She simply needed to hear something different, and Tough obliged. "Piece of cake," he assured.

Nancy appreciated the lie. It made her smile.

56.

Walter was going to be cutting it close. A million things needed handling before he left the city and he only had a couple of hours to accomplish them all. First, he needed to stop at home and gather a few things. On the way there, directly from his meeting with Tots, he mentally tallied the items he would grab and their whereabouts. As soon as he hit the door, he went to work.

In the closet near the front door, he gripped the only small bag he owned. In it, he stuffed one change of clothes and his pistol. He then scavenged the house, raiding all of the hordes of cash he had hidden over time. There wasn't much, but it would be foolish to leave any hard currency behind. A few bills were in a dress shirt, a few in his galoshes. There was a larger stash in the kitchen, stuck between two coffee cups, and another wad strapped to the bottom of his desk. Finally, the largest and most important cache was kept in a blue-and-silver Farrah's Toffee tin, under a rug in the hall, beneath two removable floorboards. From the tin, Walter removed some cash—nearly six hundred dollars—and a necklace that used to belong to his sister Sarah. He replaced the slats and rug and was finished with this stop. He paused a moment at the front door to say goodbye to his old home. The sudden feeling of sadness that crept in was confusing, as he never really liked the place all that much. The homey feel he wanted from it just never materialized, even after several years of occupancy. Still, he found the old saying held true. Parting was sweet sorrow.

The next stop was his office. Here, he gathered several

important client documents, contracts and such, and packed them into a large box. He planned to take them to Peter's for safekeeping. The last thing he needed was stolen client information that would likely lead to some form of litigation. It had been years since he retained the services of an attorney and he wasn't about to get involved in that racket again. Into the box he also slid a plaque awarded by the city commissioner, the photo of him with Cara and a small clock Mrs. Wedge had bought him. Everything else in the office, however, like at home, was immaterial. The couch and desk, his bed and table could stay in place forever or float away tomorrow. Right now, he was indifferent to their fate.

Tots had agreed to assign one of his men to keep watch on both Walter's home and office full time. Tots also agreed to find work for Mrs. Wedge that would assure her a steady income. This would certainly be a hard sell considering Tots' reputation and Mrs. Wedge's uncommonly high moral standards. However, Tots had plenty of "straight" work to pass around, and money rarely lost an argument, even to integrity.

Walter laid all the cash on his desk and began to divvy it into piles. The bulk would go to Tots to make lease payments on the office and cover any necessary expenses the home may incur. There wasn't enough to pay indefinitely, but Tots didn't mind. He told Walter they could settle matters whenever he returned. He was a great friend!

Walter left a small amount of money for Mrs. Wedge as a well-deserved bonus. He put it in an envelope along with a letter he wrote thanking her for her wonderful service over the years. No doubt, she would initially reject the "handout" and pledge never to spend it. So in his note, Walter made his expectations clear. "Spend this money on yourself, Mrs. Wedge. Quickly! I insist!"

He intended to take some of the cash with him for the trip. A pocketful would do, seeing as Cara's account would be more than sufficient. What remained was for Charlie. He assembled another box that would include cash, Sarah's necklace and a yet-to-be-written letter. The cash went in easily, the necklace was harder to let go. Walter held it in his hand, smoothing it, making one last connection to his sister. The gold chain was modern, purchased for Sarah's sixteenth birthday. It was shiny and pretty, heavy too, but merely a vessel to hold the real prize, the emerald.

The jewel was small but handsome and brilliantly green. It was said that Cortez plundered the stone from nearly the same ground on which Charlie currently walked, then returned to Europe with it as part of his gift to the Spanish royals. A few hundred years later, Walter and Sarah's father procured the stone at auction shortly after he made his first million. It probably would have been given to Sarah even if her birthday wasn't in May, but since it was, the shoe fit even better. She wore it nearly every day after and it quickly became her signature ornament. When her sickness gained strength, she imparted it to her brother as the vultures began to circle. Namely James Murray and his minions. Walter hid it away, protecting it with all he had, as the final piece of his beloved sibling.

Before he left, however, he thought it proper to give it to Charlie. The boy needed a token by which to remember his mother more than Walter deserved to remember his sister. Besides, if times got bad, which they would, the necklace would bring enough to get Charlie back above water. To send it to him was the right thing to do. Now all that was needed to complete the care package was the letter. This part proved exceedingly difficult.

Walter cried repeatedly as the letter poured from him. Admitting defeat is a grueling task that punishes a body more than the most strenuous physical effort. It scars like the deepest cut. It damages like a stroke. Some never recover from it. Walter prayed he would, in time. Cara would certainly help in the matter. Nevertheless, he would be forever altered, less in some ways, more in others. He tried his best not to apologize in the letter but near the end, he couldn't resist. It, too, was the right thing to do.

With the two boxes in hand, Walter made his escape. He didn't turn back to give a final farewell to this room as he and the space had always had an understanding. The relationship was professional, nothing more. Quickly, before the boxes' heft became too much to bear, Walter hired a brougham and gave the driver Peter's address. Once there, he instructed the man to wait while he completed his business.

Peter, as usual, was supportive, sympathetic and drunk. He agreed to keep the documents secure as long as Walter agreed to bring back a bottle of Glen Ord single malt scotch upon his return. It was a fair price and therefore, an easy accord. Peter grabbed his friend as he tried to leave and hugged him severely. He asked Walter to wait for a moment, ran to his study, then emerged holding two small crystal shot glasses, filled to the brim with a "superb spirit." Peter gave one of the glasses away and held the other in the air. Walter did the same.

"To the bravest and the boldest man I have ever known," slurred Peter. "To Walter!" The two men clinked glasses and with a mighty jolt, emptied the contents. Walter waited for the spasm that usually followed, but it never came. Instead, the liquor was smooth and warm, with a delicious spicy aftertaste. It was superb indeed.

Walter climbed back into the carriage and this time, gave the driver directions to the slip where Cara's family kept their boat. It was a bit of a journey, especially with the ever-increasing evening traffic, so Walter reclined and enjoyed the effect of Peter's sendoff. Outside, the city of Boston passed, and Walter labored to fill his eyes with memories of home.

Other carriages, broughams like the one he rode in and smaller, two-wheeled hansoms filled the streets. Shouts, curses and whip cracks cut the air. Vendors sold at the corners where they stopped. Their voices, loud and foreign, intermingled with the hoofs and wheels pounding the street, making it impossible to focus. The brick and stone buildings towered above like giants and bounced the sounds off one another again and again. The scents of food and manure mixed with the smell of fish and the nearby harbor, creating a smell distinctly Boston. It was bedlam. Filthy mayhem. But it made Walter smile realizing he loved every dirty inch and always would. It was his city, warts and all. And he would be back. It would simply be impossible to stay away forever.

When he arrived at the pier, Walter paid for the ride, then watched the horses and carriage turn and exit. He stood alone in the dark, holding his cane and a solitary bag like a man on the run. It was less hectic near the big boats but still loud. The engines droned low and full, even at idle, and the ground all around vibrated from the power. The stone road sloped down toward the water at a comfortable angle, leading to the boarding ramp of Cara's vessel. To get there, Walter would turn his back on the city one last time. He gave it a moment, then, with a nod adieu, he headed for Cara.

A few steps into his journey, he saw her. She was on board, her hair a mess from the wind, but she was glowing in the waning orange sun. She looked beautiful. The choice validated. Surrounding her, several men tended to her wishes, crew preparing to sail, shipmasters checking manifests. There was another group too, which, until Walter was near the top of the gangplank, he didn't recognize. Once at the top though, and too late, the faces of the other men registered and rang the bell. The color vanished from Walter's face and his stomach wrenched. Daniel Murray turned to greet his uncle with a cynical and scary smile. Walter stood stunned and couldn't move a muscle. His eyes were all that would work, and as they scanned the rest of Daniel's clique, he wished they were frozen as well. Boyd was there too, silent, fiendish. Another quote entered Walter's mind but this one proved to be completely inaccurate. All reunions are certainly not a type of heaven. This one was hell.

57.

Since substituting for the inept bombardier crew, Cook's raid had been flawless. In Quindaro, buildings were burning and fires were spreading. Every ten minutes or thereabout, a fractured structure failed, erasing it from the landscape. And with more and more shells being sent airborne every minute, there was no end to the destruction in sight. The town was dizzy from the constant pummeling and seemed ripe for the taking. Soon, the order to charge would come and the well-deserved beating would continue on a more personal level. Happy would see to that.

The soldier knelt on one knee at the base of the hill, surrounded by other men who wouldn't or couldn't shut up. The talk was incessant and painful, mainly concerning questions of strategy or enriching the group's esprit de corps. Most were ready, tired of the wait and welcoming of the fight. Some, however, were simply whistling past the graveyard.

Happy ignored the conversations, contributing nothing but the occasional dirty look. He opted instead to keep a sharp eye on Cook, reading movements and signals, looking for tells. He knew the leader well as he had ridden with him for some time. He had studied his boss' habits over the years and had learned much in the process. Consequently, he generally knew the impending order before it was officially delivered. This attentiveness, coupled with a natural instinct to harm, had made him an invaluable asset to Cook and his quest. It was the reason he was first in line, first up the hill. He earned his spot and held it with pride.

Happy watched as Cook's gray stallion aggressively

hopped in place, jolting its rider from side to side with violent shudders. The animal, appearing to feel the temperament of the moment change, tipped the coming command. Knowing what would follow, Happy stood up and secured his rifle and two pistols. It was time. Looking back, the horse suddenly settled, calm and poised, as his master regained the emotional advantage. All was calm now. Cook was in control and prepared. Blue was summoned, an order transmitted.

As the messenger approached the front, Happy started his climb. He didn't need to hear the official command to begin. He was a few steps into the hill when from behind, Blue's words rang out.

"Clear the town, boys!" he yelled. "Careful on the way up. Cook said it's even steeper than it looks. Give 'em hell!" A deafening affirmative shook the ground.

The men started up the steep incline, slow at first then quicker as the slope became familiar. The march was organized for the most part, but no one would confuse the throng with an official military unit. Most were local farmers or ranchers who joined the fight for the pure devotion to their Missouri homeland. Others were transients, shipped in from the southern states to be used as cannon fodder. Many had served at one time or another, and they understood the basics —chain of command, marching drills, firearms, etc. Nevertheless, most were out of practice and it showed.

An order to "hold fire" was given so all weapons would be ready once the targets were in range. It was also important to preserve any surprise element that still existed. The farther up the hill the men could get before the town fired on the lines the better. However, a few of the overzealous fired anyway, sending useless bullets into thin air and leaving their rifles impotent. The unit commanders chastised the practice with the customary name-calling and degradation that quickly helped to regain order. But from the front, Happy could see the damage was done. The offensive was exposed.

A small group of townsfolk had taken notice of the advance and started to send volleys down the hill. Their bullets, aided by gravity, were able to cover the necessary distance. The shots arrived steadily, leaving gaps as men fell out of line. By the time they met their targets, the falling lead pellets were traveling slowly and made a peculiar sound when they tore into an empty chest cavity. Almost like a stone thrown into a pond. The countermeasures were effective but only temporarily slowed the line. The sheer number of invaders was more than the pickets alone could rebuff and the advance continued, nearly unabated.

The ground Happy won was substantial. Leading the charge, he passed the first of the buildings and was gaining more ground by the second. He weaved around corners, peeking in doors and windows along the way, making sure the houses and offices were devoid of Kansas dogs in need of eradication. Thus far, every building had been empty. Nothing to kill. The misanthrope was getting itchy.

Finally, ahead, near the mill, a group of men stood by a large pile of hewn logs stacked higher than most of the buildings. Happy scanned the area for reinforcements, someone protecting his opponent's flank, but saw none. It was too easy. The men at the mill would be the first to die. He yelled behind him, "This way," then angled his ascent toward the area where the land flattened and his targets were assembled.

The climb remained steep and slow but a destination and a known objective boosted the attacker's motivation. Happy kept a close eye on the targets, scrutinizing as he climbed. There were eight total, all men and half too old to worry about. The aged would go quickly. The younger, able rivals would suffer a bit more. They would experience the savagery. Especially the fool with the city hat.

This one swung a heavy hammer with all his might,

pounding away at a stake near the base of the pile. The others kept their distance but remained fascinated by the undertaking. They screamed instructions, each adding a couple cents to the ante. It was silly at first but not for long. Suddenly, Happy stiffened. The pieces flashed in his mind, each separately, like flashcards. The stake, the pile, the goddamn hill!

He stopped in his tracks and yelled for everyone around him to do the same. They didn't hear him. His head turned left and right, looking for the closest safe spot but by his calculations, he was dead center. Back up the hill, the sledge swung one last time, striking the metal stake, releasing it from the ground. It sounded like a nail being driven into a coffin.

The moment the energy turned kinetic, the man in the city hat died. The pile ate him instantly. In mere seconds, thousands of tons started to gain speed, momentum and power. The men around Happy scrambled, running like his chickens back at the farm. It was no use. They would all die anyway.

Happy stood still and watched the logs tear and flatten everything in their path. A house, about the size of his own, blew to pieces in front of him. For a moment, the belongings were exposed and a purple quilt caught his eye. His grandmother had stitched the exact version years back and his wife, Maggie, still used it for cover every night. He suddenly saw her lying in bed, covered in the purple blanket, laughing. That was the day she told him he was going to be a father. The news made his heart sing. They celebrated that evening, unable to keep their hands off each other, the impending family fulfilling all their aspirations. Despite the fact that the child never came, that was the best day of his life. He smiled, thanking the almighty for the memory and giving him one last moment of joy. He watched the purple vanish in slow motion, rolled up in the ball of debris. His hand instinctively grabbed for the rope draped around his neck and he held it tight as he washed away.

58.

With Parkville in its wake, the *Otis Webb* navigated a sharp turn south and chugged toward Quindaro. While dodging fire from English Landing, the *Webb* hugged the southern shore and was forced to make the turn bogged down in the slower inside current. Normally, if given the opportunity, Webb would have taken the outside path of the turn since the flow could move several knots faster there, taking half the time. However, that wasn't an option today since a course any closer to the north side would have resulted in a Swiss cheese hull and a trip to the muddy bottom of the river. The captain pushed hard to get the vessel back into the middle of the channel to take advantage of the water's natural power. In doing so, smoke roared from the stacks and the motor's voice was deafening.

David yelled above the noise, assigning work to Charlie. They needed Lazarus propped but horizontal. Portable but stable. In the open but protected. David's orders were difficult to follow and marginally confusing, mostly because he wasn't sure just what he wanted. The situation ahead was unknown so the plan, above all else, must be fluid.

As far as David was concerned, there was only one certainty. Once the ferry turned the final bend to approach town, he would have mere moments to assess the situation and take the important first shot. After that, their presence and position would be exposed, making them and the ferry a crucial target. Time would be of the essence and in short supply after that. Therefore, a meaningful first strike was imperative. It had the potential to save countless lives in town. Friends. Like Tough, Cuff and the cousins. And Nancy. Whose loss was unimaginable. To David, nothing was more important. The preparation was priority one.

Charlie ran in circles, through, around and over the crates, moving and rearranging items at David's behest. His frustration grew but was irrelevant. And his suggestions, when offered, were ignored. Finally, the second-guessing became too much and David briskly reinforced the kid's role with two assurances. One, David would know the deck was right when he saw it. And two, Charlie would continue to do as instructed or he would find himself in the river again. Only this time, Cuff wouldn't be there to save him. The threat, although more real than Charlie believed, did little to quell his apprehension.

As the vessel hit the straightaway, the current picked up and so did their speed. A south wind, dropping from the steep hills ahead, smacked them head-on and carried with it the sounds of explosions and the smell of fire and sulfur. The sounds grew louder and the smells intensified with each turn of the paddle wheel. David counted the booms and guessed at the firepower, in awe of Cook's strength. If a solitary building still stood in Quindaro, he would be surprised. They needed to hurry.

Charlie screeched and David nearly jumped a foot when from above, the horn belted. Looking to the wheelhouse, they noticed the captain pointing to shore and they followed his finger. There, in a clearing, not far from the edge of the bank stood Dux. A bonfire raged near her, the flames reaching above her head, the smoke billowing all around. She was drenched in sweat that poured from her head and drained down her neck, soaking the gown she wore clear through. She circled the blaze holding a smudge in one hand and a feather in the other, chanting as she moved. She took turns, facing north, south, east and west, paying homage to the four directions, asking for help and guidance from every god that would listen. She was in deep.

David walked to the edge of the boat and watched in earnest with the rest of the crew. Dux's eyes were tightly closed during her ceremony and for a moment, David thought they would pass without notice. But just as they pulled even with her, her eyes opened and locked with his. Her arms snapped horizontal in front of her and began to make tiny circles in the air. The smoke rings from the burning sage appeared from nowhere, slowly lifted, then were gone. Her chants grew more concentrated, the mumbles becoming shouts. The yelling grew and grew, reaching a final crescendo. Then with a sudden exhale, all her movements halted and she dropped to her knees to catch her breath.

The look on her face changed, softening, her gaze still fastened on David. He thought about waving, but it suddenly seemed futile. As if she couldn't see him anyway. It wasn't until her head shook, just slightly, that David understood the purpose of the dance. Her ceremony, albeit a sign of hope and strength, ended with what he recognized as a blessing. The blessing of a soul gone forever. Despite the fact that right now, standing on the deck, his body and soul were still attached, and he was alive and well, Dux considered him dead already. She knew something he didn't. She was afraid, afraid for him. And since he couldn't remember a time when she knew fear at all, this was a bad sign.

As she faded in the distance, Charlie approached and asked, "What was that about?"

David didn't think it fair to lie at a time like this. "It means we're in deep shit."

59.

By the time Walter's sense of hearing returned to normal and his brain was again capable of processing information, it was too late. His time had run out while he stood motionless, frozen by fear and confusion, waiting on the final verdict between fight and flight. The muffled voices—Daniel and Cara, perhaps—mixed with the blurred movements around him helped facilitate the loss of motor skills and lack of awareness. He was out of control.

He wondered for a second if Cara had betrayed him. How else would the Murrays know about the trip? She could have done to him what Calvin had done already—played a joke on a joke. That's what he was, after all. A laughingstock. This was the proof. But she seemed upset. Didn't she? His surroundings were too muddy to make a definitive call. Maybe, because of the way he reacted when invited, she decided to ask Daniel to leave with her as well, to cover her bases. Now that both had shown, she would be forced to take her pick of traveling partner. Of course, Daniel would win that contest outright. Wouldn't he?

The sudden calm along with the arm around his waist brought him back. Daniel's eyebrows were arched as if he were awaiting an answer to a question Walter had missed. The arm was Cara's, wrapped tightly, holding onto him with all her might. It felt great! She was with him. Walter opened his mouth and tried to restart the conversation on his terms. Unfortunately, he was allowed a mere two words, "I'm sorry…"

Quickly and without warning, Boyd broke through his brother with a blackjack in hand and smashed it against the left side of Walter's head. The monster wasn't going to let the question be repeated. Instead, he planned to beat Walter until he talked or died, whichever came first. And that was to begin immediately.

Walter never saw it coming. He collapsed, bringing Cara to the deck with him. Two of the crewmen came to Cara's aid but Boyd gave them both a brutal reprimand. The first took a punch to the throat and fell over choking. The second was hit in the temple and was unconscious before his body crumpled into a pile. Daniel and the two goons with him spread out, looking around for potential witnesses or would-be heroes. There was only one but he ran like a rabbit, nearly tripping over his own feet as he scampered to safety. Walter and Cara were alone and at the mercy of the merciless.

Cara knelt next to Walter, holding his head as the stars cleared from the blow.

"Get her up," Daniel ordered. Cara screamed as the two men lifted her away. In the air, she kicked at her assailants but did little damage. The men were strong and experienced in holding someone against their will. She was no match. They covered her mouth, veiling the curses she spewed toward her ex-lover. Daniel, still close to his brother who was towering over Walter, only smiled as he gave his muscle a piece of advice. "Watch her, fellas, she bites."

Walter was nearly to his knees when the first kick came. Boyd's boot connected sternly with his uncle's ribcage, sending the older man tumbling. When Walter settled, another kick, this one a bit harder, followed. A sharp crack accompanied this strike as a rib bone gave way under the force. A final kick, this one to Walter's exposed cheek, sent him to his back, bloody, battered and beaten.

Daniel knelt down and began to speak to his wounded uncle. "We don't need Charlie now, Walt. We have other plans already. Now it's just the principle of the matter." He patted

Walter's chest, intensifying the pain that radiated from the broken bone. It seemed to give Daniel a boost of power. "We tried asking nicely earlier. Remember? And you lied to us, Walt. We know that now. You helped our baby brother disappear, and now you're trying to do the same damn thing." The last three words were whispered in Walter's ear, spat in tandem with three finger pokes to the fracture. The pain shot up Walter's neck as his body jolted in reflex.

Boyd pulled a blade from his boot as he knelt too. He pressed the knife against Walter's face and spoke coldly. "Where's Charlie, Walter? I won't ask again."

Daniel pulled a revolver, cocked it and then chimed in. "Give him an answer, Walt, and you go in an instant. I promise. If not," he nodded to Boyd, "you may not believe it, but this can get worse."

Walter wasn't sure if it could. Pom Shipping was all but gone. His father's legacy, his creation, would soon be erased from existence. And Charlie, his only blood relative, would be on his own forever. Cursed and on the run for the rest of his life. Finally, the life he thought would begin only minutes ago—a life of pure happiness, pure pleasure—ended before it began. His wonderful, promising future with Cara would never be. All was lost, everything in total. Nothing would remain after today. He had failed in it all and all equally. He began to cry.

It was obvious the answers weren't coming so Boyd prepared to go to work. He shifted his body to get a better angle on the first incision, pushing his brother out of the way. Daniel gave room but remained close enough to watch his brother's talent play out. Boyd was an artisan, after all. Cara screamed in horror at what was to come. She shut her eyes, not able to bear witness to the pain inflicted on the man she loved. Walter lay still, numb to the impending torture. His agony peaked, he could suffer no more.

Suddenly, the crewman who ran for cover earlier, the fleeing rabbit, sprinted from the galley corridor followed by ten or twelve other boatmen, including the vessel's captain. All were armed with a rifle, a pistol or a broadsword. The captain, an honest man and former member of the Queen's Royal Navy, shouted to the four trespassers. "Gentlemen, you will unhand that woman and step away." He looked to the Murrays. "And you there, you will not harm that man any further."

The crew surrounded the Murray gang and took aim. Cara was set free instantly as the two hired guns recognized the futility in resisting. They were clearly outnumbered and the pay wasn't nearly high enough to take on this fight. The Murrays, less inclined to bow to threats, hesitated. Daniel smiled as he stood, his charm coming on full force. His initial inclination, to cut a deal with the captain, was quickly rebuffed by the brusque Navy man and the warning further reinforced.

The captain spoke loud and clear. "Mr. Murray, under Admiralty Law, I have the responsibility to protect every passenger aboard this vessel and I will do so without hesitation. You have accosted four souls while unlawfully aboard this ship, a crime that is punishable by incarceration, fine and death. However, out of respect for your name, I will allow you to disembark now under your own power. But this arrangement is valid only for the next three seconds." He turned to his crew and gave the order. "Gentlemen and crew of the *Frontier*, be advised. If these two men do not attempt to go ashore within my countdown, you are to fire at will with sanctioned deadly intentions. And you will do so until ordered to cease. Is that clear?"

The men shouted in unison, "Yes, Captain, sir."

Then the countdown began. "Three!"

Daniel sent the hired goons away and followed slowly. Boyd continued to stare at Walter, debating his options.

"Two!" yelled the captain.

Daniel called to his brother, who reluctantly stood. As much as Walter earned it, his final punishment would have to wait. The old man would live. For now. But the clock was ticking. Boyd gave one last menacing look to the captain and turned to leave. Daniel thanked the crew for their hospitality and apologized for the disruption he and his acquaintances had caused. He took out a wad of cash from his front pocket, counted out a few bills and tossed them cheerfully onto the deck. The gang of four turned to leave, escorted to the ropes by the affronted seamen.

Cara raced to Walter's side, tears rushing down her face. She grabbed him, infuriating the cracked bone and amplifying the pounding inside his skull. Although once in her arms, Walter never felt better. The captain ordered his medic to assess the wounded man and make accommodations below deck. He wanted Walter's wounds documented for his account of the matter and round-the-clock monitoring of his progress. The ship would leave port as soon as Cara gave the word that Walter was comfortable and settled.

The men rolled Walter onto a blanket for transport, then lifted him to leave. Cara walked beside the bundle, holding Walter's hand along the way. As they neared the stairwell to enter the ship's quarters, a voice yelled to them from halfway down the gangplank. "Have a nice trip, Uncle Walt," Daniel laughed. "And have fun." He looked Cara up and down. "I know I did."

Walter squeezed her hand and lightly shook his head, trying to keep her from engaging the foolish young man. The jab didn't hurt him. Not at all. Not anymore. Cara understood and was thankful. She addressed the captain. "We're ready when you are, Captain Stone."

"Yes, madam," he answered.

"And thank you," she whispered.

"Don't mention it, Cara." He patted her shoulder and disappeared.

The heckling continued until the Murrays reached the ground. There, from a safe distance, their courage returned and promises of reprisal were made. Loudly. Daniel's bark, delivered to make Shakespeare proud, would have continued, no doubt far into the night, or at least until the ship took its leave. However, the tantrum was suddenly interrupted by three tremendous blasts, followed by three equally large fireballs. The financial district, a few blocks west, shook to its very foundation.

60.

The log pile was devastating. From a distance, Cook watched as the giant projectiles wiped out the entire first wave of invaders, the opening charge stopped cold. Nearly a hundred men lay crushed or impaled on the northern hill of Quindaro. It was a huge setback. Screams and moans of the dying echoed through the trees, causing an initial rush for survivor recovery. However, after the first few men pulled from the wreckage died within minutes, Cook called off the search for more. He'd be damned if another ounce of energy would be wasted collecting bodies of men who were already consumed. His order was clear and callous. Leave the bodies where they lay. From this point forward, doctors and priests were useless. He needed fighters.

The pile of debris fell into a heap near the bottom of the hill. A mass of building materials, splintered logs and household items acted as both a barrier to further offensive movement and a tomb to the dead. It would need to be moved. At the very least, a path must to be carved to allow access from the north once the south attack was launched. Otherwise, the belligerent hug Cook planned for the town wouldn't work.

From his horse, Cook quickly delegated the task of clearing the road to Blue, who recruited several dozen helpers. Teams of mules and horses were unhitched, led toward the pile and put to work. They heaved the giant timbers and large pieces of wall and roof still intact, causing avalanches that sealed the fate of those still alive and trapped in the mess. The men worked frenetically and before long, made noticeable progress. Cook was impressed.

He pulled his spyglass and again scanned the hill. Nothing remained. Every tree, every building, hell, even the large sedimentary stones scattered about were gone, moved by force to the very bottom. The hill was clear. The path laid bare. Cook's imagination began to grind.

From behind, a rider approached with word from the southern brigade. Earlier in the day, an order was issued to locate the position of any member of the town's leadership council and/or war chiefs. Most vital being Colonel Tough, Nancy, her husband Abe, Clarina and of course, Sorter, if he somehow returned in time. After an exhaustive search, a scout finally spotted Tough stationed on the southern plain, taking cover within the newly dug ditches and trenches. He led a small attachment that included the freed black and the traitor cousins. They weren't much of a threat, but they were entrenched. And heavily armed.

Unfortunately, the princess's exact location was still a mystery. However, word was she and her husband were farther north, in town and stationed in a makeshift command center near the demolished mill. The messenger apologized for the uncertain information but promised he would relay any updated intelligence received. Cook dismissed the rider with a nod and an idea formed.

His plan to attack from both directions seemed too complicated. The south, manned by Tough and his crew, would fall easily. That is to say, it should fall easily. Unless another surprise was waiting. He learned his lesson from the log pile, a mistake not to be made again. Maybe a better move would be to stay in the north. The hill was clear, not a single obstacle in the path. Sure, his men would take fire as they climbed the steep slope, and there would be some loss. But if every long-range gun and cannon took aim at the top of the hill, any resistance offered from above would be in the open as well. The rebels could be trounced from afar giving the foot soldiers time to close. The more he thought about it, the odds of another booby trap on the north hill was small. And there was a chance the pile was the town's best and only countermeasure. If that was the case, they had played their ace and presently, were sitting ducks.

Furthermore, a small regiment could stay south and keep Tough occupied. Without that nuisance, the north would fall even easier.

It was brilliant!

Cook yelled orders at the top of his lungs. "Mobilize the cannons," he screamed to the confused men surrounding him. The men in the south were to rotate this way, rear first. Finally, the path through the debris needed to be widened to make room for the larger force to pass. He pulled a pistol from his belt and fired it in the air as he shrieked. For the gamble to work, he needed to go now, by God. And the men would meet his wishes and meet them swiftly or there would be hell to pay.

61.

Luke was the first to notice the ominous development. The wounds to his forearm and thigh had worsened due to the hard ride in from the prairie, so for the time being, the only suitable role he could fill was as lookout and warning bell. He took cover in a deep rut on the south side of town, his eyes peeled, gun at the ready while resting his sore body. His cousin Lee, Cuff, Colonel Tough and the Six Mile mercenaries continued to reinforce the earthworks and ramparts, getting ready for a fight with what promised to be a resilient and voluminous enemy. They were assholes and elbows, making the most of the break in the cannon's barrage, and understandably missed the subtle indications of a mass troop movement. Luke's inability to help physically, an issue he had yet to acknowledge completely, finally showed dividends.

Fires in the woods below smoked relentlessly, showing signs of swift and chaotic extinguishing. A clear line and order, moving from north to south, indicated camps breaking from the rear, detachments leaving their posts. The front line swelled, pushed from the rear as caissons and coaches were turned and redirected. A few horses acted defiantly and gave away their positions with wild whinnies as they moved out. More telling was the chatter. The hum swept up the incline and intensified as the news passed from man to man like small-town gossip on a Sunday. Upon learning of the updated directives, the cheers and hurrahs from the delighted and compliant force gave away their excitement. Something big was about to happen.

Luke called his cousin over and the two of them discussed

the movement. Lee asked a nearby sentinel for the use of his spyglass and found the answer when he looked into the brass tube. Through a small gap in the trees, Lee could just get a glimpse of boots and wheels as they moved with intent back through the woods, circling toward the northern hill. He shared the telescope with Luke and yelled to Colonel Tough to give the news. There was a good chance they were preparing for a fight that wasn't coming.

By Tough's assessment, the town was vulnerable on either side. With the amount of men Cook boasted, a charge from the south would triumph just as easily as the north. However, considering the destruction in the town proper from the shelling and booby trap, cover from fire would be nonexistent on the other end. If Cook came from the north, the cannons could eat them up with little to no resistance. It was smart. A bit bolder than Cook's normal tactics, but Tough was forced to give credit where it was due. The old man had the town in check.

"We need to move, get into town and sound the alarm," said Tough. "The real fight will be over there."

"If we all pull out, they'll see it and start this way," Cuff interjected, nodding down the hill. "Some of us need to stay here."

The colonel agreed. A quick head count yielded the sad news. The manpower necessary to reinforce the north left little to spare to hold the south. Those who stayed behind would face incredible odds and would likely be overwhelmed in a matter of minutes if the enemy made a run this way. To stay was suicide. And Tough knew it.

So, too, did Lee. Rather than wait for Tough to reach an impossible decision, the young man spoke up, volunteering both himself and his cousin for the dangerous undertaking. "Dumbass there can't move anyway, so we might as well stay put," he said, pointing to the injured Luke. "We'll take these three fellas here too, if it's alright." He picked his help. "We'll do as much damage as we can for as long as we can."

Tough verified the choice with Luke, who agreed with a nod. "We'll be fine," said Luke. "Take care on the other side. And come save us as soon as you can," he joked.

The humor was wasted on the colonel. Tough called the others in the area to arms, pointing to weapon caches and ammo he wanted mobilized. He planned to make one trip and when started, he wasn't going to stop until they reached the area around the mill. If anyone was separated on the way, they were instructed to head in that direction and meet up near the flats. He didn't bother asking if his message was understood.

The team was ready in a matter of minutes and the first batch started north. Tough yelled from behind to step lively. "And if the cannons restart, whatever you do, don't stop. Run for your lives."

Cuff jumped from a trench after stocking Luke with as much ammunition as they could spare. He knelt and gave the wounded young man a pat on the shoulder, a silent appreciation and wish of good luck. He nodded to Lee as well, then told Tough, "I'll see you over there." He hoisted all he could carry and ran away, joining the others on the march.

Tough was last to leave. He paused, trying to find words to express his pride in the cousins and the small group of fighters he was leaving behind. Their will was inspiring, their courage unmatched. And they needed to hear it from someone. If David were here, he would have expressed his gratitude with eloquence and passion and somehow would have made this parting feel as if it were a triumph of sorts. Hell, David could have enticed the five men to lead their own charge downhill. But Tough didn't possess the same gifts as his friend. His words were simple and direct, but they would have to do.

"I'm proud of you, boys," he said. He swallowed hard. "Don't miss."

Luke answered, poised and confident. "We never do, Colonel."

62.

The Boston skyline as seen from the wharf glowed fiery red and orange. The buildings in the foreground seemed larger than they did only moments ago, the backlighting causing the illusion of grandeur and height. The smell of burning paper and wood filled the city as gusts of wind from the harbor blew smoke between buildings, down alleyways and into open windows. In the distance, sirens howled, calling firefighters and volunteers to the area to combat the blaze. Confusion reigned for now. Chaos and terror would soon settle in.

Everyone at or near the docks felt the shockwave of the blast and the heat as the burning intensified. Longshoremen emerged from every building in the marina, asking questions no one could answer, then joining the others merely staring in awe at the dreadful sight. The crew of the *Frontier* stood at the rail, sweating in their mackintoshes. Cara and her injured beau, too, clung to the metal barriers at the edge of the vessel, Walter limping but driven by a sudden second wind. The Murrays and their squad spread out to get a better view between buildings and over warehouses. Being on the ground made it difficult to appreciate the magnitude of the upheaval, so Daniel sent his helpers aloft to find out what happened.

The cobblestone loading area where he and his brother Boyd stood was slanted but smooth. As smooth as stones can be cobbled, anyway. It offered a wondrous view of the ships as they left port but little else. Looking toward the water, Cara's family yacht filled the scene, an imposing colossus looming overhead. While Daniel awaited word from the climbers, he found Cara and his uncle at the ledge, holding one another. It was sickening! But he couldn't look away.

Daniel hated allowing Walter to leave. Not only had his uncle not given up Charlie, he also was about to embark on what was sure to be a lavish trip with a beautiful, wealthy woman who chose the decrepit sheep over the robust wolf. She was a stupid bitch. It wasn't fair. The old man was a nuisance and the Murray boys probably should have dealt with him much sooner. To be sure, things would have ended differently. It was a hard lesson learned. A bitter bite.

To alleviate the sting, Daniel rationalized that at the end of the day, Charlie's whereabouts mattered very little to the overall deal his father had secured. It would certainly be nice to tidy up loose ends and simplify the family's affairs before everything finalized. But that would have to wait. They would find Charlie at some point and he would be handled. Matter settled. And as for the pleasure cruise, Boyd's kick to the brittle ribcage would make the journey more work than play. Daniel and everyone else present heard the cracking bone. No doubt Walter would be nursing wounds for most of the trip, leaving Cara frustrated. She would have plenty of time alone to second-guess her decision. That would show her. Finally, once the Ringgold deal went through, Daniel would have the funds to take his own trip, on his own boat, with any woman he chose. Hell, he could take two or three women if the mood struck him. That was more like it. So overall, things weren't that bad. Or were they?

Daniel yelled to the men whose climb put them atop a two-story outbuilding used as the shipping hub for a local candy manufacturer. "What happened?" he asked. From the heights, they were his eyes.

"One hell of a fire, boss," the report began.

Daniel looked to Boyd, shaking his head. A silent *no shit*! "I figured that, idiot. What's burning? Can you tell how it started?" he asked.

The man looked closer, trying to help, but it was all too jumbled. It was pandemonium. "Looks like the whole damn block is ablaze, sir. And it's spreading. Fast too," he replied.

"What block?" asked Boyd. He walked through the map in his head and an uneasiness crept in. Daniel was a bit behind but he caught up quickly. The Murrays knew the answer before it came back.

"Your block, sir," he started. Their anxiety was validated. "The bank and the offices next door. They're screaming hot. And Ringgold's place, hell, that whole street is a goner."

The man continued describing the wreckage, but neither Murray was listening. Instead, they stood motionless, staring at each other, both putting it together, working toward a conclusion. What if Calvin was in the building? Was the bank vault compromised? Were any of the documents lost? This was bad. The meeting with Ringgold, scheduled for the next morning, was surely out. Where did that put the deal? Postponed, at the least. At worst, cancelled outright. This was really bad.

One of the men above suggested that the Murray contingent should vacate the area. And quickly. The whole district was at risk and if they didn't leave now, they may not get another chance. The fire was spreading like mad, eating everything in its path. The load-bearing masonry, usually quite fire resistant, unfortunately wasn't the sole structural system in the financial district. Bricks, which made up most of the at-risk buildings, didn't handle tension well, so the floors and ceilings were generally made of wood, a fire's best friend. The destruction of the wooden interiors, coupled with the swelling of the heated brick, caused irreparable spalls and cracks. The structures collapsed one by one, shaking the ground like a tripped giant. The messenger was scared and it showed. He and his companion started their descent down a rusty ladder strapped to the corner of the warehouse. Although their combined weight was probably more than the ladder could handle, neither man was willing to wait. It was time to move.

Retreating to their custom brougham, the Murray brothers consented to their predicament. However, like most people who find themselves in a tight spot, they looked for someone to blame. And to punish. A list of names, made of enemies, disgruntled partners and jealous associates rushed through the two Murray brains simultaneously. Try as they might, none of the would-be offenders completely fit the profile. The move was too bold, the strike too harsh. No one in their right mind would endeavor to deal a blow of this nature to an organization run by the likes of the Murray clan. It was either a chance disaster of natural origins or the work of a fool with no concept of repercussions. This wasn't chance, the timing was too coincidental. Someone had started a war. Or... Could it be something else altogether? Could it simply be the work of someone with nothing to lose? Someone like...

While everyone else aboard the *Frontier* stared at the fire, Walter's gaze remained fixed on his nephews as they walked silently across the limestone ground below. His rib was screaming but between the railing, Cara and the explosion, he was more comfortable than he had been in years. He waited patiently for the sign he knew would come eventually. The Murrays were horrible boys who had grown to become even more horrible men, with very little to offer as far as positive attributes go. They were, however, as much as Walter hated to admit it, extremely bright and naturally quick thinkers. They were apex predators. The pieces would fall into place any second now. And Walter would have his moment.

The two Murray boys halted in unison a few steps away from the carriage. They shared a quick glance through squinted eyes; then, stunned by the notion, turned again toward the yacht. There on the deck they caught the stare of their uncle. A smile broke out across the old man's face, a smile he was physically unable to control. It was confirmation in its purest form. It was the swagger of a conqueror. A victor. It was obnoxiously shiny and toothy. Unbelievable. It was fucking Walter Pomfrey!

63.

Cook's attack resumed. Upon hearing the distant roar of the cannons, Nancy and those with her took cover behind what remained of the sawmill. The scared group of stragglers hid, counting the dreadful two to three seconds as the projectiles climbed the hill. They shook with fear, awaiting the hellfire. But it never came. The explosions, along with the cries of terror that followed, occurred elsewhere, at the other end of town, on the south side. The reprieve from the shelling brought a strange joy, a relief almost, that was difficult to reconcile. The small group that huddled near the flats was temporarily safe from the bombing, for which they were grateful. However, not a mile away, others, friends even, fellow townsfolk, were being beaten to death by the heavy fire. Being safe, even for a moment, felt wonderful. But it brought with it the guilt of living and the shame of fortune. To smile would be gloating; to thank God, undignified.

Nancy could feel the heaviness of those around her. The others were despondent, confused and dangerously tranquil. They needed direction and motivation, and Nancy was bursting with both. She spoke up excitedly, rejoicing in the current lull, seeing the perfect opportunity to strategize and pillage supplies. Not that far away, in the wake of the log pile, the dead lay with their supplies free for the taking. Some of Cook's departed were so close they could be scavenged without descending the hill more than a few dozen yards. They were sure to be carrying rifles, pistols, knives and precious ammunition that the town could use against the next wave. Nancy directed the group to mobilize, clapping her hands loudly as she did so. Luckily, they responded! They leapt to their feet absolved, ready to reap the lifesaving crop of stray firepower.

As the group diffused, Nancy walked to the threshold of the steep hill, looking for a body she knew was nearby. She found Chris Kelley lying at the base of the structure that once held the giant logs. He lay twisted at the waist, his torso angled downhill. His face was smeared with dirt and turned away from her approach. The bowler hat lay under his head, propping it a bit. His blue eyes were open wide.

The injuries that took him were obvious. The right side of his chest and that arm were crushed, the bones flattened under his vest and half-open shirt. From the looks of it, death likely came fast with little or no pain, for which Nancy was thankful. After all, she was responsible.

She kept him here, in town, to assist in the fight. She had also picked him to man the trap that sent him to the next life. The choices that led him to die in battle were hers alone. She pulled the strings that put him here, in harm's way, to fight and kill and ultimately sacrifice his very self. As much as it hurt to lose such a valuable piece, it was obvious Nancy's intuition was spot on. He was the man for the job, one of the very few who would have played the part willingly. His actions were proof enough.

By all accounts, Chris died a hero. When the last stake holding the pile refused to give way, he grabbed a sledge and pounded it until it surrendered. When the pile rolled, he tried to get clear but failed. Moving in front of the logs was foolish and everyone around him knew it at the time. But he went anyway, driven by the task, driven to prove his worth to himself and maybe her as well. Nancy could have taken responsibility for that too, but she refused. She never promised this man anything, regardless of how he chose to interpret the budding relationship. His drive, for whatever reason, was what she recognized. His strength and will were his real value, not his beauty or his charm. These traits were superfluous. The internal prowess to fight was why she picked him, why she used him. And at the end of it all, these qualities and her ability to identify them saved countless in town and shocked the enemy to their very core. It was worth it. There could be no doubt.

She knelt beside him and stroked his cheek with her soft hands. Thanks to the sunshine, he was still warm and almost felt alive. She closed his shirt and buttoned it toward the top to keep it fastened, then quietly asked the spirits to take him gently and protect him for all eternity. She made a promise, to both Chris and the ghosts, that the body would receive a proper burial to guarantee the soul's safe passage elsewhere. Finally, she reached down and closed his eyes, smiling at how much better, how more at ease the closed lids made him look. He was at peace. So was she.

A local farmer who had taken cover with Nancy near the mill approached with an armful of rifles and pockets full of shells. "Look there, Mrs. Brown," he said. He pointed with a nod behind her to the south.

It was Tough and his band coming from the southern edge. The cannon fire surrounded them as they weaved around demolished buildings and jumped over massive craters trying to stay alive. As they made their way toward Nancy and the mill, the bombing followed, drawing it closer and closer to this end of town. It was time to take cover again and fast.

Nancy and the others ran toward the flats, waving at Tough and his troop to follow. Once there, Tough took a head count that came up eight short. Nancy was furious and wanted answers. The men lost on the journey through town were valuable commodities and Tough's decision had cost the town dearly. What was he thinking?

"Why are you here?" she demanded.

Tough cut her off before she could continue her rampage,

ducking as the explosions zeroed in on the new sanctuary. "Cook's rolling this way. All the men from the south are about to hit this hill and march straight up through us. The fight will be here," he answered.

Nancy looked to the bottom of the hill and saw the army as it began its ascent. It was terrifying. The town was outnumbered three to one. When she accounted for the mortar shells as cover, the odds were long. Impossible, almost. Tough was right, he and the men he brought would be needed here. The losses crossing the open divide were irrelevant. She took stock of the spoils the townsfolk collected but by her calculations, they were still short. Way short. But it didn't matter. The fight was about to start whether she was ready or not. It was time to make a stand.

64.

Cook and Blue watched with anticipation as Tough and his faction sprinted to the north. The southern cannons summoned earlier had yet to arrive but were close. They were currently stalled behind the mass of men as they, too, marched north through the woods, anxious to make the climb and attack. The cannons present and forward, however, fired furiously at the scurrying roaches as they ran at the top of the hill, ducking and dodging the explosions all around. Cook yelled at and cheered on the artillerymen, pushing them faster and harder in hopes of dropping just one consecrated shell on top of Colonel Tough's boorish skull. The spongers and rammers moved frantically, preparing the barrels for the powder and projectiles that were hastily sent up the hill at a thousand feet per second. The hard work had already paid off, as several of the targets had been hit causing losses the town could ill afford. But Tough still moved, still lived. And if he made it to cover, a golden opportunity would be lost.

"Hold! Hold!" Cook yelled as the elusive colonel disappeared near the flats. The firing slowed, then stopped altogether as the order spread down the lines. "Son of a bitch!" he said to Blue. "I knew it was too good to be true."

"At least we got a few of them, sir," replied Blue.

"I guess," was all Cook could muster.

"Nice work, men," he said to those near him and expressed his reverence to those able to hit a moving target from this distance. It took a fair amount of skill and focus, and he made sure his men knew he was proud of their work. Inwardly, he knew the direct hits were eighty percent luck, maybe more. But it never hurt to stroke the egos of the dim-witted, to boost their vanity and keep their minds from wandering. Besides, luck and skill were cousins, and Cook valued both equally. The effect was plain—Tough lost valuable resources. The cause was immaterial.

It seemed odd that Tough and his men could disappear from open ground so suddenly and be clear of the danger of the long guns so effortlessly. Cook was confused and looked for answers.

"Where did they go? How do they disappear right around there?" he pointed to the last spot Tough was seen.

"The ground there, behind the sawmill, flattens out." Blue explained. "They can sit there and be out of range. And out of the line of sight."

"That doesn't work," thought Cook aloud.

"No worries, sir," offered Blue. "If they're serious about putting up a fight, they'll have to show themselves. There's no way they can defend the hill, the entrance, from the flats. They'll have to come out in the open, right about there." He pointed to the hill's crest. "Our guns will reach them easy. As long as they didn't run off for good, they'll be finished today."

Blue's clarification was sufficient and appeased Cook's inquiries. His plan to attack the town's north edge remained relevant and his cheery demeanor returned.

The river of manpower flowed around him at his post, and with a break in the action, Cook took the time to acknowledge and inflate his army. He returned salutes like a trained theater actor playing Napoleon or Hannibal to a full house of enthralled fanatics. He bounced majestically on his rambunctious dapple gray, waving his hat in the air as he shouted words of encouragement spiked with insults aimed at the enemy forces. He gobbled up the *hurrahs!* that came back to him and used the fuel to raise the stakes. He, like most, was at his best when things were lined up in his favor. And seeing as matters hadn't looked this good in years, he was going to make the most of it.

"Head on up, men!" shouted Cook. "Get up that hill and take it to 'em!"

East of the Quindaro docks, a large passage had been cleared through the logs and debris, and the men marched through. Cook thought about holding a moment and sending everyone at once, but word from the front line changed his mind. The bodies and body parts inundated the area and the longer the men stood there, the more their nerves would waver. It was a mess. So rather than dawdle at the hill's base, the mass started hiking into the sky, assured by their leader there would be no more surprises.

Finally, the last two cannons arrived and were quickly put into position. The other guns were being cooled to protect the integrity of the barrels and assure they would last through the final assault. All the guns were to hold until Cook said otherwise, and then they were to fire until he ordered them to stop. He hoped against hope to see the town emerge from the safety of the flats and attempt a stand. If they did, he would open up on them like never before. He would finish them before they ever had a chance to defend the hill. He couldn't wait. It was a dream come true.

65.

Time was up. The fight for survival would start shortly and most, ready or not, had come to grips with the awful reality. The men climbing the hill inched closer every second and would soon be within firing distance. The booby-trapped log pile that worked so well earlier had left behind a smooth, unimpeded path that would be nearly impossible to defend. The move had bought time and for that, all were thankful. But the aftermath brought unforeseen consequences that now set the town up for failure. Cook had recognized the weakness and capitalized. His men were closing fast, bringing the fight to the town and its people. And everyone knew how that would end.

A large contingent of townsfolk had gathered near the mill, joining Nancy and Tough as they prepared to step out into the open and form their line. Clarina was there, armed but mystified. Her son Tom was present as well along with Reverend Mills, Abelard, young Billie Cody and Andrey, the Russian chef. Most of the band were locals, shop owners, teachers or farmers whose bravery far exceeded their experience or aptitude. Their drive, fierce and rigid, was their greatest attribute. Their will and determination, fueled by a common, agreed-upon belief, would have to be enough. It was all they had.

Taking stock of those assembled, Tough found more to work with than he anticipated. He still had several bona fide fighters in the mix in the form of Cuff, a couple Six Mile hired hands and Chris Kelley's goons. These men, Nancy and Tough himself, along with the fifteen or so Jayhawkers still alive could do a ton of damage. They could handle the heavy lifting and leave the cleanup for the civilians. Ultimately, there was little doubt who would take the field today. But even if it was the last thing Tough did in his life—and it probably would be —he would make sure the asshole at the bottom of the hill suffered a bit too. The cannons would surely do his side in, but they would kill like maniacs until that happened. And the men coming up the hill would pay severely for their trespasses. Tough was ready to fight.

Nancy appraised the group and had a different take altogether. Abe was a political marvel, with important and wealthy contacts back east. He could be an integral part of the coming power structure of the Free State of Kansas. If he survived. He was important to the cause and could do so much more than die in a stupid firefight. He shouldn't be here.

Clarina's value too was high. Her writings describing the area and its struggles were invaluable. Over the last couple of years, her words were reprinted in larger eastern newspapers, where she shared so eloquently the life and times of a city lost in the wilderness and surrounded by the unholy. Even across the Atlantic, her descriptions were alarm bells warning of what would surely be a cataclysmic era in America's near future. Her understanding of the times, her assessment of the wrongs and her demand for change concerning slaves as well as women was the mirror the country needed to truly see itself and take measure of its declared righteousness. She could be the voice, the conscience of an entire country. And she would be if Nancy could help it.

"Tough," she yelled. "A word, please."

She pulled the Jayhawker away from the crowd and quietly expressed her wishes. Abe, Clarina, young Billie, the Reverend and a few others from town needed to be set free.

"The battle today," she said, "although important, is not worth losing the war. Those who make it out will live to fight another day, stronger than before and more motivated." She paused before she stated what she really wanted. "They will need safe passage through Six Mile, it's the only route safe from Cook's forces."

Tough balked.

The sight of a small but notable tiff caught the attention of both Clarina and Abe, who moved close and joined the sidebar. Against Tough's better judgement, Nancy allowed it.

"Can you get them through, Colonel?" asked Nancy. She squeezed the soldier with her stare, gripping him with all her might. It took everything she had to keep him still.

His eyes bounced from Nancy to Clarina to Abe and back. None offered the comfort he looked for so desperately. Nancy knew the answer before she asked the question. His reply, especially in the presence of the oblivious, would open doors that should remain closed. He nodded, dejected by her public implications and what was exposed.

"Will you get them through?" she asked, barely above a whisper. "Please, William."

He held her eyes for a moment, solemn from the coming surrender. Her plan was selfish and foolhardy. It would bring questions of loyalty and honesty. And virtue. Questions he and his associations never wanted to answer. And never thought they would. He was stuck.

Nevertheless, Nancy was right, as usual. Abe was tired and obsolete, but that seemed to be what most of the world looked for in a leader nowadays. And Clarina, beneath her sturdiness, was cultured and soft. She couldn't help it. Both would offer more in a state house than on a battlefield, so theirs was no great loss. They could go. Billie, however, would be hard to replace.

No formal answer came. Tough called one of the Six Mile refugees over and issued the new orders into his helpless ear.

The man leaned in and out as the instructions came in violent waves of varying volumes and intensity. Tough clapped the man on his shoulder, pulled him back and forth by the shirt, driving his instructions and opinions home. The man nodded constantly, trying to prove his understanding so the abuse would wane. It did, but only after Tough and his directive was understood.

In the meantime, Nancy let the others in on the plan and had them prepare for departure. Clarina was relieved but still afraid for her son. She went to him immediately and delivered the grandest embrace of their lives. Billie refused to leave outright until Nancy was able to convince him his service as a bodyguard was essential. "The group may need a fighter, Billie," she said. "And you are the only man for the job."

The boy agreed.

Listening to the plan to evacuate, Abe assumed Nancy was coming along. She used the word "we" just enough to put him at ease, postponing the inevitable dispute that would commence once her husband realized she was staying to fight. "We need to get through Six Mile and then make it to Grinter's ferry to cross the Kaw," she said. "From there, we'll make Lawrence with little trouble."

Abe agreed and reached for her rifle. "I'll carry this, you can saddle up with the others," he said.

But she held firm to the weapon and her decision. He knew instantly. She wasn't coming. He tried to change her mind, speaking firmly at first, explaining a wife's place was with her husband. Making no headway, his argument shortly devolved into begging and pleading for her to reconsider. That didn't work either.

Hearing enough and with time running out, Nancy quieted Abe with a kiss, deep and firm. She caressed his face and stared into his eyes as their lips met for what could be the last time. After, he tried again to speak but she stopped him, touching his bearded lips with her fingers. Her head shook slightly, a sign she had heard enough. It was time for him to go. A tear rolled through the dust gathered under his eyes and he said the only thing any man could. "I love you, my sweet," he said. She kissed him again and turned away.

Tough appeared with the newly arranged guide, Billie, Clarina and the others who were bugging out. "Time to go," he said. "Travel safe."

Abe, still a bit puzzled and increasingly suspicious, spoke up. "He'll get us through Six Mile?" he asked, pointing to the guide.

"Yep," replied Tough.

"Just how is that going to happen?" asked Abe. Clarina listening intently, wondering the same thing. However, an explanation wasn't part of the deal. Tough shook Abe's hand, hugged Clarina, then rejoined Cuff and the others to prepare for battle. Without answers and no likelihood of clarification, the group to be preserved started out with the guide and Billie leading the way. They crested the hill quickly and disappeared from sight.

"You should have gone too," said Tough to Nancy. "He'll never forgive me if something happens to you."

Again, she took the other side. "David will be proud of my resolve," she said. He knew her like no other, always understanding and respectful of her tempestuous spirit. "Thanks, Tough," she answered. "For everything. You're a good man."

"Hardly," he replied.

66.

Every gun in his arsenal took aim at the tiny group that formed a picket near the top of the great hill. Poised, they waited for the order to sound. Cook's hands shook as he held the spyglass to his left eye, the good one, barely able to control his excitement. He stood in the stirrups as his horse quivered beneath him, the animal's instincts spiked by the building tension and enthusiasm. Everyone and everything was quiet as they waited for the leader to set it off. The moment was at hand, and it would be his finest yet.

The prey, the scoundrels he'd hunted for so long, the cause of so many headaches and heartbreaks, filled the lens in his hand like a baby bird he could crush at his whim. The princess was there. Colonel Tough and his thieving Jayhawks too. Cook squinted, trying to see the looks on the faces of those who soon would be blown into obscurity, dying to see any sign of fear or regret. That would make the moment all the better.

He pulled his pistol while keeping his eye glued to the scope and raised the gun to the air. The hammer pulled by muscle memory, the trigger readied. He wouldn't miss this for the world.

All of a sudden, the stillness, the eerie calm and serene ambience caused by the anticipation was interrupted, sullied by a quiet, distant *boom*. Cook heard it, his men did too. Confused, each looked to his neighbor for answers neither had.

Lowering the spyglass, Cook was the first to speak but wasn't able to finish his thought. "Did you hear...?"

From the heavens, a missile landed midway between

two artillery batteries, igniting their powder and exploding shells. The detonation was massive and shook the ground beneath before completely swallowing the two closest guns and every crewman in the vicinity. There were screams of terror but they lasted only a second before the eight-hundred-degree fireball choked off all sound as it filled open lungs and brought sudden death. Those nearby ran on impulse into the woods north and south, hoping they were escaping in the opposite direction of the attack. Since no one knew from where the shell came, all were lost and scrambled like blind mice. At once, order turned to chaos.

A few of the bold scampered toward the crater left by the explosion to offer help and assess the damage but found nothing to save or anyone to console. The guns and men were a total loss. Cook, whose composure never failed him, steadied his spooked mount and searched his surroundings for the instigator. He quickly ruled out sabotage, conspiracy and accident. The attack originated outside of his camp, but from where was a mystery.

Gazing up the hill again, Cook became indignant. Not only had his shrewd position been sucker punched, but also his crusade that hitherto had been a raging success seemed to have stalled. The men who had reached the top were dispatched harshly by the townsfolk. No surprise there. It was a numbers game and he had them. The tide would turn eventually. However, the others, the reinforcements that would assure his victory, had stopped halfway and now stood stupid, gawking and pointing backwards toward the river. Cook's scrutiny moved in that direction and he found the culprit.

Coming down the river was the *Otis Webb*, and on its deck sat a twelve-pounder. Two tiny men swarmed around the gun, loading and aiming. To get the whole story, he moved the glass to his good eye. When he did, the vein in his neck nearly burst.

"Goddamn Sorter," he mumbled through gritted teeth.

Cook immediately went to work forging a plan to deal with the new threat, but he didn't get far. On the boat, a puff of smoke materialized at the barrel's end, followed a half-second later by the booming sound. Another round was on the way.

"Oh shit!" Cook whispered to himself. "Take cover" barely left his mouth before the second shot hit pay dirt. Fifty yards south and tucked in the forest, the three-inch howitzer and its artillery crew paid the price. Nearby trees shattered and fell, smashing those unfortunate enough to be standing close to the target.

More men, this time many from the front, began their unauthorized retreat, running right past their fearless leader in the process. Cook, furious, chastised the cowards and ordered them to halt and return to duty. He fired his pistol at a few, hitting a couple in the back as they ran for their lives. Again, pandemonium reigned.

Cook moved his horse into the path of the next batch of runners and stopped them cold, both pistols pulled and aimed to harm. The men, knowing their leader's insolence, listened with all their might. Their job was simple yet vital. Sink the *Otis Webb* and kill every living thing riding the wretched boat or they themselves would be in a shallow ditch within the hour. The men hastily retraced their steps back toward the river's edge to return fire. They had no choice.

Cook, satisfied his policy on desertion had been clearly reaffirmed, yelled behind them as they marched away. "Once more unto the breach, you sorry bastards!"

67.

The first volley fired from the *Otis Webb*'s deck missed its mark by nearly a hundred yards. David and Charlie grimaced as the shell neared the land, caught an updraft and sailed. However, as luck would have it, the punch delivered a more destructive outcome than the original target area ever could have. By complete accident, they hit something. Something big. It was Sorter magic. The explosion in the woods was awesome and seemed to grow exponentially, gobbling up everything in the vicinity. The two men shared a smile and a shrug, knowing they couldn't have asked for a better way to announce their appearance. Then they reloaded.

"Hold here!" David shouted to Captain Webb. The ambitious boat jerked intensely as its engine revved to reverse its wheel. The wooden paddles groaned as they dug backwards, deep into the muddy river, bringing the vessel to a halt. Stationary, they were more vulnerable. Nevertheless, David needed to take the risk to improve the accuracy of his secret weapon. Firing while moving wasn't easy.

The first shot was a miss but could be used as a benchmark for what should be a well-targeted second try. Charlie finished with the ram and fine-tuned the aim to David's discretion. He shortened up the barrel two or three inches, then hustled clear of the gun to ready the fire. More men lay hidden in the woods and another shot, this one closer to the river proper, would surely help the cause. Best case, in David's words, they would put this one "up Cook's sorry ass!" And as the round left Lazarus, it looked as though they may have done just that.

The second shot flew farther than intended but hit something valuable just the same. Charlie jumped for joy as another fire began to roar on shore.

David was less exuberant. Two shots and two hits were certainly a great start, but no one was that lucky. Not even him. As he and Charlie began to load another round, David wondered aloud, "How many goddamn cannons does he have down there?"

Looking up the hill, he found his answer. The town was gone. Everything. Buildings, trees, even the grass, vanished. The ground smoldered black. Fires large and small still burned, some fresh with large orange flames consuming newly destroyed tinder. Others, old and tired, were dying from a lack of fuel. These caused the most distress as it became apparent the bombardment had been going on for a long time. The town was devastated. So was David. If Nancy were alive on that hill, it would be a miracle.

Near the docks, a large contingent of Cook's army stood poised to climb the barren landscape where the town used to stand. Through a clenched jaw, David gave Charlie their next objective. "Swing it around, kid. We're going to put one right in the middle of those pricks right there," he said, pointing out the target area for Charlie.

The two made the adjustment, reloaded and let it go. The exploding shell hit higher up the hill than they wanted and as a result killed only a few of the most unfortunate. However, the round still made an impression. Several in the rear of the line turned and began a not-so-orderly retreat, running past Cook and a small group of sharpshooters standing at the edge of the bank and spilling over onto the large rock wharf. From their position, Cook's conscripted squad had an unobstructed view of the exposed battleship. And their bullets were en route.

David's next shot would have to be better if he wanted to turn the tables. The bullseye would be in line with the last attempt, but down the hill and into the mass of flesh gathered there. He shouted his intentions to Charlie as he reached for the next ball. It was then he noticed something funny. He gave his left arm the simple task of reaching out and helping the right one lift the heavy projectile and carry it toward the mouth of the cannon. However, the arm was strangely uncooperative. Instead of following orders, it swung loosely at his side, dead clear to the shoulder. And it suddenly ached. Badly.

The deck of the *Webb* helped put the pieces together as it was awash with a fair amount of dark red splatter. David was hit. And evidently losing a lot of blood.

Surprised, he stood still, tracing the blood to the original wound. Just then, something whizzed by and bore into a crate stacked a few feet behind the gun. Wood shards dashed high in the air like a mirror that had been hit with a hammer. A second later, David felt the sting in his rib cage. Dammit! He was hit again. Somewhere on his side, in the back. This wound knocked the wind out of him and made it hard to stand. On impulse, he fell to all fours, gasping frantically to refill his lungs. It took a moment, longer than it should, but his insides came around, his breath regained.

David had been shot before, plenty, and in worse spots. He would live if he got help soon enough. Probably. But he was out of the fight.

Charlie ran to David's aid and pulled him to the back of the deck behind the barricade of crates at the base of the wall beneath the wheelhouse. The younger man did his best to dress the gunshots and lean David into a more comfortable position, all the while unconsciously mumbling under his breath the desperate need for the ferryboat to get back upriver and out of range. The way Charlie moved was scary, and David knew the signs all too well. Shaking hands, loss of motor skills, manic speech. Charlie was on the verge of breaking down. And David needed to slow the spiral before it was too late.

"Stop a minute, Charlie," said David. It was the first time he remembered ever saying the kid's name aloud and it must have done the trick because Charlie froze like a statue. David reached out with his right arm, the one still following orders, and held Charlie's shoulder before he continued. "Settle down now, everything's going to be fine. I'm hit but I'll live, trust me." Charlie's eyes darted to the deck, then to his hands—the blood was everywhere. "Trust me," David repeated gently.

Charlie settled for a moment but began to slide again once he started to speak. "We need to get out of here," he said. "I'll tell Webb to back it up, we can't…"

"Nope," David interrupted. "Listen…" Charlie continued his rant but David persisted and finally won. "Listen to me! We're not going anywhere, you hear? We need you. Me. The town. All of us. We need you to take that shot," he said, pointing in the direction of Lazarus. "Because if you don't, we lose. It's that simple. Cook takes the town. The ground. He takes it all. And all those dead bodies on top of that hill were for nothing."

Charlie tried to argue but David was resolute. "We need to make a stand, boy!" Charlie fell quiet. "And you're all we've got left."

David was right. The town had been great to Charlie and he felt at home there. He would have to fight for it if he wanted it to last. He was sold.

He closed his eyes, trying to remember the sound of his mother's voice, the voice in his dreams, his memories. She would get him through, not David or the town. Sarah held the power and Charlie needed her. Just her.

Finally, her words flashed in his head. The only words that ever worked. "Get. Your. Bearings." Charlie focused, letting the courage build that would drive him to finish what he and

David started. The Jayhawk leader continued to chatter away, giving last minute instructions and advice about angles, gunpowder and wheel chocks. However, Charlie wasn't listening. Not to David, anyway.

Ignoring the warnings regarding the sharpshooters on the docks and the potential movement of the ferryboat, the kid rose and moved boldly to the cannon. There were a few steps yet to complete before the gun was ready, so Charlie went to work. Mentally, he checked off items, step by routine step, as he meticulously fulfilled the requirements necessary to turn Lazarus into a proper killing machine. Once complete, he double-checked his work; satisfied, he turned to the most vital undertaking—aiming.

Charlie looked to the hill, locating with ease just where the last shell landed. He remembered the adjustment made between shots one and two and decided something similar would suffice. It may not be perfect, but it would have to work.

Suddenly, a bullet ricocheted off a piece of iron railing directly in front of Charlie on the starboard side of the vessel. His reflexes took over and he hit the deck hard, crawling behind a large crate filled with bags of flour and cornmeal. A second later, two more bullets found the backside of his shelter, and although their momentum stopped somewhere inside the crate, the thud resonated down Charlie's spine, giving him a chill. As he leaned against the wooden box, he closed his eyes again, took in a deep breath and whispered to himself, "Get your bearings. Get your bearings. Get your bearings." The growing fear kindly tapered for the moment.

Charlie knew all he needed was to touch the fuse with the fire chord and the shot would be off. He just had to live long enough to make it to the rear of the cannon and finish the job. He opened his eyes, looking for the best and easiest route to take across the deck and was shocked to see the figure of a man positioned between the spoked wheels of the gun. It was Oliver. And Charlie freaked.

"Oliver!" yelled Charlie. "Get down!"

The deck was showered again with bullets fired from the shore, pinging and crashing all around. One shot missed Oliver by mere inches. Strangely, he never flinched.

Charlie yelled another warning, trying to convince his friend to take cover but soon realized it was all for naught. Oliver wasn't listening, nor did he show any signs of being apprehensive about the incoming slugs. Instead, he gazed over his glasses, looking downriver, using his thumb and index finger to measure distance and height. Then he studied and compared the movement of tree branches, from one side of the river to the other, getting a feel for the direction and speed of the hot, gusting wind closer to the target.

Another bullet from Cook's men struck near Oliver's boot but again, he paid no mind. He knelt and untwisted the mechanism to lower the barrel, then, looking through the sights, nodded his silent approval.

Oliver stood, looking downriver one more time to the target area, then yelled toward Charlie's hiding place. "You're all set, son," he said. His accent was gone. Alex was back. "If you light it up quick, I think you'll like what happens." He gave Charlie a wink. "I'm heading back up top," he continued, pointing to the wheelhouse. "When I do, make your way right here, where I'm standing, the very spot. It's the mercy seat." Another wink. "Then unleash it, you hear?"

Alex turned and made his way to the ladder leading back to the captain's nest. David stared hard at his brother as he walked past, hoping for a moment, a second even, of something familiar. A flash of awareness or recollection was all he needed. But he wouldn't get it. Alex was already gone, his work complete.

Charlie scampered low to the back of the cannon as Alex instructed and put the fire to use. He jumped clear of the recoil, taking cover again behind the crate of ground grains. Just in time, he covered his ears to shield them from the sound of the blast that rocked the boat and thrust it backwards. Charlie peeked around the corner of the box, curious and hopeful that his effort wasn't in vain. Through the smoke, he found the projectile in flight and watched as it cut through the sky, its arc perfectly in line with its objective. With a roar, it hit the mark. It was perfect!

Cook's men who lived through the blast dropped their weapons and ran. Some were covered completely in fluids blown from their compatriots, amplifying the horror and despair. This retreat was swift, total and unreserved. And nothing, not even Cook's swearing and threats, could bring it to a halt. Charlie had blown the fight right out of them.

The last straw was a charge down the hill led by Nancy, Tough and Cuff. The rest of the town followed close behind, screaming like banshees, shooting and killing everything in their path. They chased Cook and his men to the edge of the woods, then the riverbank, and finally to the barges used to cross the river into Missouri. Cook's force was beaten, to a man. The fight was over. Charlie owned the field.

68.

The Quindaro docks, or what remained after the Missourian's attack and Charlie's counter, erupted. Not in flames, but in jubilant, euphoric celebration. Captain Webb pulled hard on the whistle, blowing nonstop shorts and longs, all the while poking his head out of his perch and screaming curses at the fleeing "mangy dogs" of Cook's army. Oliver enthusiastically joined in the slighting but unfortunately, his slurs came off much more polite than intended. It was probably the accent. The townsfolk fired their guns in the air and although new to the measure, hollered loud enough to make their southern foes jealous. Grown men hugged, wives kissed their men and hats of all sizes took flight like scattered quail. It was a remarkable victory indeed!

Tough and Cuff led the rest of the Jayhawkers into the woods to make sure nothing was left of the invaders and to complete the rout. At this point, it was a mere formality.

Nancy fell out of line as the *Otis Webb* landed with no other thought than to get David in her grasp. While the boat bounced against the wharf and before the onlookers could secure the ropes, she jumped the railing, boarding the vessel that held her knight. She stopped as she reached Charlie and snatched his face in her hands. Without a word, she affectionately kissed his cheeks, then his forehead and finally his lips. As quickly as she seized him, she let him go with a brisk, playful slap on the stunned kid's flushed face.

Behind the wall of wooden boxes, she found David struggling to get to his feet. She closed on him like a mountain lion and once she had him in her arms, she kissed him just as violently. Between the loss of blood and the power of Nancy's embrace, David's knees buckled and the two stumbled against the wall of the ferryboat, the kisses continuing all the while. They spoke faintly, words only they could understand, then sealed the joyous reunion with a monstrous hug that neither wanted to end.

David and Nancy stood in silence, knowing their time together now was short. He breathed deeply, inhaling the smell of her hair, her clothes, her skin. She, too, held tight, moving her hands slightly, feeling his body, memorizing the moment she knew wouldn't last. As expected, almost on cue, they heard a familiar voice.

"Nancy, Abe's coming this way," said Clarina.

Nancy turned, surprised to see her friend.

"We didn't make it far," Clarina offered in response to Nancy's inquisitive glare. "He didn't want to leave you either," she said of Abe. "And to get Billie to leave was simply impossible. My goodness, that boy is a handful!"

Nancy turned back to David and gave him one more kiss. "He's hurt," she said over her shoulder to Clarina. "Put him back together, will you?"

"I'll take good care of him," replied Clarina. "Now get up front before it's too late."

Nancy thanked her friend with a hug before she was shooed away. Then she went to greet Abe and rest of the town while Clarina went to work on the wounded warrior.

Back in the open, the merriment continued.

Lee had made it on board and was congratulating Charlie on his triumph. His cousin Luke, limping badly, was unable to make it down the hill but was waving fervently from above. "I see he's feeling better," said Charlie.

"He'll be just fine," said Lee. "You may have to help me hunt for a couple weeks though. He's probably going to have to rest a bit."

"Deal," said Charlie with a handshake. He couldn't wait.

Oliver and Captain Webb emerged from behind the wall of crates, carrying David between them. Clarina directed the route and upon seeing Lee, began to issue her orders to the young man. The doctor must be found, a bed prepared, fresh water and linens, and everything else that was necessary. Lee listened intently and once assured of his list of to-dos, took his leave to tackle the assignments.

Tough and the gang returned from the woods and he, along with several of David's regulars, relived the captain and Oliver from the duties of transporting their leader.

Tough addressed his comrade. "You made quite an entrance," he said.

"Did you like that?" asked David.

"It was glorious," replied Tough. "Saved the day. Again."

"That's what I do," joked David with a shrug that turned into a grimace. As his men lifted him clear of the railing, he yelled back to Charlie. "Hey kid." A wink. "Nice shot."

An arm flung over Charlie's shoulder and a familiar voice rang in his ears. "Nice shot indeed, my boy. Nice shot indeed!" said Oliver. "You certainly put those maniacs in their place. A bloody victory for the ages, I'd say."

Charlie laughed a little. "Yeah," he said. He looked at Oliver, wondering if any of the memories of the fight and his part in it were there, but nothing registered on his face. As happy as he was to have Oliver back, he felt just as miserable for David's loss. With as much insinuation as he could marshal, Charlie replied, "I had plenty of help. There's no way I could've done it alone."

"Oh, don't be silly, young Charles," said Oliver. "Of course you could have. Because you, young man, are exceptional!"

69.

The weeks following Cook's attack were bittersweet for the town of Quindaro. The rebuild would take a Herculean effort that would test the mettle of every survivor regardless of age, gender or status. But a newfound sense of pride and self, brought on by the unlikely victory and taking the form of comradery and determination, would fuel the machinery. Small wins, like a personal memento found in the rubble, would garner wild hoots and hollers that sometimes far exceeded the significance of the actual prize. Larger milestones, like the day the sawmill reopened, nearly shut down work for an entire day. The celebrations were exaggerated and at times, almost hollow. But no one seemed to mind. The festivities were the manna for those still lost and doing without, and they would be indulged. The wins were sweet indeed. As sweet as chocolate bars and just as necessary.

The bitterness was there too, however. In spades. Beneath many of the fallen structures lay the kindred, smashed and smothered, cold and dead. When found, the work ceased while the friend or family member was rushed off to a hasty funeral before the body began to smell and the soul to wander. Large craters created by the bombardment made for easy burials where the fallen were stacked close together to save real estate and breed efficiency. Over time, these mass graves would be lost to the living. But those below would lie beside one another for all eternity and forever share stories of the day the Missouri Huns were beaten back, and their meek town was saved.

The first few days were the hardest, of course, and dealt

mainly with water supply, triage and self-defense. A small, willful group of Cook's men along with an even smaller, sober contingent from Parkville continued to launch annoying and mostly ineffective raids against the town. During his recovery, David forged a plan whereby Lazarus would be posted atop the hill on a cleared path, ever moving and alert, an orbiting sentinel. Since this latest band of Ruffians instigated their attacks from across the river, they were no match for Lazarus, which chased them away from its perch in the sky. A second gun, one of the three-pound howitzers commandeered when the original group of attackers bugged out, was stationed at a lower elevation and helped with the smaller details. After a few tries, these Ruffians, too, decided to regroup elsewhere, and the town was free to move into full-time salvage and construction pursuits.

Quindaro buzzed like a beehive from first light until deep into the late summer evenings. The nights began to cool and were combatted by campfires that lit up the hillside like fireflies. Everyone worked to their own level of exhaustion, but few worked as hard or as much as Charlie. Though he lacked experience and offered little in the way of advice or technical know-how, he made up for it by supplying what he could—grit and sweat. It seemed that every day, a new task was set out for him, each a little different from the day before. But the kid never complained. In fact, he was constantly learning something new and loving it.

After the battle, Charlie became a celebrity of the highest order. He was hounded around the fires at night and forced to retell his story ad nauseum to what seemed like the same audience time and again. They couldn't get enough. He heard his story told back to him many times as well and with each successive version, he himself seemed to become more allegory than truth. Almost overnight, Charlie had morphed into the hero of a real life western tall tale.

When Charlie walked through town, he was accosted regularly, his hand shaken violently, or his ribs crushed by unrelenting bear hugs. He rarely went a day without receiving some sort of baked goody of either the savory or sweet variety and got lost more than once trying to return an empty dish to its rightful owner. Between the hugs and kisses, the delicious gifts and the multitude of introductions to his admirer's unattached nieces and daughters, the cousins Lee and Luke were never wanting of an excuse to tease their new best friend. They were ruthless at times; however, they were careful not to damage Charlie's "delicate mannerisms" too much so as not to lose their place in the cookie, pie and biscuit cavalcade.

Charlie tried several times to set the record straight, but no one seemed to care about the factual recollection concerning his pounding, fearful heart or his on-the-job cannon training. The outcome made the hero, not the path taken to get there. Charlie sometimes wondered if this were true of all heroes and what his story would sound like in a hundred or a thousand years. At the current rate of growth, he would be Leonidas by fall and Alexander by spring next year. Maybe these men were products of circumstance too, lucky winners who ended up on the right side of history. Who knows, George Washington may even have been human.

These were the thoughts that kept him up at night. Usually by day's end, Charlie's body was finished and sore, ready for the shutdown. His mind, however, teemed with invaders that kept the healing sleep at bay. He tried reading a few of the books found in the rubble but nothing worked. Instead, he typically found relief in the letters sent to him by his uncle Walter, letters delivered by Captain Webb only a few days after the battle. In them, he found solace.

The first letter was a warning about Chris Kelley and his gang. Charlie had been on the prairie when they arrived in town, so the danger was never as real as Walter described. But that was merely due to good timing. Since he and David missed most of the fighting, Charlie learned the details of the battle from those he worked alongside daily. He heard about Tough's sprint across the deadly, open ground, Nancy's brutal revenge on The Whistler and of course, the devastating log pile, a success made possible by the deceased hit man himself. At the service for Chris Kelley, Charlie stood five feet from the two surviving Irishmen who were sent to hunt and kill him. Afterwards, the two men left Quindaro to return to a small Ohio village that reminded them enough of home to entice their return. As far as they were concerned, the job they were sent to do was complete. Charlie was off the hook for now.

The second letter was Walter's goodbye, and Charlie read it nearly every night. The letter was long by Walter's standards and like the author, its emotions were thinly veiled. It started with sorrow, moved to anger for a short time, then finished with a quiet acceptance that never failed to mend Charlie's nightly aches. His first read-through was like a punishment and nearly broke Charlie in two. But with each subsequent reading, although it remained taxing, the letter helped Charlie understand his uncle in ways he never had before.

Charlie smiled most nights as he finished reading, simply staring at the paper itself. He noticed in places, usually when mentioning the Murrays, that Walter's furious pencil nearly cut the paper clean through. In other places, most notably near the end, practically on top of the most unnecessary apology, the graphite had smeared by what was surely drops of tears cried by his uncle as he closed this chapter of his life. Walter was moving on and so would Charlie. Despite the mention of a plan to disrupt the transaction, Pom Shipping was almost surely gone by now, sold and severed into a hundred pieces. Therefore, Charlie would make his own way from now on, and he planned to do so here in the West.

The dream, recurring and fantastic, started the night he first read Walter's farewell. It began the same each time with Charlie as a young boy at his grandfather's estate on the Connecticut River. The grand Georgian home, nestled between

Amherst and Sunderland, was surround by fertile farmland, lavish river views and sage forests ruled by ancient American sycamores. One of the giants on the property, the oldest of the bunch, rivaled the famous Buttonball Tree located in Sunderland proper. The tree was enormous, with a canopy stretching more than a hundred feet high and a trunk of more than twenty feet around. It was here, in the cool shade of this beast, where Charlie's subconscious journeyed to feel secure, to revive and find harmony once again.

His grandfather made the first appearance, standing in the clearing nearby, expounding on his reverence for the grand trees he admired so extensively. The man stood proud, hands gesticulating as he retold the story of the signing of the Buttonwood Agreement of 1792 which formed the basis for the New York Stock Exchange. This momentous act was tellingly fulfilled beneath an everlasting sycamore. He told stories of his childhood climbing and playing in and around the same organisms alive and well to this very day. His favorite lesson, though, dealt with the unmistakable mottled bark, flaking and peeling from the massive trunks as they grew, showing the white beneath. "Nothing," he would say, "shows its growth more openly, more proudly than the sycamore." Stretching and tearing, every difficult stage is on display for all to see. Moreover, it never stops, even after they become giants and tower over their sprawling realms, the growth and the ugliness that comes with it continues. Nightly, he would fade into a mist, declaring in his own renowned, dramatic fashion, "We should all be so bold!"

Next, his mother Sarah would arrive, healthy and carefree. Young Charlie would curl up next to her at the base of the tree, peeling chunks of loose bark, listening as she read from the New England masters—Emerson, Longfellow and Hawthorne. Her eyes would sparkle, her voice changing as she recited the works as she understood them, bringing the stories and poems to life. Shelley's monster, Dumas' count and Dickens' ghost were all on display, along with Shakespeare and of course the Holy Bible. Daily newspapers filled the spaces between the classics, relating the newsworthy details of the Millerites' Great Disappointment or the tragic ending of the Donner expedition. Slowly, as the dream evolved over time, the reports were updated, and Charlie's own exploits took over as front-page news to be shared and enjoyed.

Nightly, Charlie filled his eyes with the glorious image that was his mother, soaking up the moments as she read how her heroic son saved a small western town from annihilation. She wiped away tears, delicious tears that all parents hope to taste, seasoned with pride and approval as she learned of the deeds attributed to her only child. She was overwhelmed! And Charlie was bolstered and rebuilt.

Sarah, too, would fade into mist every night, joining her father in the unknown. She seemed to sense her impending departure, however, and never failed to leave her son with the gentle words that made the coming dawn inspiring. Most mornings, her parting words, "I love you too, my sweet boy. I'll see you tomorrow," were still in Charlie's ears as his body roused and the day began. He would awaken refreshed, soothed and willing. His new life, with his new family, in his new hometown, restarted every morning. And it was a gift to be cherished and protected.

There would be difficulties for sure, learning curves and the like. But Charlie would be ready for the challenges and use every opportunity to further impress those watching over him, his angels. He would try to grow, bravely and openly, careful to display the consequences no matter how unpleasant. Charlie was a man in progress, and he would wear it for all to see.

70.

Charlie was initiated into the Independent Order of Odd Fellows with a grand ceremony. Every member of the small Quindaro Lodge was in attendance along with visiting dignitaries from towns around the territory including Lawrence, Lecompton and Manhattan. Attendance was mandatory when welcoming a new member, of course, as per the current Order bylaws. But you would be hard pressed to find anyone willing to miss Charlie's induction and the subsequent festivities regardless of rules, regulations, time or distance.

The ceremony was long and sober and filled with pomp and rigorous circumstance. The themes of the evening swung wildly from the truly meaningful to what could only be described as downright confusing. But Charlie, heeding the advice David passed to him before the official meeting began, "played along." The benefits and responsibilities of his membership were still sketchy, and he hoped at some point to be filled in on the details and such. Even so, when the final vow was repeated and the formal proceedings were complete, Charlie, for the first time in his life, felt accepted. He was officially a member of the town and the territory and it was wonderful. His smile lasted all night.

That evening, Charlie was introduced to a man from the abolitionist stronghold of Lawrence who invited the young hero to his river town, promising more introductions to even more influential allies. A trip out of town sounded nice and the timing couldn't have been better considering conditions in the area had returned to normal rather quickly, and once again, folks were killing and dying on a regular basis. That, coupled with the news of a bounty placed on Charlie by Cook himself, made a trip farther into the territory sound even better.

Charlie wanted to start his expedition west with Captain Webb aboard his ferryboat, as he'd never taken the turn at Kaw Point and traveled on the smaller Kansas River. In fact, Charlie hoped to work for Webb at some point, taking trips to the border towns and learning firsthand the geography of the Missouri valley. However, David nixed both the travel arrangements to Lawrence and the full-time employment on the river due to the likelihood of Charlie being "spotted, captured and gutted" by the enemy forces that would surely be monitoring river travel. It was a disappointment for Charlie, but he acquiesced. Sadly, he would travel to Lawrence by land, at least as far as Grinter's ferry, and he would find work somewhere in town upon his return.

As the journey neared, Oliver, along with the cousins, felt the brunt of Charlie's frustration. The Brit consoled his young friend by explaining it as the natural balance of things, "the yin-yang, if you will," and it was the adoration Charlie earned from Quindaro itself that was the very culprit. It was, after all, impossible to be only loved. No matter how hard one tried, an equal amount of disdain existed somewhere in the universe and it would forever. It was Newton's third law. Charlie was lucky, as far as Oliver was concerned, that the subject of his scorn wasn't hidden, waiting to show itself. No, Charlie could simply look across the river and see it.

The cousins, by contrast, offered no solace whatsoever, stating only that what David says, goes. Lee did, however, agree to accompany Charlie to Lawrence and took care of most of the preparations. The first of which was his insistence that the pair should leave in the wee hours of the morning to make it through Six Mile in the small window that was both too late and too early for the crazies to be a menace. Promptly, the trip was set. They would leave in the morning.

Charlie hadn't returned to Six Mile since his meeting with the strange man on the throne, so his end of the bargain struck on the way to recover Lazarus had yet to be squared. Creepy invitations were delivered now and again, both reminding Charlie of his agreement to return and promising a wonderous evening that would include a quiet, intimate meal along with "other pleasantries to be explored." The thought of returning to Six Mile was frightening, to say the least. And the "other pleasantries" were positively terrifying. But Charlie knew he would have to return at some point, either on his own or taken by force. And his time to choose the course was running short.

Lee and Charlie set out for Lawrence just as planned. They made it to Six Mile, the woods around it anyway, and were waiting for their opening. Charlie shivered as he looked at the door leading into the king's lair. He and Lee were crouched behind a hedgerow just north of the tavern itself, fully hidden by a small group of shrubs growing between the tightly grouped tree trunks. One day soon he would again walk through that door, but it wouldn't be today. Thank God! Today, he and Lee would sneak through the spider's web, quickly and quietly, without making contact and without incident. That was the plan, anyway.

Lee led his horse by its bridle to the end of the row, cocking his head to the right, giving Charlie a silent direction to follow. There was an open area they needed to cross, then a steep but short decline fifty yards or so past the rearmost point of the building. Once there, they should have enough cover to ride unseen back into the woods on the other side of town. Lee scouted the route, happy to see his timing was spot-on, as the village was silent and the coast was clear. Then he turned and whispered to Charlie, "Let's go."

Lee stepped out into the open, still leading his horse and using the animal as a shield in case he was spotted. Charlie followed closely behind, doing his best to keep up. The trek across the clearing seemed to take forever but finally, the slope came into view. Lee was a skilled rider. As he approached the drop, he mounted his horse in one fluid motion and disappeared down the slope.

Charlie tried to follow Lee's example but suffered a much different result. As he jumped toward the saddle, his boot slipped from the stirrup, he lost his grip and tumbled to the ground in a heap. The horse he was leading, unmoved by the wreck, trotted onward, following the leader as instructed, leaving Charlie bruised and in the open.

Ignoring the pain in his ass, his shoulder and his wrist, Charlie scampered on the ground toward the top of the hill. Once there, he rolled down a bit, landing on his back, staring upward, trying to catch his breath as he listened for movement behind him. He watched as Lee neared the woods and his own horse followed. Charlie was stranded.

"Get your bearings!" he insisted. He moved slowly, pulling off his hat so it wouldn't give him away and climbed back to the top of the hill to assess his predicament. He expected to see a hundred naked weirdos running toward him, ready to cut their prey to pieces or barbecue him alive or worse. But looking over the hill, his mind was steadied, and his heart slowed. The trespass and subsequent fall had gone unnoticed somehow. Remarkably, Six Mile remained still and undisturbed.

Charlie rolled over again onto his back, took a deep breath and nearly laughed out loud. He looked in the distance at the woods where Lee was waiting, and this time, his laugh couldn't be suppressed. He had one hell of a walk ahead of him with some pretty bad bruises forming.

As he rose to catch up with his partner, he heard something behind him that brought the fear crashing back. He hit the ground again, peeking over the hilltop searching for the source of the commotion. It only took a second for his eyes to find the singular movement on the horizon. It was at the back entry of the king's tavern. A door had swung open and a person, a woman by the looks of it, had stepped out and lost her balance navigating a crude set of wooden stairs.

She was clearly tipsy, held a near-empty bottle in her right hand and was laughing at her own momentary lack of grace. However, once she regained her composure and began sauntering back toward the stairs and the still open door, it was obvious that she lacked little else. The outline of her figure, the movement of her feminine body, bathed in the aura of the waning moonlight was, even from Charlie's distance, energizing. Her being was familiar, her essence one of a kind. It could only be Nancy.

Charlie froze as he watched her climb the stairs, approaching the door that swung outward, blocking his view of the person standing in the entryway. She spoke as she moved but the night breeze took the words, leaving soft and sugary mumbles directed at what was unquestionably a lover. Charlie strained to hear the conversation to no avail.

Upon reaching the doorway, Nancy leaned in, her voice falling to a whisper, then she went silent. The kiss that followed made her body sway and her arms go limp, the passion so robust it forced Charlie to look away.

Nancy pulled back, her parting words again a jumble in the wind. She reached out with her empty hand and teasingly pulled the hat from the head of the man in the doorway. Charlie recognized it instantly. The long, dangling feather was unmistakably the showpiece of the Six Mile king's crown. The devil himself was in attendance!

Before Charlie could process the situation and put some sort of meaning to it all, things suddenly turned from bad to worse. As the king leaned into the night to retrieve his signature hat, a lantern in his hand illuminated his face from below and, despite the spooky shadows cast, revealed his identity to the flabbergasted onlooker.

Charlie swooned, overwhelmed by a wild mix of emotions. Confusion led the way, followed closely by indignation, sorrow and wonder. Each burst mixed together with another, stirring and blending with the slightest splash of what could only be described as jealousy. Charlie was lost in space.

Thankfully, Lee shook him awake verbally, whispering loudly from the bottom of the knoll. He had returned with Charlie's horse and was pressing hard to complete the breakthrough.

"Are you alright, Charlie?" called Lee.

Charlie nodded his head slowly but said nothing.

"Can you ride?" Lee asked.

Again, only a nod.

"Then let's get out of here, dumbass!" Lee belted. "You waiting around to get yourself killed or something?"

Charlie rolled down the hill and climbed atop his ride. The two men pushed the animals hard until they reached the woods and were safely through the danger zone. Lee asked several times during the journey if Charlie was hurt and needed to see a doctor. Each time, the reply was a short "No." But Lee knew differently and decided he would set up an appointment for his friend as soon as they hit Lawrence. He was sure Charlie was hurting more than he let on as the poor kid sulked the whole way.

Sadly, there wasn't a doctor alive who could set Charlie straight. The vision of Nancy placing the feathered hat on David Sorter's head caused damage of a permanent nature.

ACKNOWLEDGEMENTS

I would like to say thank you to everyone who helped along the way. Some were hands on while others helped without knowing. Either way, it took many people and a lot of effort to make this book possible. In no particular order, I would like to thank: my mom, Shirley , my sisters, Gina and Stacy, my dad, Paul, Linda, Connie, Dave. Kansas Historical Society (kshs.org). Chris Malcolm and his friend in Colorado for saving the data on my computer (always backup your work!). Christie Stratos for the proofreading and polish (check out her work at christiestratos.com). The early readers, you know who you are. Ashton, Ethan and Maggie for being the best children they could possibly be with me as a role model. I love you guys so much! And my wonderful wife Christa for pushing me to finish what I started. I love you like crazy!

Finally, thank you, reader for choosing my book, I truly hope you found something in it worthwhile. I appreciate any and all feedback so feel free to reach out to me with any thoughts or questions. If you get a sec, a review on Amazon would be wonderful and a recommendation to a friend greatly appreciated. See you soon!

www.AAJohnsonworks.com

Made in the USA
Coppell, TX
31 October 2019